**"I'M A _____**
**WHAT'_____ND."**

Beaudry continued in a husky voice, "And right now, you're on my mind."

Mattie's cheeks reddened and she leaned back, well away from him. "I don't understand."

"I think you do. You're a widow—you know about a man's needs, and you're a powerful temptation." When shocked indignation widened her eyes, he grabbed her wrist. "Listen to me before you run off in a huff. I want you, Matilda St. Clair, but I won't take anything you don't want to give."

"Then you won't be getting anything!"

Her spirited reply made him chuckle. "Even when you're saying no, those eyes of yours blaze like lightning, tempting even the saints. And I ain't no saint, lady."

"I may be a widow, but that doesn't mean I'm easy pickings for a drifting man," Mattie said stiffly. "And you don't have anything I need—or want."

# MAUREEN McKADE

# Outlaw's Bride

AVON BOOKS
*An Imprint of* HarperCollins*Publishers*

This is a work of fiction. Names, characters, places, and incidents are products of the author's imagination or are used fictitiously and are not to be construed as real. Any resemblance to actual events, locales, organizations, or persons, living or dead, is entirely coincidental.

AVON BOOKS
*An Imprint of* HarperCollins*Publishers*
10 East 53rd Street
New York, New York 10022-5299

Copyright © 2001 by Maureen Webster
Inside cover author photo by Bezy Photography
ISBN: 0-380-81566-4
www.avonromance.com

First Avon Books paperback printing: February 2001

Avon Trademark Reg. U.S. Pat. Off. and in Other Countries, Marca Registrada, Hecho en U.S.A.
HarperCollins® is a trademark of HarperCollins Publishers Inc.

Printed in the U.S.A.

10  9  8  7  6  5  4  3  2  1

For my critique group—
Karen, Paula, Pam, Deb, and Carol—
for the encouragement, laughter, and friendship.
You all helped more than you know.
Thank you.

In memory of my grandfather,
who possessed the soul of a cowboy.

# Chapter 1

*Late July, 1887*
*Green Valley, Colorado*

**T**all, dark, and very, very dangerous.

That was Matilda St. Clair's first thought when she saw the black-clad stranger leaning in her boardinghouse doorway, his long fingers curled around a low-slung gunbelt.

He lifted one hand and tipped back his wide-brimmed hat, allowing the latigo string to hold it as it slipped down his back. Cool green eyes and long blond hair added to the aura of danger that fitted him as snugly as his dark trousers.

Apprehension shivered down Mattie's spine and she tightened her grasp around the broom handle. She met his stoic gaze without flinching, though her heart slammed against her breast. "May I help you?"

"Are you Matilda St. Clair?" he asked.

His deep, tobacco-roughened voice caressed her like velvet across bare skin and Mattie blinked the disturbing sensation aside. She nodded curtly. "I'm Mrs. St. Clair."

His languid gaze roamed from her face down to her toes and back up. Though angered by his bold scrutiny, Mattie couldn't help but wish she'd worn something other than her faded black skirt and patched blouse. She smoothed back the damp tendrils from her forehead, then was annoyed at herself for that small feminine vanity.

"My name's Clint Beaudry, and I'm looking for a room," he said with a slight Texas drawl.

"For how long?"

"A couple days"—he shrugged negligently and his hair brushed across his shoulders—"maybe a week."

Mattie coolly studied Beaudry's whipcord-lean body in turn, from his scuffed boots to his tanned, rugged features. Her gaze paused on the concho-studded belt around his slim hips and the gleaming revolver in the holster tied down around a muscular thigh. Her mouth grew dry at his blatant virility and she damned her body's unwelcome reaction.

Clint Beaudry was definitely dangerous, in more ways than one.

Mattie swallowed back the rise of bitterness. "What business are you in, Mr. Beaudry?"

A corner of his mouth quirked upward, giving his features a boyishness at odds with his deadly weapon. "I'm in between jobs right now."

Mattie tightened her grip on the broom until her knuckles whitened. "You're a hired gun."

His expression hardened. "No, ma'am. My gun isn't for sale."

Mattie wanted to believe him, but the tied-down holster told her otherwise. "I won't have a killer staying under my roof."

His eyes narrowed and he spoke in the coldest voice she'd ever heard. "I'm not a killer." He glanced around. "Besides, from what I've seen, you can't afford to be picky."

Beaudry's arrogance sparked Mattie's temper, and she raised the broom as if wielding a sword. "How dare you come into my house and tell me how to run my own business. Get out!"

"I'll pay double your rates," he said, as if she hadn't even spoken.

Money would be of little concern to him. A man like him thrived on the power of the gun he carried—the power of life and death. She met his insolent gaze, which only made her angrier. Raising her chin defiantly, she said, "Not at any price."

He took a step toward her and her heart leapt at the intensity in his face and eyes. "Look, you need the money and I need a room. Simple as that, ma'am."

Simple? Nothing was simple with a man like him.

His piercing gaze didn't waver and Mattie had the terrifying feeling he could see straight to her soul. She averted her eyes, taking in her comfortably furnished front room, from the knickknacks and framed pictures to the needlepoint pillows on the sofa and chairs. For the past ten years, this had been their home, thanks to Ruth Hendricks and her generosity. Beaudry's money would allow her to make a few needed repairs around the place.

*Blood money.*

Mattie shook her head and dragged her attention back to the gunman. "You heard me, Mr. Beaudry. I said no and I meant it."

Something that looked suspiciously like admiration flared in his eyes, then a grim smile lifted his lips. "Whatever you say, ma'am."

He reached back to bring his weathered black hat onto his head. Touching the brim with two fingers, Clint Beaudry left.

"Who was that, Ma?"

Mattie whirled around to see her ten-year-old son standing in the doorway leading to the kitchen. "What have I told you about listening in on folks' private conversations, Andrew St. Clair?"

The boy slipped his hands into his overalls pockets. "I didn't mean to. I was just getting a cookie when I heard him."

Mattie's temper ebbed, and she walked over to her son. "I didn't mean to yell at you, sweetheart. That man made me a little nervous, then you startled me."

"I saw him sitting out in front of Billy's Saloon a little while ago." Andy's hazel eyes lit up. "Everyone was makin' a wide circle around him, like they was scared of him."

"Were scared of him," Mattie corrected as she brushed his long bangs off his forehead.

"Why do you think they were scared?"

"Because he's a dangerous man." She started sweeping, trying to banish the disturbing stranger from her mind. "Have you filled the woodbox in the kitchen?"

"Yes, ma'am." Andy paused, then looked at Mattie questioningly. "Why didn't you want him staying here?"

"He carries a gun and uses it to hurt people."

Andy's eyes saucered. "Like one of them fast guns in a dime novel?"

Mattie laid a hand on her son's shoulder and spoke firmly. "You know what I think of those stories, Andy."

"I know, Ma, but they're fun to read."

Worry squeezed Mattie's heart as she gazed at her son, who looked exactly like her husband Jason, the man Mattie had foolishly fallen for—hook, line, and wedding ring. Thank heavens Andy had taken after her in temperament. She only hoped he would grow out of this fascination he held for gunmen. "Are you going fishing?"

Andy's face lit up. "Gotta. Herman said they were bitin' good this morning. He came back with a whole string of trout."

"Just be home before supper."

"Can I take some cookies?"

"To use as bait?" Mattie teased.

Andy grinned. "Nah. Herman said the fish are crazy for worms."

Mattie made a face. "Yuck. Fine, but only two cookies. And you can take two for Herman, too."

"Thanks. He says you make the best oatmeal cookies ever."

"Tell him flattery won't get him any more."

"I will, but he won't believe me, since he only got one last time." Andy dashed into the kitchen, leaving Mattie shaking her head tolerantly.

Herman was seventy-five if he was a day and had a bad habit of telling Andy more than his share of tall tales. He'd been living at the Hendricks's place for years. The old man had obviously thought the world of Ruth. When she had passed away four years ago, Herman had remained, extending his friendship and loyalty to Mattie and Andy.

She walked across the room to the fireplace and gazed at the shiny music box that sat on the mantel. With a shaking hand, she lifted the lid and the achingly familiar strains of a waltz surrounded her. In her mind, Mattie pictured her mother and father, forever young in her memory, dancing to the music box's melody.

She closed her eyes and her parents' image was replaced by the gunslinger, dressed completely in black, which made the contrast of his green eyes and blond hair all the more striking. Men like Beaudry attracted trouble like honey attracted bears and she would have been courting danger if she had allowed him to stay.

Mattie dropped the lid back in place, silencing the music. She had chosen the wrong man to waltz with, and would never make the same mistake again.

The following morning, Clint Beaudry tightened the saddle cinch on his sorrel mare and drew a hand along the horse's cream-colored mane. He'd spent the night under the stars instead of renting a room above one of the noisy saloons. Listening to the working girls cater to their customers in the neighboring rooms hadn't appealed to him. Hell, for that matter, none of the whores had appealed to him, either. After a month of no female companionship, he should have welcomed the feel of a woman's soft body, but he hadn't wanted any of them.

As he rolled up his bedroll, his thoughts took him to the widow woman at the boardinghouse. Now, *there* was a lady he wouldn't have minded taking for a tumble between the sheets.

Those sparking violet eyes of Mrs. St. Clair's had set his blood near to boiling and damn near set his hide ablaze. He smiled, recalling her ripe curves and passionate fury, and imagined she'd be a lively bed companion if he could get past her self-righteousness. She had even turned down his impetuous offer of twice her going rate. His impulsiveness must have been provoked by those riveting eyes and the hope that he could slip into her room when only the moon lit the night. Just imagining her lying beneath him, her black hair fanned across a pillow and her eyes clouding with desire, made him grow hard with lust.

Sighing, he reluctantly banished the erotic image from his thoughts. It was a damned shame she was as cold as an undertaker at a hanging. He tied his blanket to the back of the cantle and took one last glance around the camp to make sure he hadn't left anything behind—not that he owned much. For the past year he'd traveled light and far. There was little need for anything but the clothes on his back, his gun, and his traveling gear—except for maybe a glass or two of whiskey in a friendly saloon and the occasional company of an agreeable woman to satisfy his needs.

He stuck his boot toe through the stirrup and hauled himself into the saddle, then lifted his gaze to the blue sky and touched the brim of his hat respectfully. "Maybe today, Em."

Since his wife's death a year ago, he greeted every day the same. One of these days his swiftness would fail him and he'd join Emily. Until then, he would pursue the man who had raped and murdered her . . . to hell, if he had to.

The leather creaked beneath his shifting weight as he tapped his heels against his horse's belly. Dakota leapt ahead, as eager as Clint to be on the trail again.

Suddenly Clint felt himself catapulted forward, like he'd been struck in the back with a tree branch. He fell across Dakota's neck and slipped to the ground, hitting the earth face down with a bone-jarring thud that knocked the air from his lungs. Struggling to breathe, Clint sucked in air mixed with mud and coughed. Agony stabbed through him. He managed to turn his head slightly so he wasn't eating dirt and tried to catch his breath.

Warm moistness seeped across his torso and back, and Clint figured the bullet had gone right through him. No doubt about it—he was hurt bad, maybe even dying. What cowardly bastard had shot him in the back?

The sound of a horse's hooves made him freeze. Had the bushwhacker come back to finish the job? Clint painfully reached for his Colt. He clutched the weapon's butt and hoped he had the strength to pull the gun from its holster.

He listened to the person dismount, and through nearly closed eyes he spotted a pair of shiny black boots approaching him. He prayed his would-be murderer would figure he was dead.

"Looks like I got you before you got me, Beaudry," the stranger said. He nudged Clint with his toe and Clint barely restrained the moan that threatened to escape.

The man squatted down beside him and laid a hand on Clint's shoulder, and Clint held his breath. His ruse must have worked because the man withdrew his hand and straightened. He grunted something, then turned around and strode back to his horse. Leather creaked and the man's horse passed within a few feet of Clint. It was a palomino—like the one the man who'd killed Emily had ridden.

Hatred gave Clint the strength to roll onto his back, but not the power needed to raise his Colt. The receding rider and his golden horse doubled and blurred. Violent shivers overtook Clint and the

Colt slipped from his numb fingers. To be so close to vengeance and have it stolen away . . .

Pain ebbed and flowed through his body, and consciousness wavered. He didn't want to fight anymore. He was tired of battling the darkness . . . the pain.

*No, not yet. Not until I make the bastard pay.*

Andy jiggled his fishing line and sighed heavily. He glanced over at Herman, who sat with his back against a tree and a fishing rod in his gnarled hands. The old man's eyes were closed and he could have been sleeping, but Andy knew better.

Nothing was biting, and he wished he'd gone into town to play marbles with Buck and Josh instead. He shifted his numb backside and stifled another sigh.

"Stop movin' around like a hen on a griddle there, boy. Remember, you gotta be smarter'n them trout in order to catch one."

Sometimes it seemed Herman could see straight through his eyelids.

"We've been here since before sunrise and we haven't had a single nibble," Andy complained.

"That's 'cause them critters know we're here. If we stay real quiet, we'll trick 'em into thinkin' we left."

Andy didn't think so and felt ornery enough to argue. "I reckon they took off upstream to spawn or whatever they do."

"That's in the spring, not the summer. Nope, they're down there. I can smell 'em."

Andy sniffed the air, but all he could smell was fishy water and Herman's pipe tobacco. But if Herman said the fish were here, then they were. The old man had an uncanny sense when it came to fishing. Still, it would be just Andy's luck that Herman was wrong today.

The sound of a gunshot nearby interrupted a gray jay's scolding and sent a squirrel into a chattering fit above them.

Herman opened his eyes. "Hunters."

"How do you know?"

Herman removed his pipe and used a finger to tamp down the smoking tobacco in the bowl. "It was a rifle shot and that's what folks use when they go huntin'," he explained patiently. "Now, iffen it was a revolver, I'd be a mite suspicious. Course I remember a fellah once who used a Navy Colt for huntin'—could hit a prairie chicken from a hundred yards."

Andy tried to imagine such a feat, but couldn't. His ma wouldn't even let him touch a gun, much less shoot one. He was ten years old—nearly a man. Most of his friends already knew how to use a rifle and some of them had handled a revolver, but all Andy had was a pocketknife his ma had given him for Christmas two years ago. *If I had a pa*, he'd *teach me how to shoot*.

He glanced at Herman—maybe he would show him how to shoot.

Herman sat up straight and his white eyebrows drew together. "There ain't been a second shot."

Andy looked at Herman, puzzled. "What do you mean?"

"Usually there's a second shot to put the critter down." The spry old man rose and tucked his pipe in his overalls bib pocket, then pulled in his line.

"What're we gonna do?" Andy asked as he copied Herman's motions.

"You stay put. I'm gonna go see what that hunter got."

Andy shook his head. He wasn't going to stay behind and miss any potential excitement. "I'm coming, too."

Herman fired him a warning look, which Andy ignored. He wouldn't let Herman treat him like a baby, too.

Carrying his fishing rod, Andy followed the old man across a path through the sparse woods. A few minutes later, Andy heard a horse nicker and the path opened to a small clearing. Herman stopped abruptly and Andy nearly bumped into his back.

"Damn," the old man muttered.

Andy stepped around him and stopped, shocked. A man lay on the ground with blood staining the green grass around his body. Andy put a hand to his mouth, hoping he wouldn't lose his breakfast.

"You gonna be okay, boy?" Herman asked.

Andy's throat wouldn't work, so he nodded. He forced himself to look again at the man dressed in black, but this time he lifted his gaze to the man's face, rather than his blood-soaked shirt. The boy's stomach flip-flopped as he recognized him. "That's the gunman who stopped by the house yesterday."

Herman stepped closer and scratched his gray-bearded chin. "Yeah, I seen him in Billy's last night havin' a drink."

The stranger groaned and Herman quickly knelt beside him, placing a hand on his chest. "Looks like the Reaper ain't got him yet." He pulled a wad of cloth from his pocket and pressed it against the man's side. "Andy—catch that horse and ride back for help or this feller's gonna die."

Andy's heart pounded in his chest as he tiptoed toward the horse, trying not to scare her. He finally got close enough to grasp the reins that hung to the ground. Leading the mare to a stump, Andy mounted the animal, then gave the horse's sides a kick with his heels. The sorrel leapt forward, almost unseating him. The boy had to grip the saddle horn with one hand as he used the other to steer the horse.

Ten minutes later, he drew the mare to a halt in front of his ma's boardinghouse. She'd know what to do. He slipped to the ground and his legs almost collapsed beneath him. He had to wait a moment until his knees stopped wobbling.

"Ma!" Andy hollered as he ran up the porch steps and into the house. "Ma, where are you?"

Mattie rushed into the foyer as she wiped bread dough from her hands. Seeing her son in one piece, she breathed silent thanks, then took hold of his shoulders. "What's wrong, Andy? What happened?"

"We . . . f-found a man . . . hurt bad. He was shot," Andy said in between gasps. "Need help."

Mattie removed her apron and tossed it over the banister. "You stay here while I go get Dr. Murphy."

Mattie raised her skirt hem as she dashed out to the hitching post. Though Green Valley was a small town, it was large enough to have both a full-time doctor and a lawman.

Mattie soon dismounted in front of Kevin Murphy's office and flew in without knocking. The young doctor glanced up from his desk, his somber gray eyes magnified slightly behind round spectacles.

"You have to come quickly," Mattie exclaimed. "Andy says there's a wounded man outside of town who needs help."

Kevin rolled down his shirtsleeves and grabbed his jacket from the back of his chair. "What's wrong with him?"

"Andy said he was shot."

Kevin met Mattie's gaze. "You'd better get Sheriff Atwater, too. If there's been foul play, he'll have to look into it." He leaned over to snag his medical bag from the desk. "I'll need your help. Meet me in the livery."

Fifteen minutes later, Mattie sat on the wagon's hard seat beside Kevin as they rolled into her yard. Sheriff Atwater rode beside them on his horse, his forehead creased with more wrinkles than usual.

Mattie couldn't blame him for being worried. Gunplay was rare and murder even rarer in these parts. The last time anything this serious had occurred was over ten years ago, when her husband had been killed.

"Where is he?" Mattie asked her son.

"I'll show you," Andy replied.

"No, I want you to stay here. Just tell us where."

Andy shook his head stubbornly. "I'm going." He climbed into the back of the wagon and held on to the seat to keep his balance. "Follow the road for a little ways."

Mattie's gaze collided with Kevin's and she shrugged helplessly. "Let's go."

A mile down the main road, Andy directed them to a turnoff. A few minutes later, he pointed ahead. "Over there, where Herman is."

A few hundred yards more and they arrived at the site. Andy jumped down from the wagon before Mattie could stop him. She climbed down and joined Kevin, who knelt beside the wounded man.

Recognition struck her immediately—Mr. Beaudry. She pressed a palm to her mouth.

"It's that gunslinger, Ma," Andy said.

She nodded faintly. "Clint Beaudry." The severe lines of his brow had disappeared, smoothed by unconsciousness, and his pale complexion gave his features a marblelike appearance. He no longer appeared dangerous, only . . . vulnerable.

Mattie shook aside her sympathy. Beaudry was no better than an outlaw.

"Mattie, I need your help," Kevin said urgently.

Herman moved aside so she could kneel on the other side of Beaudry. "What do you want me to do?"

"The bullet went right through his side, so he's got two open wounds. When I sit him up, I need you to dress the entry wound while I take care of the exit wound," Kevin said with calm authority.

Mattie took the thick dressing from his outstretched hand and helped him raise the stranger to a sitting position. She detected woodsmoke underlying the metallic tang of blood and realized the stranger must have camped out last night. Guilt gnawed at her conscience. If she hadn't turned him away, maybe he wouldn't have been shot.

Working together, she and Kevin removed Beaudry's ruined shirt. Her breath caught at the ragged hole in the gunfighter's side. Blood oozed from the wound, and Mattie pressed the thick dressing over the bullet entry.

"Wrap it up, bringing the bandage around his waist and covering the front dressing to hold it in place, too," Kevin instructed.

Mattie leaned close to Beaudry to wrap the four-inch-wide cloth around his torso, and his long hair brushed her cheek as his masculine scent invaded her nostrils. Her stomach muscles clenched and her chest grew tight, forcing her to take shallow breaths. She concentrated on her task, but her gaze flitted across his smoothly muscled back. A scar marred his left shoulder—a mark of his violent profession.

She hastened to finish her task. "I'm done."

Kevin nodded in approval and lowered the

injured man—right into Mattie's lap. Her arms instinctively moved around Beaudry's shoulders.

Herman and the lawman joined them.

"You figure it was a Colt or Winchester that got him, Doc?" the sheriff asked.

"Probably a Winchester. There's no powder marks and the bullet went all the way through," the doctor replied.

"I heard a rifle shot 'bout ten minutes afore me and Andy found him," Herman added.

Kevin pressed his spectacles up on his nose and glanced around. "If I had to guess, I'd say this man was shot by someone in those rocks up there."

Sheriff Atwater nodded. "That's what I figured, too." He pointed to the sorrel tied behind the wagon. "There was blood on the horse's neck."

"Are you saying he was ambushed?" Mattie demanded, desperate for anything to take her mind off Beaudry's warm skin searing her with awareness.

"That's exactly what we're sayin', Mattie," Herman said. "There's horse tracks leading away from this fella."

Unwanted compassion tugged at her heart. Even a man like Beaudry didn't deserve to be shot in the back.

"I'm gonna follow the tracks, see who I find at the end of them," Atwater said.

Kevin stood. "Before you go, help me get this man into the wagon. We have to get him back to town."

"I can help, too," Andy said.

Mattie had forgotten about her son. With a sinking heart, she realized she couldn't always protect him from the brutality guns were capable of inflicting.

Kevin smiled at Andy. "You can spread those blankets I brought in the back of the wagon so he'll be a little more comfortable."

The boy nodded earnestly and hurried to carry out his task.

Kevin squatted down beside her. "I have a favor to ask, Mattie."

"What?"

"There's an influenza outbreak over in Minton, and I was just getting ready to leave for there when you came to get me. Can I leave this patient at your place?"

Although Mattie had done the same for many of Kevin's patients in the past, she didn't want the gunman in her house. Before she could refuse, Beaudry groaned and his muscles tensed beneath her arms. He opened his eyes, and in them Mattie saw agony so raw she had to look away before his pain became hers. He tried to sit up, but groaned again and fell back against her, consciousness leaving him once more.

Mattie took a shaky breath. In that moment, she'd seen more of the man's soul than she'd wanted—and God forgive her, but she couldn't turn him away.

She raised her gaze to Kevin and nodded slowly, praying she wasn't making an even bigger mistake than the one she'd made with Andy's father.

# Chapter 2

"**A**nd remember to change the dressings every few hours," Kevin instructed.

Mattie crossed her arms below her breasts. Clint Beaudry lay in bed, his face the color of the white muslin sheets. There was little resemblance to the menacing man who'd stood in her doorway yesterday. "Will he live?"

The doctor shrugged. "I truly don't know, Mattie. It was pure luck the bullet didn't pass through any major organs." He lifted a hand and raked his fingers through his thinning brown hair. "Most men wouldn't have lasted this long after losing so much blood."

Mattie didn't know whether to be reassured or not.

"I'm sorry to leave him with you," Kevin said apologetically, as if reading her mind. "But you're a good nurse and I know you'll take good care of him."

She shook her head, wondering what Kevin would say if he knew just how uncharitable her thoughts were toward this patient. "The fact is, I don't like Beaudry staying here, and I don't like exposing Andy to a man who lives by the gun."

"He's unconscious," Kevin reminded her gently. "And in all probability, he won't recover."

She curled her fingers into fists at the thought of Beaudry dying, then hated herself for caring. It shouldn't matter to her whether he lived or died.

Kevin retrieved his black bag from the night-stand, leaving three rolls of bandages along with a couple of brown bottles. He held up the one labeled CARBOLIC ACID. "Dilute this and use it to clean out the wounds every time you change the dressings."

"I've done this before," Mattie said, barely restraining her impatience.

He smiled self-consciously and set the bottle down, then picked up the other one. "He's going to be in a lot of pain when he wakes up and this laudanum will help him sleep."

*If* he wakes up. She shoved the unpleasant thought aside. "How much should I give him?"

"Two teaspoonfuls to start with. As he gets bet-ter, you can give him less."

She nodded.

Kevin rested his palm against her back and she reluctantly allowed him to guide her out of the darkened sickroom and downstairs to the foyer.

"Remember to send Andy for the sheriff when Beaudry regains consciousness."

Mattie pressed her fingertips against her throbbing temples. "I will."

"Are you all right?" he asked in concern.

She gave him a shaky smile. "I'll be fine." Skepticism remained in his face. "Really, I will."

"If this influenza outbreak wasn't so bad, I wouldn't go."

"I know." She reached out and smoothed his shirtfront. He had become a stable influence in her life the last year, even making her reconsider her decision not to remarry. Kevin was nothing like Jason had been. "I'll miss you," she said.

"I'll miss you, too." Kevin brushed her cheek with the back of his hand, a gentle touch that did little to calm Mattie's fears. "I hope to be back in a week or so, then we can move Beaudry to my spare room at the office."

Only a week—she could tolerate the gunman in her house for seven days. Fewer if he died. . . .

Mattie thrust that thought aside and managed another smile. "Be careful."

"Don't worry. As long as I know you're here waiting for me, I'll be extra prudent." Kevin kissed her cheek lightly. "Good-bye."

Mattie listened to his footsteps echo across the porch and down the wooden steps. Then it was silent except for the clock's pendulum, but the steady rhythm failed to comfort her as it normally did. Clint Beaudry's presence unnerved and frightened her. But she'd proven she could survive on her own. She'd turned this place into a boarding-house and learned how to manage a business by herself. She could handle this, too.

Her gaze moved up the stairs. She should go and sit with Beaudry, but the thought of being in the same room with him made her palms sweat and her mouth go dry. Why was she afraid of an unconscious man who already had one foot in the grave?

Andy and Herman entered, and her son asked, "How is he?" His hazel eyes were wide and his face anxious.

"Still alive," Mattie replied. She glanced at Herman, who puffed his pipe as if he didn't have a care in the world. "Do you know this gunman?"

The old man shook his head. "Nope, never heard of him."

"I thought you knew all the fast guns this side of the Mississippi."

"I do, which means this feller ain't one."

Mattie couldn't accept that. She'd seen Beaudry's well-oiled gun and tied-down holster, and both those told her he wasn't a typical drifter. "I'm going to sit with him for a little while. Think you two can find something to eat in the kitchen?"

"Got any more cookies?" Herman asked, a twinkle in his rheumy blue eyes.

Mattie smiled. "I think there might be some left. After you eat, would you keep an eye on Andy for me?"

"Aw, Ma," her son grumbled.

Mattie laid a hand on Andy's narrow shoulder.

"I'll feel better knowing you and Herman are together."

"Don't you worry 'bout a thing, Mattie. Me and Andy'll find somethin' to do," Herman assured her.

"How about fixing the corral?" she suggested, trying not to smile.

Herman shuffled his feet like an overgrown kid caught with his hand in the candy jar. "That ain't what I had in mind."

Mattie coughed to hide her laughter. Herman would rather be staked to an anthill than engage in manual labor, and she often wondered why Ruth had put up with him. She should insist he do some work around the place for his meals, but his genuine fondness for Andy made up for his lack of ambition. "Don't be at the fishing pond too late," she said, surrendering to the inevitable.

Then Mattie climbed the steps and paused in the dim room's doorway. She gazed at Beaudry's still-as-death figure, and the back of her neck tightened as a sharp ache started in her temples. His lean, almost gaunt features blurred, replaced by Jason's too-handsome and too-confident countenance.

Mattie swayed and she leaned against the doorframe, taking a deep breath. Clint Beaudry brought back too many memories.

*Get a hold of yourself, Matilda St. Clair. Clint Beaudry probably won't last the night.*

She'd been strong for ten years—she wouldn't let Beaudry turn her into a silly girl again. Steeling herself against the déjà vu that threatened to suffocate her, she crossed the room to sit in the chair beside the bed, then leaned forward to moisten a cloth in the pan of water sitting on the nightstand. Beaudry's eyelids twitched and Mattie tensed as her breath faltered in her throat, but his eyes remained closed.

She folded the moistened cloth lengthwise and laid it on his forehead. Heat radiated from him and his face was flushed with fever. Unwanted compassion made her throat tighten, and she rested the back of her hand against his whisker-roughened cheek. The heat of his skin created a sudden awareness of the man, and she jerked her hand back.

Twining her fingers together tightly, Mattie rested her trembling hands in her lap and leaned back in the chair. She lifted her gaze to the white curtains that had tiny violets scattered across the material. How often had she sat in this room reading to Ruth, or sitting with her and talking? Ruth had given her two precious gifts—friendship and understanding. And when Ruth had died, she'd bequeathed her home to Mattie and Andy, giving them a security Mattie hadn't even dared to imagine.

Beaudry shifted and moaned, drawing Mattie's attention once more. She removed the cloth from his forehead and rinsed it in the cool water, then returned it to his fevered brow. Her fingertips brushed his thick, sweat-dampened hair and she smoothed back a few strands from his face. The sun slanted in the window, gilding his blond hair and lending him the visage of an angel.

A fallen angel.

She remembered how Beaudry had wrapped his fingers around that leather belt, insolence in his sharply drawn features as his gaze had raked across her. Mattie's stomach muscles clenched and her camisole suddenly seemed too snug across her breasts.

"Stop it," she rebuked herself. It was his fault she was thinking about things she hadn't dwelt upon in years. Things like the feel of a man's whiskered cheek against her palm, the texture of a man's hair between her fingers, and the touch of a man's lips—

Abruptly, Mattie stood and stepped over to the window. Her entire body throbbed with sensual remembrance and she damned the loss of control. Hadn't she spent the last ten years ridding herself of such irrational yearnings? Even Kevin, who had been courting her for a year, hadn't produced such wanton images in her mind. She had to distract her mutinous thoughts before she drove herself insane.

Pushing aside one of the flowery curtains, she stared down into the yard. Jewel, the milk cow, grazed in front of the porch. Andy must have moved the animal's picket line while she and Kevin had taken care of the gunman's wounds. Several hens clucked and scratched in the dirt not far from Jewel.

Living a quarter mile from town allowed Mattie to have a cow and some chickens so she didn't have to buy milk or eggs. It also gave her fresh food for her boardinghouse guests. Not that she had any right now, but autumn would bring a few people looking for places to hole up for the winter. Until then, she sold the milk and eggs and took in laundry, to buy clothing for her fast-growing son and food staples like flour and sugar.

Beaudry groaned again, and Mattie returned to her chair and rewetted the cloth on his forehead. His brow seemed even hotter than it had been earlier and worry gnawed at her. As much as she despised what he stood for, she couldn't wish his death.

The gunman's fever continued to rage into the night and she cooled him down with a damp towel, drawing it across his broad chest and down his muscled arms. She took more time to cool his neck and wrists, like Kevin had taught her. He'd also told her that cool cloths on the groin area helped bring a fever down. Mattie raised the sheet and steeled herself. Carefully, she laid the cool cloth across his masculinity, and her traitorous gaze remained on him a few moments longer than necessary.

*I've been without a man for too long.*

Mrs. Hotzel at the orphanage had always said Mattie had the devil in her—and had punished her more often than any of the other children. Ruth had pshawed such a notion and told Mattie she was merely a woman with a passionate nature, which was nothing to be ashamed of. However, Mattie couldn't bring herself to accept that explanation. Her wicked thoughts proved Mrs. Hotzel had been right.

The clock downstairs chimed two in the morning and Mattie took a moment to sit and rest her aching muscles. She leaned back and rocked as she listened to the man's raspy breathing. Occasionally his breath stammered, and her own heart missed a beat. As much as she hated to admit it, she didn't want him to die.

"No . . . don't hurt . . . her."

Mattie awakened immediately to the man's pain-filled voice, surprised that she'd fallen asleep. She scooted to the edge of her chair and looked into his sweat-slicked face.

"Leave her . . . be," Beaudry murmured, his eyes still closed.

Mattie realized he was lost in fever dreams. "It's all right, Mr. Beaudry. You're safe here," she said softly.

He muttered something she couldn't understand, and she placed a hand on his shoulder. She'd been around delirious patients before and often a human touch would soothe them when nothing else would.

Beaudry's mouth twisted into a grimace and he tried to rise, eliciting a groan. Mattie stood over him and wrapped her fingers around his arms, holding him down. "Don't move or you'll injure yourself further."

Corded muscles flexed beneath her palms and Mattie used every ounce of strength to keep him from thrashing around and opening the fragile scabs on his wounds.

"No . . . have to help," Beaudry slurred.

"Everything's all right. You don't have to help anyone," Mattie said calmly, hoping he would understand her through his feverish haze.

"Emily . . . needs me."

Surprise shuttled through Mattie. Who was Emily? A sister? A wife?

"Em!" he cried out.

"I'm right here," Mattie said, not knowing what else to do. "I'm all right, Clint."

His eyelids fluttered open, jolting Mattie with the intensity deep in his startling green eyes. He stared up at her, but Mattie knew he was seeing someone else. Beaudry stopped struggling and Mattie eased her grip on his arms as her muscles trembled with exhaustion.

Tentatively, Beaudry raised his right hand and his fingertips grazed her cheek. She remained motionless as he cupped her face in his palm, and for an insane moment, Mattie wanted to press her cheek closer to his callused skin.

"I thought . . . you . . . were dead." He coughed and a spasm convulsed though his lean frame. "Em, I'm . . . sorry."

His anguished voice cut through Mattie's defenses, and her chest tightened. "It's all right." Her voice shook.

He blinked a few times and moisture filled his eyes, and a tear rolled down the side of his face into his tangled hair. "God, I'm . . . so sorry."

The agony in his eyes tore a hole in Mattie's heart. She felt a tear burn a trail down her cheek to fall onto Beaudry's bandage.

He closed his eyes, then his hand slipped down onto the mattress.

Mattie's knees collapsed and she dropped into her chair. Obviously Emily had been someone Clint Beaudry had cared for a great deal. Why had he told her he was sorry? What had he done to her?

Mattie had never seen such anguish in a person's eyes . . . except in a mirror ten years ago.

The next three days passed in a blur for Mattie. She only left Beaudry's side to cook meals and tuck Andy into bed. For the first time, she was glad she didn't have any boarders. Her life seemed to revolve around the gunslinger and his fevered ramblings that continued sporadically as she fought to keep him alive.

She caught snatches of sleep sitting in the chair beside him when she couldn't hold the exhaustion at bay any longer. Herman had volunteered to stay with her patient so she could get some rest, but Mattie had the horrible feeling that if she left Clint for longer than an hour, he'd slip away, so she refused Herman's offers.

By the evening of the fourth day, Mattie's mind had grown sluggish and her body ached. However, Beaudry's fever had steadily dropped and he'd gone nearly eight hours without slipping into a delirium.

"Here's the water, Ma," Andy said softly.

Startled, Mattie glanced at the doorway to see her son holding a pitcher in two hands. She managed a smile. "Thanks. Go ahead and set it down."

Andy entered and placed the pitcher beside its matching bowl on the nightstand. Curiosity etched his young face. "Do you think he's going to live?"

"I don't know." Mattie had difficulty getting the words out. "But he's got a better chance now than when you first found him."

Andy placed his hand on the rocker's arm. "Did my pa look like him?"

Warning bells clanged in her mind, obliterating the cobwebs. "Why do you ask that?"

Andy shrugged. "You don't ever talk about him."

Because she didn't want to be reminded of Jason's foolish bravado. Stalling, she dipped the cloth into the water and placed it back on Beaudry's forehead. "No. He had brown hair and dark eyes."

"How did he die?" Andy pressed.

Mattie placed her arm around her son's shoulders. "I've told you before, he was shot by outlaws."

Andy gazed at the pale man in the bed. "Is Mr. Beaudry an outlaw?"

"I don't know," Mattie replied honestly.

"Why are you taking care of him?"

*Because I saw something in him I can't forget.* "Because it's my Christian duty."

Andy shifted his attention to the gunbelt lying on the dresser and Mattie saw envy glint in his expression. "When can I learn how to shoot?"

Fear slid through Mattie. "You know how I feel about guns, Andrew."

Defiance flared in his face and he drew his hand

away from hers. "All my friends can shoot. If I knew how, I could hunt deer and rabbits so you wouldn't have to buy meat. Why won't you let me learn?"

"You know why."

"Because Pa was killed by a gun."

"That's right," Mattie said firmly. She wouldn't tell him his father had goaded the man into a gunfight. "Time to get ready for bed. I'll be along in a few minutes."

"You don't have to tuck me in, Ma. I'm not a baby anymore." Andy whirled around and charged out of the bedroom.

Mattie rose to follow him, but Beaudry's groan stopped her. She laid the back of her hand against his cheek—the fever had finally broken. She breathed a sigh of thanksgiving.

Beaudry shifted and his eyelids fluttered. He opened his eyes, then closed them and reopened them. For the first time, she saw awareness in his expression.

"How are you feeling, Mr. Beaudry?" Mattie asked softly.

He studied her silently, as if trying to figure out who she was.

"You're safe here," she said.

"Where . . . the hell . . . am I?" His voice was raspy, but his tone left no doubt it was a demand and not a polite inquiry.

The dangerous gunman had returned.

# Chapter 3

Clint stared up at the woman's moonlight-tinted face and recalled violet eyes and black hair—the widow who owned the boardinghouse.

"You're in my home," she answered flatly. "Would you like some water?"

He nodded.

As she filled a glass, Clint studied her slim back and rounded hips—hips that would fill his hands nicely. When he'd ridden out of town, he had spent some pleasant moments imagining the body she hid beneath the plain black skirt and baggy blouse, and suspected her curves would fit against his own body just fine.

She turned back to him. "I'll help you."

Her hand slipped behind his neck and she raised his head so he could drink. The water slid down, relieving his parched throat. He didn't stop swal-

lowing until he'd emptied the cup. As she eased
him back down to the pillow, her slender fingers
cool against his nape, he noticed the shadowed circles beneath her eyes. Guilt twinged his conscience.
Nobody had cared for him in a long time.

Slowly, he became aware of an ache in his
side—an ache that became a sharp piercing pain.
He closed his eyes tightly and focused on control-
ling it.

"I was shot?" he asked, damning the weak
tremor in his voice.

"That's right." The woman's corn-silk tone gave
him something to focus on other than the red ants
that scurried through his insides. "You don't
remember?"

He concentrated, shoving aside the curtain
shrouding his memory. The recollection of a man
wearing shiny black boots and riding a golden
palomino slammed back. "The sonuvabitch back-
shot me."

Her lips thinned in irritation. "You'll refrain
from that kind of language while under my roof,
Mr. Beaudry."

In spite of his rage that his wife's killer had
escaped, he chuckled. "Next to you, a cactus
would seem downright friendly, lady."

"My name is Mrs. St. Clair," she said curtly.

Though he couldn't see her blush in the dimness, he knew it was there. He had no problem
calling to mind the color in her cheeks and the violet eyes that flashed with fire when she'd rebuffed
him . . . yesterday? "How long have I been here?"

"Four days."

Damn, he must have been hurt bad. "Bullet out?"

He saw her nod. "It went through your left side. A few inches higher and you'd be lying in a pine box."

*Just like Emily.*

"A man's gotta die sooner or later," he said quietly. A coughing fit caught him off guard and agony streaked through him.

"Shhh, take it easy. I'll get you some laudanum for the pain." Mrs. St. Clair's gentle voice and her soft hand across his brow eased Clint more than any medicine.

"No," he rasped out. "No . . . l-laudanum."

"It'll help you sleep."

"D-don't want—" he coughed again and clutched the sheet in tight fists—"t-to sleep." His wife's murderer already had too much of a lead.

"Sleep is the best way to heal, Mr. Beaudry." She withdrew, leaving Clint feeling cold and desolate. A moment later, she held a spoon to his lips. "Take it."

He tried to keep his mouth closed but didn't have the strength to resist, and the bitter liquid spilled across his tongue, forcing him to swallow. Then her hand slid behind his neck again and he drank more water to wash away the caustic taste. She rested his head back on the pillow and her fingertips whispered across his brow. He caught a whiff of roses.

"Sleep now, Mr. Beaudry."

Her voice floated around him, like an angel's. No—a woman who looked liked her was no angel.

"Who are you?" he asked.

"I told you—Mrs. St. Clair."

He gazed at her fine, silver-gilded features and his vision blurred, softening the severe line of her mouth and the creases in her brow. "*What* are you?"

Her lips puckered as if she had bit into a lemon. "Your nurse, for now."

"And later?" Clint lifted his hand and his fingers grazed her unbound hair and the firm breast hidden beneath it.

She gasped and jerked back. "If you do that again, Mr. Beaudry, I'll throw you out by way of the window." Her husky voice was breathy with anger.

He would have laughed if he had the strength. "Always . . . d-did like a woman . . . with s-some spirit."

Clint tried to stay awake, but the medicine was dragging him down . . . down into a dark cavern. The widow became fuzzy and faded into the blackness, leaving him with only the lingering scent of wild roses.

Mattie's heart slowed its rapid beat as she examined Beaudry's bandage. After his paroxysm, she wasn't surprised to see fresh red blood staining the white material. Now was a good time to change it, while the laudanum was in effect. As she removed the old bandage, Mattie was careful to keep from touching his skin any more than necessary.

When his fingertips had brushed her breast, she'd nearly jumped out of her skin. Her nerves had hummed like bees after their hive was disturbed. It was impossible to deny her unwanted attraction to Beaudry, but that didn't mean she had to surrender to it. Only weak women gave in to such carnal feelings.

Weak like she'd been.

She mixed the carbolic acid and water, and cleaned the wounds. Beaudry groaned softly and Mattie worried her lower lip between her teeth. She hated hurting him, but the solution would keep an infection from setting in. After cleansing the injuries, Mattie attached clean dressings and wrapped them. She tucked the end of the bandage between his skin and the gauze, then re-covered him.

Mattie laid her palm against his forehead—still normal. She kept her hand in place a few moments longer, prolonging the contact with the unsettling man, then she jerked her hand away, embarrassed by her shameful indulgence.

Exhaustion—that explained her actions.

She should go tuck Andy in, then climb into her own bed and get some much-needed sleep. Yes, that's what she would do. . . .

If only he hadn't revealed such anguish concerning the mysterious Emily—now she felt bewildered and unbalanced. What other secrets did he harbor? Was he a Robin Hood in disguise, stealing from the rich and giving to the poor? Or perhaps Don Quixote, willing to slay windmills for his Dulcinea?

Impatiently, she flung her long hair over her shoulder. This insane conjecturing had to be a product of her overtired mind. She spun around and marched to the door, only to pause and gaze at him one last time, but her gaze was sidetracked by his gunbelt. She stalked back to the dresser, then picked up the holster and gun as if it were a rattlesnake.

She couldn't take the chance of Andy being tempted by the weapon. Since Beaudry wouldn't be needing it for a while, she would hide it in her own room.

Right beside her husband's, which she hadn't touched in over ten years.

Mattie straightened slowly and stifled a yawn. After the long days of sitting and watching over Beaudry, standing for two hours ironing clothes was sheer torture. Of course, she could have made bread or mended clothes or cleaned and filled the lamps, or one of a dozen other chores she'd neglected because of her uninvited guest.

She finished pressing the last shirt and flattened her palms against her back, then stretched and popped her spine. If she could only lie down and rest for just a few minutes . . .

Attuned to the slightest sound from upstairs, she heard Beaudry's bed creak. Remembering Kevin's admonishment to get Sheriff Atwater as soon as Beaudry regained consciousness, Mattie called out the back door, "Andy!"

"I'm coming," came his faint reply.

A few moments later, Andy raced around the corner of the house.

"Run into town and get Sheriff Atwater," Mattie said.

"That gunman finally wake up?" Excitement lit Andy's expression.

"He just woke up. Hurry, now."

Andy nodded and tugged his hat down on his head, then dashed away.

She returned to the house and mounted the stairs, pausing outside Beaudry's door to bolster her defenses against his magnetic lure. When she entered his room, her gaze clashed with his piercing green eyes. Her breath faltered and she resolutely reined in her galloping heart.

"I was wondering when you were going to wake up," Mattie said, her tone more brusque than she'd anticipated, then added lamely, "It's nearly ten o'clock."

"Some water?" he asked.

Ashamed of her attitude toward the injured man, Mattie poured him a glass and raised his head so he wouldn't choke. His long hair tickled her fingers and she sternly kept her thoughts from straying. After he'd finished drinking, Mattie settled him back against the pillow. "I need to check your bandages."

Beaudry remained silent as she drew the covers off his chest and folded them down to his waist, high enough that she didn't embarrass him. One look at the glint in his eyes made her amend that thought—so *she* wouldn't be embarrassed. Her fingers, usually so steady, betrayed her and she fumbled with the end of the bandage.

Beaudry grimaced. "You ever done this before?"

Mattie's hackles rose. "Never," she replied sarcastically. "I've had my ten-year-old son change them the last few days."

"Maybe you should get him, then." His tone matched hers.

Mattie bit the inside of her cheek to keep from continuing the childish verbal duel and removed the old bandage. Aware of Beaudry's cool gaze, she leaned closer to make certain both the entrance and exit wounds were free of purulence.

"It looks like your luck is holding."

Beaudry snorted. "You call getting a bullet in the back lucky?"

"It is when you survive and the wound doesn't get infected," Mattie shot back. The man's lack of gratitude galled her. She poured some carbolic acid into the basin and added some water, then cleaned the open wounds carefully.

Beaudry inhaled sharply. "Sonuvabitch, lady, you trying to finish the job that bastard started?"

Mattie froze for a moment. The ungrateful man didn't deserve her apology for hurting him. "What did I say about swearing in my home?"

"Shit."

Mattie narrowed her eyes. If he had any sense, he'd know she hadn't meant to hurt him and would restrain his offensive language. But he was probably so accustomed to people jumping at his commands that he didn't care how he treated them.

A few minutes later, Mattie tied off the fresh bandage and washed her hands in the basin.

Beaudry opened his eyes. "You finally done?"

"Yes." Mattie dried her hands on a rough towel and averted her gaze from his chalk-white face. "Are you hungry?"

"Yeah," he replied. "Got a steak?"

"You'll have bread and chicken broth to start with," she said firmly.

"That'll be fine, ma'am," he drawled.

Surprised by his unexpected politeness, she managed to nod. "I'll be back in a few minutes."

Mattie forced herself to ignore the tingle at the base of her neck that told her Beaudry's gaze followed her out of the room. The gunman could drive a teetotaler to drink.

While the broth heated, she sliced and buttered some bread for him. Once the thin soup was steaming, she scooped some into a bowl and carried the meal up to Beaudry.

She paused in his doorway. He'd fallen asleep again. For a moment she debated leaving him be, but he needed food to rebuild his strength. And the sheriff would be coming to talk to him. He could sleep after that.

Mattie set the tray on the nightstand and lightly touched his shoulder. His hand shot out, grabbing her wrist with bruising intensity, and his eyes flew open, wide and terror-filled. Stunned, she could only stare into his face. What could frighten a man like Clint Beaudry?

Abruptly, he released her and she stumbled in retreat, the back of her knees bumping the night-stand and nearly toppling his food.

"Don't . . . ever do that . . . again." Though his voice was husky, it was also colder than a January day.

Outrage overtook her shock. "I was only waking you so you could eat."

Something flickered in Beaudry's eyes. Remorse? Panic? "Next time, just say my name." His gaze shifted to her breasts and back to her face, and a crooked smile danced on his lips. "I wouldn't mind waking to your voice anytime."

Heat licked across Mattie's skin. She should be outraged by his brazenness, but her body had other ideas. Damn the man for stirring long-extinguished embers to life. "Don't get used to it, Mr. Beaudry. Once you're able, I want you out of my house."

*And my life.*

She turned away. "Can you feed yourself?"

He raised his hand, then dropped it back on to the bed. "No." A heavy dose of frustration was packed into the single word.

She scooted the chair closer to his bed and sat down. After dipping the spoon in the broth, she held it up to his lips. As he opened his mouth, she couldn't help but notice his straight white teeth, a rarity among men around here. He swallowed the broth with a slight grimace.

"What happened to the man who shot me?" Beaudry asked in between helpings of bread and soup.

"Sheriff Atwater tried to find him, but he lost his tracks."

His eyes grew stormy. "Do you know where he was headed?"

"The sheriff said north, to Grand Junction."

He ate the remaining food in silence, and Mattie could tell he was thinking about the man who'd tried to kill him. "He's probably long gone by now," she said. "There's no reason to go after him."

Beaudry lifted his gaze to her. "Yes, there is."

Mattie trembled at the intensity of his voice and the hatred in his expression. She'd been right—he was a killer. Sickness crawled up her throat.

"Where's my gun?" he suddenly asked.

She stiffened her shoulders and met his gaze. "Somewhere safe."

"I want it."

"You'll get it when you ride away from here and not a moment sooner."

His jaw muscle knotted. He was angry, and Mattie wondered why she wasn't frightened. Maybe because she somehow knew he would never hurt her.

Surprised by her conviction, she concentrated on feeding him until the bread and broth were gone. Taking a corner of the napkin, she dabbed the broth from his chin and the corners of his lips. She tried to tell herself this was no different than when she'd fed Andy as a baby, but the grizzled whiskers that rasped her knuckles and Beaudry's steady gaze on her face made that impossible.

Footsteps downstairs were followed by the sound of creaking wood as someone climbed the steps. Mattie drew away from Beaudry and busied herself with cleaning the tray. A few moments later, Sheriff Atwater's wide frame filled the doorway. He removed his hat and held it against his chest. "Mattie."

"Hello, Walt," Mattie greeted too brightly. "Kevin said you wanted to talk to Mr. Beaudry when he regained consciousness."

"That's right."

She stood and lifted the tray. "I'll go downstairs and leave you two alone." She started toward the door, but Beaudry's voice made her pause.

"I'm not a murderer, Mrs. St. Clair."

"Whatever you say, Mr. Beaudry," she said coolly.

Helplessly, Clint watched Mrs. St. Clair slip past the sheriff. She didn't believe him. He sighed. Why did her opinion matter, anyhow? Nobody's assumptions had ever concerned him before.

"You feelin' up to answerin' some questions?"

Clint eyed the lawman, noting how similar every small-town sheriff looked. Most of them were as dim-witted as they appeared, and he generally steered clear of them. But he couldn't walk away this time. "Sure."

"What happened?"

The throbbing in Clint's side intensified with the

rise of his temper. "I got shot in the back by a man wearing black boots." He wasn't going to tell the local lawman about the palomino—it was too rare a breed in these parts and Clint wanted to take care of the man himself.

"Who was he?"

"Somebody who shined his boots a lot."

Atwater's eyes narrowed. "Look, Beaudry, you were shot in my jurisdiction and I want the bastard who did it. You should, too."

Clint eyed the husky lawman with grudging respect. "I wish I could help you, Sheriff, but like I told Mrs. St. Clair, I don't remember much."

Atwater heaved a sigh and glanced out the window. "I know who you are."

"Who am I?"

"You're a U.S. marshal, and a damned good one, from what I heard."

"I turned in my badge a long time ago."

The sheriff brought a sympathetic gaze to bear on Clint. "Because your wife was murdered. And you've been trying to find the man who did it ever since."

Clint couldn't conceal his surprise. "How did you find out?"

Atwater shrugged. "Your name sounded familiar, so I sent a telegram to a friend of mine—Pete Dodge down in Amarillo."

"He shouldn't have told you anything. My business is my own." Clint shifted, and regretted the movement when his side protested.

The sheriff leaned over to adjust the pillows

behind Clint's back. "Take it easy, son. I tracked your backshooter for about twenty miles, then lost him when a hard rain hit. He was headed toward Grand Junction, though."

"Mrs. St. Clair told me." Clint had no reason to treat the lawman rudely, and added, "Thanks."

"Don't thank me, Beaudry. I was just doin' my job." He shifted his weight from one foot to the other. "You try to go after him too soon and you're gonna wind up dead."

"As long as the bastard dies alongside me, I don't care."

"Hatred only begets more hatred," the sheriff said thoughtfully.

"I like 'an eye for an eye' better."

"That's revenge, not justice." The sheriff placed his hat on his balding head. "You once upheld the law, Beaudry. Breaking the law ain't gonna bring your wife back." He turned to leave.

"Sheriff." The man turned back to Clint. "Don't tell Mrs. St. Clair."

After a moment, Atwater nodded. "If'n that's what you want." He aimed a forefinger at Clint. "But I don't want you hurtin' her—she has a heavy enough burden without you addin' to it."

Anger flared in Clint. "I don't hurt women."

"Maybe not intentionally."

Clint stared at the man's back as he left. Atwater's comment had struck too close to home. If Clint had quit his marshal's position like Emily had wanted, his wife would still be alive. Instead, he'd gotten her killed. Unintentionally.

He closed his eyes against the moisture welling within them.

Mattie heard the sheriff's footfalls on the steps and wiped her soapy hands on her apron. She met him at the bottom of the stairs. "Well?"

Atwater paused and leaned on the balustrade as he removed his hat and scratched above an ear. "He's got a lot of anger inside him, Mattie."

She crossed her arms as a chill went through her. "Tell me something I don't know."

"He's not a killer."

Mattie hadn't been ready for that one. "How can you be so certain?"

"Trust me."

She studied his face and reluctantly recognized his sincerity. She had known Walt Atwater for a long time—he'd taken over as sheriff after Jason had been killed. He was tough, but compassionate and fair. But she had a son to think about. . . .

"What about Andy—is Beaudry a threat to him?"

"Depends on what you mean by threat." He shrugged. "Beaudry won't harm him, but Andy's hungry for a man's attention, and Beaudry's someone a boy's gonna look up to."

Mattie understood only too well. "I'm going to have to keep Andy away from him."

Walt laid a weathered hand on her arm. "Don't. I got a feelin' they can help each other." He donned his hat. "I'll be stoppin' by from time to time to check on how things are goin'. 'Bye, Mattie."

"Good-bye, Walt."

She listened to his footsteps on the porch and the faint sound of him talking to Andy. Despite the sheriff's reassuring words, Mattie wasn't going to accept Beaudry's innocence so readily. Maybe he wasn't a murderer, but his Colt told her he was a man who lived by the gun.

And a man who lived by the gun, died by the gun.

Clint shifted on the too-familiar mattress and stifled a groan of impatience. Since he'd regained consciousness, all he'd done was lie around and sleep. At first that had been fine. He'd been overwhelmingly weak and his body hungered for rest. But now it was more than a week since he'd been shot, and all he wanted to do was get the hell out of these four walls before he suffocated.

Mrs. St. Clair brought his meals and changed his bandages, but otherwise she steered clear of him. Hell, it was probably a good thing she did. Though Clint could have eaten his meals by himself now, he allowed her to believe he was still too weak, so she continued to feed him. His fascination with her was fast becoming an obsession. He'd never met a woman more closemouthed or cantankerous than Mattie St. Clair. Nor one so unaware of—or indifferent to—her own beauty. Since she was a widow, he was surprised she hadn't guessed his uncomfortable reaction to her closeness. A man could only take so much of lush curves, even a man in his condition.

Her secrecy about her past gnawed at him, too. When he'd asked her about herself, she'd given him a frigid look that could have frozen a brass monkey's balls. The only information he'd gotten from her was that she had a son named Andy.

He moved and swore under his breath. Nature had a way of calling at the worst possible time. He knew he should holler for Mrs. St. Clair, but even after eight days of her nursing, he felt a keen sense of embarrassment when she helped him with the personal task. Maybe he could handle things on his own this time.

He spotted a boy with hair the color of Mrs. St. Clair's peeking into his room. The kid had to be her son. "C'mon in, Andy."

The boy appeared startled, shot a glance down the stairs, then entered the room furtively.

"How'd you know my name?" the kid asked in a low voice.

"Your mother told me," Clint replied. "What were you doing out there?"

Andy slid his hands deep in his trouser pockets. "I just wanted to see if you were a bad man."

A smile tugged at Clint's lips, but he restrained the impulse. "And?"

"You don't look so bad. Not like the fella Sheriff Atwater arrested for peein' in the street the other day."

This time Clint didn't stop his grin. "Pretty bad fella, huh?"

Andy's cheeks reddened. "He *looked* bad—badder'n you, anyhow."

"Thanks," Clint said dryly. The boy's story reminded him of his own discomfort. "You want to help me up?"

"Ma said you're not supposed to be getting out of bed."

"I don't plan on going for a walk—I just need to use the necessary."

"Oh." Andy thought about that a moment, then nodded. "All right."

The boy stepped over to Clint's side and swept back his covers. Bracing himself with his hands on the mattress, Clint pushed himself up while Andy put a helping arm around his waist. Nausea ripped through Clint as his head swam in dizziness. Sweat popped out on his forehead and chest.

Andy planted his anxious face in front of Clint. "Are you all right, Mr. Beaudry?"

"I'll be fine, kid," he managed to say. "Just . . . give me a minute."

Clint wrestled with his weakness as he debated having Andy call his mother. Finally the light-headedness passed, and with the boy's help, he was able to relieve himself without passing out. Andy helped Clint back to bed, then tucked away the chamber pot.

"What's going on?"

Mrs. St. Clair stood with her hands planted on her hips as she pinned her son with a stern gaze.

"It wasn't the boy's fault, ma'am," Clint spoke up. "I asked him to come inside to help me."

"With what?" the woman demanded.

"He had to—" Andy started.

"I had to relieve myself," Clint broke in, irritated that his private business had become everybody's business.

Mrs. St. Clair's cheeks flushed, which gratified Clint.

"Oh." She straightened her shoulders and fixed her strict gaze on the boy again. "You're not allowed in here, Andrew. Go on."

Andy's mouth opened, but closed abruptly. "Yes, ma'am."

After the kid left, Mrs. St. Clair transferred her disapproval to Clint. "I don't want you talking to my son, Mr. Beaudry. Is that clear?"

"Why not?"

"Because of what you are."

The lady didn't pull any punches. "Anyone ever tell you you're a hard woman, Mrs. St. Clair?"

She dipped her head, but not before Clint caught the pain in her eyes. "He craves a man's attention. He never knew his father." Raising her proud gaze, she said softly, "Please, Mr. Beaudry, don't tempt him with something you can't give him." Then she spun on her heel and was gone.

Clint sucked in his breath at the sorrow her words wrought. Mrs. St. Clair was right—he could give the boy nothing.

Because he had nothing left to give.

# Chapter 4

**H**er arms stacked high with freshly laundered bedding and clothing, Mattie climbed the stairs wearily. At the top of the steps, she heard Andy's voice coming from Beaudry's room and froze. Just yesterday afternoon she'd ordered her son to stay away from him and now he'd disobeyed her, something he rarely did. She marched toward the room, her footsteps muffled by the rug.

"I think all boys like fishing," she heard Beaudry say in a tone that held a smile. She halted in the hall and listened to the man's rich, Texas-laced voice. "When I was your age, me and my pa would spend hours fishing in this little pond."

"Did you catch a lot of fish?" Andy asked.

Mattie's heart ached at his eagerness. Thank heavens for Herman, though he was more of a grandfather than father.

"Sometimes. But even if the fish weren't biting, we'd just talk," Beaudry replied.

Silence stretched out between man and boy, and Mattie was tempted to peek around the corner. Beaudry's voice stopped her.

"Why the long face, Andy?" There was genuine concern in his tone.

"Ma doesn't want you here," Andy replied. Mattie leaned closer to hear the rest of his quiet words. "As soon as you're feeling better, she's going to throw you out."

She drew back and pressed her spine against the wall, tipping her head back to stare at the ceiling. She was the villain in her son's eyes, and by the sound of it, Clint Beaudry had become the hero. How could she explain to Andy why Beaudry had to leave?

"Your ma's a smart woman."

Startled, Mattie peeked into the room and saw Andy sitting on the edge of the bed. Beaudry had a hand on his shoulder in a fatherly gesture that brought a lump to Mattie's throat. He didn't look or sound like a killer.

"She loves you and wants to make sure you aren't hurt," Beaudry continued. "That's what mothers are for."

"Then what are fathers for?"

Pain flashed across the man's angular features. "They provide for their families and build something to leave to their children." He smiled, and Mattie could tell he'd forced the gesture for her son's sake. "And they take their sons fishing."

Mattie backed away from the door and slipped into her own bedroom. She set the folded laundry down on her bed and sank to the mattress. She had done her best to compensate for Andy's loss, giving him all the love and affection she had inside of her. But was it enough to make up for not having a father? She had so many dreams for her son but hadn't come any closer to them.

She stood, her fingers curled into fists of determination. She *would* succeed; she didn't need a man to waltz with during the lonely nights.

"Ma."

Andy's voice startled her and she turned to see her son in the doorway. "Yes?"

"Is it okay if I go fishing?"

There were numerous chores to be done and her son was old enough to do many of them. But she was determined to give her son a happier childhood than the one she'd endured. She would weed and water the vegetable patch herself after she got supper started. "All right."

His face lit up and she basked in the happiness of his smile. "Thanks."

"Be home by suppertime."

He nodded, then scampered away. Mattie remained by the window to watch her son race across the yard to the barn where Herman lived in a small room. A few minutes later the two walked down the road toward their favorite fishing hole, poles in hand.

As she watched them, Herman blurred and was replaced by the tall, lean figure of Clint Beaudry.

Would it be so bad to allow Andy to visit with Beaudry?

She recalled Sheriff Atwater's assurances that Beaudry wouldn't harm her son. Maybe it was time Mattie began to trust him a little, especially after overhearing his conversation with her son.

She put the clean clothes away and resolutely walked into her patient's room. Beaudry's unreadable gaze settled on her immediately.

"Afternoon, Mrs. St. Clair," he said.

Mattie suppressed a sensual shiver at the exaggerated drawl in his voice and inclined her head in acknowledgment. "How're you feeling, Mr. Beaudry?"

"You don't want to know," he grumbled.

She couldn't help but smile, and the tension in her muscles eased. "Let me guess. You're restless, but if you move around, your wound hurts like the devil. So you just lie there, getting angrier by the minute until some innocent bystander like myself walks in and you take out your short temper on her."

Surprise lit his handsome face, then a boyish grin captured his lips and sent Mattie's heart racing. "Either you're a mind reader or you made a lucky guess."

"An educated guess. I've helped Dr. Murphy take care of other patients." She moved to his bedside, all too aware of his masculine interest in her. "And everybody I've dealt with, except Herman, who searches for reasons to sleep, has felt the same way."

"Herman?"

"He came with this place and helps me take care of Andy." Mattie motioned toward the sheet covering his chest. "Do you mind if I take a look?"

Clint had immediately noticed a change in her demeanor toward him. The fact that she'd smiled for the first time boded well for his chances of getting to know her better.

He lifted his arms off the covers. "Be my guest."

As she leaned over him to fold the blankets back, his gaze flickered to the high breasts her apron and plain clothes couldn't hide. All he had to do was raise his hand a few inches and his palm would be treated with the soft fullness of her breast. His blood heated, tempting him to touch her, but he recalled her admonition about throwing him out the window. Clint had little doubt she'd do just that.

"Have you lived here long?" he asked, hoping to sidetrack his lusty imagination.

"Most of my life. My parents were killed when I was eight, then I was placed in the Children's Home in Green Valley."

"That must've been tough." Clint and his five siblings had had two loving parents. He couldn't even imagine how difficult it had been for Mattie, orphaned and alone at such a young age.

"Yes, it was."

Her head dipped close to his and her now-familiar scent of roses tickled his nose. He concentrated on the ache in his side as she checked his wound. Her fingertips brushed his skin and blood pooled in his groin. The bullet wound certainly hadn't affected anything down there.

"What about you, Mr. Beaudry? Where are you from?" she asked in a friendlier voice.

Grateful for something to sidetrack his body's response, Clint said, "Texas. The only time I'd left was when I fought in the war."

"That was a terrible thing," she said softly. "I knew families who were destroyed by split loyalties, and others who lost all their sons."

She rested her warm palm on his chest a moment, and he was afraid she could feel the thundering of his heart. Finally, she covered him with the sheet and ended the sweet torture. He focused on his breathing to sidetrack the delicious sensations the widow had aroused.

"Did I hurt you?" she asked.

His gaze caught her concerned violet eyes. "No, that's all right."

"You don't *look* all right."

She leaned so near that he could see faint freckles sprinkled across her nose and cheeks. A few tendrils of shiny dark hair had come free of the loose bun at the base of her neck and framed her face. Her full lips were pursed in thoughtfulness, and Clint wondered how they would taste.

"I'm a man who says what's on his mind," he began with a husky voice. "And right now, you're on my mind."

Her cheeks reddened and she leaned back, well away from him. "I don't understand."

"I think you do. You're a widow—you know

about a man's needs, and you're a powerful temptation, ma'am." Shocked indignation widened her eyes and she tried to escape, but Clint grabbed her wrist. "Listen to me before you run off in a huff."

"Why should I?"

Damn, this hadn't been the answer he'd hoped for. "Because you should know this," he said in a low voice. "I want you, Mattie St. Clair, but I won't take anything you don't want to give."

"Then you won't be getting anything!"

Her spirited reply made him chuckle, but he regretted it when pain sliced through his side. He released her and put a hand against the wound. "Even when you're saying no, those eyes of yours blaze like heat lightning, tempting even the saints." An ache more powerful than his wound tightened Clint's gut. "And I ain't no saint, lady."

She studied him, her expression revealing nothing of her thoughts. "Thank you for being honest with me, and I'll extend you the same courtesy," she said stiffly. "I may be a widow, but that doesn't mean I'm easy pickings for a drifting man. You don't have anything I need or want, so I'll ask you to refrain from mentioning this ever again."

"Is there another man?"

Her gaze sidled away from his. "Not that it's any of your business, but yes, there is."

It had been foolish of him to believe a woman as beautiful as her wasn't being courted by someone. Unless all the men in this town were blind, which wasn't likely.

"All right," he ceded.

She seemed startled that he would capitulate so easily, but Clint Beaudry wasn't about to pursue a woman who clearly didn't have any interest in him. There was enough gentleman left in him to bow out gracefully.

"I heard you and Andy talking a little while ago," she said.

"It was my fault," he said. "I called him in because I couldn't stand another minute of my own company."

Her lips hinted at a smile. "I can understand that." She crossed her arms beneath her bosom and her gaze strayed to the window. "Andy never knew his father, Mr. Beaudry. He died before he was born."

"I'm sorry," Clint said awkwardly.

"It was ten years ago. I'd only been married to him a couple weeks." Her shoulders rose and fell as she inhaled deeply. "I was sixteen at the time. Jason was twenty-two and the most exciting man I'd ever met."

Clint wasn't certain he wanted to hear about the man she'd married. Especially one she'd obviously loved a great deal.

She turned around to face him once more. "Do you have children, Mr. Beaudry?"

His stomach clenched. "No."

He and Emily had wanted children in the beginning, but they'd been unable to have them. Maybe if they'd had a family, Clint would have resigned his U.S. marshal position and Emily would still be alive.

"If you ever do, you'll know why I worry about my son so much." She paused, and he looked over at her to find her eyes blazing with intensity. "Don't hurt him, Mr. Beaudry, or so help me God, you'll curse the day you ever came here. Do I make myself clear?"

A she-grizzly protecting her cubs had nothing over this woman. "I understand," he replied solemnly.

Her mouth eased into a tremulous smile. "All right. I won't forbid Andy to visit you anymore, and once you're on your feet, I'm sure he'd enjoy taking you fishing if you'd like to go."

Warmth spread into Clint's long-frozen heart. How long had it been since anyone had given him that kind of trust? What had changed her mind about him?

"I'd like that," he said softly.

She cleared her throat and turned toward the door. "If you're going to heal, you have to rest."

He nodded reluctantly, and his fingers curled into fists—he couldn't afford to stay in this bed much longer. The longer he did, the colder the murderer's trail became.

"I'll bring your supper up to you later." She walked out, leaving him alone.

He closed his eyes, and images of Mattie St. Clair dressed in a frilly white camisole and drawers with her long black hair spilling across her breasts bedeviled him. She had made her position crystal clear.

But that didn't mean he had to give her up in his dreams.

Mattie had almost an hour to weed the vegetables before supper would be ready. Removing her apron, she tossed it on a chair and grabbed her wide-brimmed hat to protect her face from the sun. She tied the ribbon strings beneath her chin, then went out to the porch, snagging her gardening gloves from the bench.

As Mattie knelt in the dark soil, the hot sun beat down upon her back. Though she enjoyed working in her garden, she couldn't help but think of the numerous other chores that had to be done, including Jewel's evening milking and the peaches she'd hoped to pick today.

Instead, she'd allowed her son to play while she toiled. She removed a glove and brushed her hand across her brow. Self-pity was a useless emotion. She'd spent too much time wallowing in it after Jason had died.

Searching for something else to occupy her thoughts, she settled on Clint Beaudry. He'd surprised Mattie by speaking so frankly. She probably should have been outraged by his outspokenness, but her feminine vanity had appreciated his honesty. Besides, now that it was in the open, temptation could more easily be laid to rest.

So why wasn't she thinking about Kevin and wondering how he was faring? When he'd left Beaudry in her care, she'd hoped he would return quickly. But now Mattie wasn't certain what she wanted.

The late afternoon's rays slanted across her back as she worked, and perspiration trickled down her brow and between her breasts. She ignored the discomfort, concentrating instead on the smell of the loamy earth and the ripening vegetables she tended so diligently.

The sound of an approaching wagon drew her attention and Mattie shaded her eyes against the sun. As if her thoughts had conjured them up, she recognized the horse and buggy as Kevin's, and her breath caught—not because she was glad to see him, but because now she might lose Clint's company.

She stood and walked over to the buggy as he drew it to a halt. Kevin climbed down and smiled, then leaned over to give Mattie's cheek a chaste kiss. "Hello, Mattie."

"Kevin," Mattie said, forcing a note of happiness in her voice. "How did things go with the influenza outbreak?"

The doctor's face grew somber. "We lost nine, seven of them children."

Mattie grasped Kevin's hands. "I'm so sorry. Are you all right?"

He nodded, his expression easing. "I'm fine, and glad to be home." He glanced at the house. "How's Beaudry?"

"He's going to make it," she replied, unable to keep the satisfaction from her voice.

Kevin smiled slightly, but the gesture didn't touch his eyes. "I knew you were the best nurse in the territory." He glanced at the house. "I'd take him back to my place, but I'm on the way to deliver a baby. Would you mind keeping him here?"

Warm relief filtered through Mattie. "No, that's fine. We've reached an understanding."

He studied her, his intense gaze making Mattie nervous. "Are you sure it's all right? I hated to leave him here in the first place."

She squeezed his slender hands reassuringly. "Don't worry. He wouldn't hurt us."

Something flickered in Kevin's gray eyes. "As long as everything is all right." He paused. "I'm sorry I can't stay longer, but I really have to go."

"I understand." She released him. "Go on. Next time you stop by, you'll have to stay for supper."

"I'd like that." He smiled. "I'd like that a lot."

Mattie watched the doctor climb back into the buggy, then lifted her hand in farewell as he rolled out of the yard.

Clint would remain here until he was well enough to travel. She tried to tamp down the happiness within her, but couldn't. It had been too long since something had made her feel this elated, and she was going to hold on to the feeling as long as possible.

Mattie carried a tray of food up to Clint's room. He lay on his back, snoring softly. His shaggy hair needed a trim and he hadn't shaved since the day he'd been shot, but he still oozed a sensuality that lured Mattie like apple blossoms attracted a honeybee.

*Fine-looking specimen, Mattie. You'd be a fool to let him get away.*

She could almost hear Ruth's voice in her head.

Ruth had not approved of Mattie's decision to never marry again. She had thought Mattie was being overly dramatic, denying herself the comfort of a man's arms simply because she'd made a mistake with the first one.

Mattie shoved the memories aside. Clint needed to eat and she'd have to wake him. She leaned over to touch him, but stopped before her hand reached his shoulder. He'd told her not to touch him, only to call his name to awaken him.

"Mr. Beaudry." His face remained relaxed in peaceful slumber. "Mr. Beaudry, time to eat," she said more loudly. He shifted and lifted his arm, laying it across his eyes. This was getting her nowhere. "Clint," she nearly shouted.

He jerked awake and drew his arm away from his face. His green eyes were sleepy, but at least they were open.

"What is it?"

"Supper's ready."

"First you tell me to get some rest, then you wake me up to tell me it's time to eat. Next thing I know you'll be waking me to tell me when it's time to use the privy," he grumbled.

Mattie almost laughed. "I can wake you for that, too, if you'd like, Mr. Beaudry."

His scowl deepened, but there was a twinkle in his green eyes she hadn't noticed before and her heart beat a little faster. "No, I don't think you need to. Waking to you that often might give me other ideas."

Her cheeks warmed, ideas of her own flitting through her mind. "I think you're strong enough to feed yourself now." She set the tray down on his thighs, much too conscious of what lay beneath the covers.

He picked up his fork as if it weighed a hundred pounds. "I'm not so sure of that."

"Fool me once, shame on you; fool me twice, shame on me."

"What about three times?" he asked, his lips quirked upward.

"Then shame on both of us," she quipped. "I'll come back in a little while to get your tray."

"You aren't even going to keep me company?"

She'd like nothing better, but the ground rules had been laid and she knew better than to tempt a man like him. "I have to set the table. Enjoy your supper."

She turned to leave.

"Mrs. St. Clair," Clint called.

Stopping, she looked at him. "What?"

"You have a smudge of dirt right"—he touched a spot on the left side of his jaw—"there."

Embarrassed, she rubbed the place on her own jaw.

"It's still there," Clint said. "Come here."

She hesitated, then crossed to his bedside.

He dipped a corner of his napkin into the glass of water on his tray. "Closer."

She leaned over him and he wiped away the dirt with the damp cloth while his other hand cupped her cheek. Her skin tingled where his fingers touched and her heart fluttered.

"Were you working in the garden?" he asked, his warm breath fanning her neck.

She nodded, unable to put two words together coherently.

"There, I think I got it." He released her and she straightened on trembling legs. "You should have Andy do some of that work."

"He likes to fish with Herman," she said defensively.

"And I'll bet you have things you'd like to do, too. Instead, you do more than your share of the chores around here," Clint said with far too much perception.

She stiffened her spine. "You don't hear me complaining, do you?"

Mattie hurried downstairs, away from the confusion Beaudry made her feel. Pausing in front of the stove, she lifted her fingers to her face where Clint had cradled her cheek in his palm. She closed her eyes as desire raced through her. Not even Jason had heated her blood like Clint Beaudry had done with such a simple gesture.

Clint was just as dangerous as she'd thought—and the danger lay in his ability to arouse her with a single touch.

*  *  *

"What are you doing?" she demanded of her patient one early morning two weeks after he'd been shot.

Clint's face was the color of chalk. "I'm getting dressed."

Mattie forced herself to remain standing just inside the doorway. She had a feeling her aid wouldn't be well received by the proud man.

She watched him struggle with a boot, amazed that he'd donned his trousers without any assistance. Though she'd often seen his bare chest, the sight of him partially clothed made her heart pound.

He pressed a hand to his side and sank back on to the mattress.

Mattie went to him to check his bandage and found fresh blood. "You've broken the wound open."

"I'm not going to lie in that bed another day," he stated through thinned lips.

"You're only going to set back your healing if you don't."

"I don't give a damn."

"Mr. Beaudry, you will *not* swear in my house."

He glared at her and Mattie met his hostile gaze with an obstinacy that matched his. After a few moments, he relinquished his glower and the corners of his eyes crinkled. "You're more cussed stubborn than my first horse."

"No doubt he was more intelligent than you, too," Mattie said in a bantering tone.

Beaudry's eyes twinkled with mischief. "That he

probably was, ma'am." He glanced down at his bandage. "Is it bleeding bad?"

"No," Mattie admitted. "But I still think it's too early for you to be trying to get up."

"Will you wrap it up tight?"

She knew it would be useless to argue with him. Cabin fever could be ten times worse than any other fever, if it went unrelieved for too long. "All right, but you have to promise me you'll only sit on the porch."

"I promise."

Mattie sighed and set to work removing the old dressing. She found that only the exit wound had broken open, and it had stopped bleeding already. She cleaned it, then rewrapped a bandage about his trim waist.

Overly aware of his close-fitting black jeans, Mattie tried to keep her attention averted, but her traitorous gaze kept returning to the bulge beneath the buttoned fly. She finally tied off the bandage and found herself suddenly faced with his chest— bare except for the captivating triangle of chest hair that tapered down to his waist.

She cleared her throat. "I'll get your undershirt." Opening a dresser drawer, she pulled out the one she'd cleaned and mended—the one he'd been wearing when he'd been shot. She handed it to him. "Here."

Clint put his arms in the sleeves, then tried to lift it over his head. He grimaced and his arms fell back to his thighs.

Without asking, Mattie helped him pull it on

over his head and tugged it down to cover the temptation of his chest and snug jeans.

"Thanks," Clint mumbled.

"You're up!"

Mattie looked over to see her son enter the room.

"You need help with your boots, Mr. Beaudry?" Andy asked.

One of them was partially on, while the other lay on its side on the floor.

"I'd be obliged, Andy," Clint said.

Her son knelt and struggled to tug on the boots. Clint's jaw muscle twitched, revealing his discomfort, but Mattie knew he'd endure almost anything to get out of this room.

"There," Andy announced as he scrambled to his feet. "You gonna have breakfast with us?"

"If your ma doesn't mind."

"As long as he can make it downstairs without passing out, he's welcome to join us," Mattie said, arching a dark eyebrow.

"You're a hard woman, Mrs. St. Clair," Clint teased.

"And here I was going to offer to help you downstairs."

"In that case, you're an angel of mercy."

Mattie laughed. "We'll see if you're thinking the same thing by the time you get downstairs."

Clint took hold of the bedpost and slowly pulled himself to his feet. His face, which had gained some color while he'd been sitting, paled again.

"Are you sure you want to do this?" Mattie asked.

He nodded without hesitation.

Reluctantly, she stepped up beside him and wrapped her arm around his waist, heedful of his wounds. He placed his right arm around her shoulders and they shuffled out of the bedroom. His harsh breathing told Mattie of the pain he was in and she gritted her own teeth in empathy. As they descended the stairs, he held tightly to the banister with his left hand while leaning heavily on Mattie on his other side.

She ached with tension and his extra weight, but the feel of his body against hers diminished her burden. Clint Beaudry was lean, but sinewy muscles gave him a strength she wouldn't have thought he possessed.

At the bottom of the stairs, Clint drew away from her, but she remained close by his side in case he stumbled. She had better things to do than spend another two weeks playing nursemaid to a stubborn fool.

Even a stubborn fool as handsome as Clint Beaudry.

# Chapter 5

**D**espite the morning's coolness, sweat beaded Clint's forehead when he finally lowered himself into a chair in the kitchen.

"You look whiter'n Herman's beard," Andy exclaimed.

"That . . . must be pretty white," Clint said as his head spun.

"You gonna be all right, Mr. Beaudry?" Andy asked, his young face worried.

"He'll be fine once he rests for a few minutes. Go on and gather the eggs, and have Herman milk Jewel."

"Yes, ma'am." Andy skipped out of the kitchen.

"So aren't you going to say I told you so?" Clint asked.

Mattie glanced at him. "Would it do any good?"

"No."

"Then I'd be wasting my breath, wouldn't I?"

Clint chuckled. There were a lot of things to admire about Mattie St. Clair. He watched her mix a batch of biscuits, content to sit in the silence of her comfortable kitchen.

Mattie's slender fingers moved gracefully as she worked. She brushed back a strand of hair from the side of her face, leaving a dusty white trail behind. Her unpretentiousness crept into Clint's chest, lodging too close to his heart. She was nothing like the sporting women he'd kept company with since Emily had died, and therein lay the tender peril.

"Here."

Mattie's voice startled him out of his musings and he glanced up to see her offering him a glass of water. He smiled gratefully and his fingers wrapped around hers as he accepted it. Her smooth warm skin ignited a spark of desire that he quickly squelched. "Thank you, Mrs. St. Clair."

Her smile could have brought a dead man back to life. "You're welcome, Mr. Beaudry."

Clint drank the water, not even aware if it was warm or cold. All he knew was that he needed to find something else to dwell on besides the lilt of her sensual voice and the light in her violet eyes.

"Would you like more?" she asked.

He nodded and she took his glass to fill it at the pump in the sink. Her slim back curved gracefully as she worked the pump's handle, and the profile of her high breasts captured Clint's undivided attention.

Mattie finished her task and returned, handing

Clint the glass. "Looks like you're getting some color back into your face," she commented. "Are you feeling better?"

*Better* wasn't the word he'd use, but it was close enough. "Yes, ma'am." This time he drank the water more slowly. It was cold and fresh; too bad he couldn't douse himself in it. Maybe he could do the second best thing. "I'd like to take a bath."

"You shouldn't be getting those wounds wet." She frowned, and her cheeks pinkened. "I can give you a sponge bath later."

His erection throbbed at the thought of Mattie's hands sliding across his body, caressing and tantalizing . . . No, that wouldn't be a good idea.

"I'd rather take a bath," he said.

"But—"

"I'm a grown man, Mrs. St. Clair, not a little boy. So if your intention isn't to seduce me, then you'd best let me take a bath on my own."

Mattie's flush deepened to crimson, and he knew he'd won the argument. "It's your choice," she said flatly.

Despite his victory, he didn't feel like gloating. His blunt talk had embarrassed her, as well as himself. His manners had grown rusty and he'd forgotten what it was like to be around a decent woman like Mattie.

After breakfast, she and Andy helped Clint out to one of the old rockers on the porch. He leaned his head back and closed his eyes, enjoying the sweet smell of freshly cut hay carried along on the breeze. It felt damn good to be alive.

With a start, he realized he'd forgotten his customary morning greeting since he'd been shot. He gazed up at the blue sky brushed with white clouds that looked like horse tails and whispered, "Maybe today, Em."

For the first time, the words seemed harsh and were difficult to speak aloud.

He could hear the sound of Mattie's footsteps as she cleaned up after breakfast. Near the barn, Andy's call to Herman startled some cooing pigeons on the roof and the beating of their wings signaled their departure. A horse nickered and Clint looked over to see Dakota prancing in the pen, the sun shining off her sorrel hide. He smiled, glad to see his old friend was being well taken care of.

Tranquillity tempted him to relax his guard and give in to the draining exhaustion that had dogged him for over a year. He'd been pushing so hard for so long that he'd forgotten there were peaceful places like this one. Maybe that's why the words were so tough to say today—they didn't belong here, among people like Mattie and her son, who were truly alive.

Unlike him, who had been dead inside since he'd found his wife's body.

Clint shifted and pain arrowed through his side. The man who'd shot him had also destroyed his life. He couldn't let anyone or anything lull him into abandoning his quest for revenge.

Mattie finished pouring steaming hot water into the tub that sat in a corner of the kitchen. Then she added enough cold water to bring the temperature down to a comfortable level. Shoving aside her nervousness, she stepped onto the porch. "If you're up to that bath, it's all ready for you."

Clint appeared startled. "You didn't have to do that, Mrs. St. Clair. I could've waited until you weren't so busy."

"Then you would've waited forever," she said wryly. "There's always something to be done around here."

"As soon as I'm feelin' stronger, I'll give you a hand with the chores."

"You're a patient and a guest. You don't have to work."

"Even paying you double your rate, it won't come close to what I owe you for everything you did for me. By helping you out some, maybe it'll come out a little closer to even."

Sincerity glimmered in his green eyes. Without his gunbelt and insolence, Clint Beaudry was a very appealing man—too appealing. "I never said you had to pay me double."

"I offered and I don't go back on my word." His voice gentled. "You earned it, Mattie."

The sound of her name spoken in his deep timbre brought goose bumps to her arms. How was she to resist him if she turned to mush every time he spoke her name?

"All right, if you insist," she relented. "Think you can stand by yourself?"

He placed his hands on the chair's arms and

tried to push himself upright. Mattie kept her arms wrapped around her waist as his face paled with pain and exertion. Finally he succeeded in standing. She unclenched her fists. "Would you like a shoulder to lean on, Mr. Beaudry?"

"Clint," he said with more breath than sound. "I'd appreciate it."

He lifted his arm so she could slip beneath it, and she helped him inside.

"Would you mind giving me a hand with my clothes?" he asked.

Mattie's heart jumped into her throat, and she chastised herself for her indecent thoughts. After he sat on a chair, she lifted his undershirt over his head, then squatted down in front of him to remove his boots.

She felt a touch on her hair and glanced up to see Clint rolling one dark strand between his fingertips. "You have beautiful hair, Mattie. Soft."

His husky voice fueled her hunger and her breath tripped in her lungs. "Thank you," she managed to say.

"You shouldn't hide it."

"Vanity is a sin, Mr. Beaudry."

"Clint, remember?"

If she called him Clint, she would surely give in to the urge to splay her palm against his muscled arm and feel the heat of his skin against hers. She removed his socks, leaving him clad only in his black jeans—his tight black jeans. Her hands shook and she cursed the man for his blatant masculinity.

"There, you should be able to do the rest yourself," Mattie said as she got to her feet.

"You aren't going to help me take my pants off?" His eyes smoldered with banked passion and the promise of fulfillment.

Mattie forced herself to take a step back, bridling the temptation to take him up on his unspoken offer. "If you need help, I'll call Andy."

He shook his head. "I think I can handle it from here."

"I'll be outside working in the garden if you need me."

"What if I only *want* you?"

Mattie's belly tensed with desire, and she pretended to misunderstand him. "Let me know what you want and I'll get it."

"Yes, ma'am," he responded dutifully with a boyish grin.

Turning on her heel, Mattie fled for the sanctuary of her garden.

Half an hour later, she set a bowl of newly picked peas on the porch. The silence from the kitchen made her uneasy. What if Clint had slipped beneath the water in his weakened condition? Or what if he'd stumbled getting into the tub and knocked himself out?

Mattie's heart thundered in her ears. She shouldn't have allowed him to take a bath by himself—he wasn't strong enough yet. If he was dead, she would never forgive herself.

Throwing propriety aside, Mattie rushed into the kitchen, only to stop abruptly. Clint still sat in the tub, his head resting against the rim. A soft snore told her he had fallen asleep.

She should wake him. So why didn't she call out his name or walk across the kitchen to him? Instead, she studied his tranquil brow and blond eyebrows, his generous mouth and strong jawline, his smooth-muscled shoulders and arms. Her gaze traveled to his bent legs in the too-small tub, which hid the rest of him from her devouring eyes.

"Like what you see?"

Mattie jumped and sucked in her breath in surprise, then the swift, burning heat of humiliation flooded her face. "I, uh, I was . . . You fell asleep," she finished lamely.

"I tried to get out by myself but couldn't, so thought I'd rest a little first. I guess I fell asleep."

"You should've called out," she scolded him, hoping to make him forget her too-avid interest in his body.

"Would you have come?"

"I would've sent Andy or Herman."

"So why didn't you have one of them check on me?"

Damn the man! "I got worried."

A strange light came into his eyes and his expression became thoughtful. "Thanks."

"For what?"

"For worrying about me."

What kind of solitary, lonely life did he live? She couldn't let him see how his words made her want to care all the more for him. "Don't get used to it. Once you're healed, you're back on your own."

"I've been on my own more years than not."

She tried not to hear the forced indifference in his voice, but it was there, as real as the dirt under her fingernails. If only he had remained a villain in her eyes, she could continue to dislike him.

"Could I ask you a favor?" Clint spoke up.

"What?"

"I'd like to shave, but my razor's in my saddle-bag."

"I'll get it." Mattie hurried up the stairs, relieved to escape his devastating presence. She unstrapped one side of his saddlebag and found a razor amid his extra clothing. Returning to the kitchen, she studiously kept her gaze aimed at his face. "Here you are."

"How about a mirror?"

"It's in my bedroom."

"Is that an invitation?"

Aghast, Mattie's mouth dropped open. "Of course not." She took the razor from his hand. "I'll shave you."

"Fine by me," Clint said with a shrug, and crossed his arms over his bare chest.

Mattie had intentionally filled the tub with only about six inches of water so his bandage and wound would remain dry. Her gaze flitted to the water's surface, and from her vantage point she could make out . . . She quickly looked away, and from the smile on Clint's face, he knew exactly what she had been doing.

Determined not to be embarrassed by his audacity, or her own, she said, "I'll add some more water."

Taking the kettle from the stove top, she carried it to the foot of the tub and added the warm water carefully. Once his nether regions were well hidden beneath the soapy water, Mattie set the large pot back on the stove.

He sighed. "That feels better. Water was getting downright cold."

"Why didn't you say so? Herman or Andy could've helped you out."

"And miss having you shave me?" He winked. "Not a chance, Mrs. St. Clair."

She smiled in spite of herself as she knelt beside the bathtub and lathered his face with soap. Leaning forward, she concentrated on dragging the razor down his cheek and across his jaw. The whiskers rasped away under the sharp blade.

Mattie's face was so close to Clint's that he could have turned his head and met her lips with his. He focused on his breathing as second thoughts plagued him. He hadn't expected her to accept his challenge and now that she had, the joke was on him.

She laid her free hand against the opposite side of his face as she carefully drew the razor across his whiskers. The discomfort of his wound was surpassed by the feel of her palm on his cheek. And if the water hadn't been covering his privates, Mattie St. Clair would know exactly what he was thinking.

He closed his eyes, enjoying the sensation while at the same time fearing it. He could get real used to this woman's touch . . . as long as he could finish what she so innocently began.

Sweat glided down his neck. Mattie completed her task and Clint opened his eyes to see her gaze locked on the bead of sweat rolling down to his chest. She drew her tongue along her lips, leaving them pink and glistening. His heart pounded in his ears as he lifted his hand and curved the palm around the side of her slender neck.

Her eyes widened and darkened with passion. She didn't attempt to escape, but instead leaned closer. Her mouth was slightly open and her warm breath caressed his neck. His need before was nothing compared to the heat that burned in Clint's blood now. He brought his other hand to her cheek, barely grazing her peach-soft skin.

Footsteps on the porch broke the spell, and Mattie jerked away.

"Well, look-ee here," Herman said with a grin. "Am I interruptin' anything?"

"Of course not," Mattie replied too quickly. "I was just shaving Cl—Mr. Beaudry."

"Looks like you was doin' more than shavin' there, Mattie." Herman's eyes twinkled.

"Nope, that was all," Clint interjected, easily injecting a note of genuine disappointment in his tone.

"I was jest wonderin' when lunch was going to be ready."

"As soon as you help Mr. Beaudry out of the tub, I can get started cooking," Mattie said, keeping her eyes averted from the two men. "I'll wait outside."

She dropped the razor on the table and scurried out of the house.

"Well, there, Beaudry, looks like you got to start mindin' your manners," Herman said.

"I—"

"Don't you try lyin' to me. I've been around for a few years and don't need no book to tell me what I just seen." Herman waved a finger in his face. "That little girl's been hurt enough—she don't need your hurtin', too."

Clint didn't like the idea of someone taking advantage of Mattie—yet wasn't that what he had almost done? "Help me outta here before I shrivel up like a damned raisin," he growled.

Herman leaned over, then cackled. "Looks like you already done turned into a raisin."

"That isn't funny. A man could be permanently damaged if he's interrupted at a—a delicate time," Clint said defensively.

"Well, there'd best not be another 'delicate time' around Mattie. I'm gonna be keepin' my eye on you."

First the sheriff, now Herman. What was it about Mattie St. Clair that made men want to protect her? Whatever it was, Clint wasn't immune to it, either. Maybe it was her pride and determination to do everything by herself.

Herman helped him up, then Clint dried himself and dressed with the old man's assistance.

"I thought you was deader'n a beaver hat when me and Andy found you," Herman commented.

Clint grinned wryly. "Me, too. By the way, I don't think I ever thanked you."

"No need. I only done what any other man would've."

"Thanks anyhow."

"You jest get better so's you can leave Mattie and Andy afore the leavin's gonna be too hard on them."

Clint's smile faded. The problem was, it went both ways—leaving Mattie and Andy was going to be difficult for him, too.

Mattie did something she hadn't done in years—she laid on her bed in the middle of the day staring up at her bedroom ceiling. After she had escaped Herman's censuring gaze and Clint's smoldering look, she'd circled the house and reentered through the front door.

Her body hummed and her nerves were sensitive to the very air surrounding her. He had warned her, but she'd blithely convinced herself she could resist the attraction between them. She should have known any contact, especially one as intimate as shaving, would only incite more temptation. But God help her, she'd delighted in the texture of his face against her palm, his breath across her cheek, and the slow burn that started in her belly.

She remembered her father allowing her to skim the razor across his whiskers and his fond laughter when she'd asked him when she could start shaving.

Who would teach Andy how to shave in a few years? If Kevin asked her to marry him, maybe he would be the one. But could she be content to wed a man who didn't fire her blood like Clint Beaudry did?

Mattie sat up on the bed and smoothed her hair back, then crossed to the oval mirror above her dresser. She scrutinized her nearly threadbare dress and her sunburned nose. Jason had told her she was the prettiest girl he'd ever laid eyes on, but that had been eleven years ago. That girl had disappeared, replaced by a widow who used all her money on her son's needs instead of a new dress for herself.

So what had Clint seen in her?

No matter how hard she searched, Mattie could see nothing in her reflection that would attract a man like him.

Nothing except loneliness.

# Chapter 6

⟨ ∽∾ ⟩

Nearly three weeks after he'd been shot, Clint awakened feeling stiff, but the pain that had dogged him for so long had decreased to a tolerable ache. He donned his clothing alone for the first time, then shaved.

After he rinsed his face with the cool water, he blindly reached for the towel, and someone handed it to him. He opened his eyes to find Mattie beside him. Her appearance in his room so early made him wish she'd been there all night, too. No doubt about it, that part of him had fully recovered.

"Mornin'," he greeted.

"Good morning," she replied in the same formal tone she'd adopted since their near-kiss.

Her gaze swept from his head down to his toes and back up to his chest. His belly tightened and his blood headed south as if her hands had followed the same path across his bare skin.

"You're dressed," she said.

He smiled and leaned with his weight resting on one leg. "I hear civilized people do it every day."

Her lips twitched, but her smile died before maturing. "It's nice to see you're civilized."

"You didn't think I was?"

"Civilized people don't need guns."

If she'd seen the violence he'd witnessed during his time as a lawman, she wouldn't be so quick to judge. "That's right, but not everyone is civilized," he said grimly.

"They would be if no one carried a weapon."

Mattie was nearly as naive as Emily had been, believing that men were essentially good. His wife had paid the price for her naïveté; he didn't want Mattie to do the same. "Do you have a gun?"

She glanced away. "I have Jason's." She folded her arms around her waist. "I haven't touched it since the day he was buried."

"Living out here alone, you should keep that gun close by."

Mattie lifted her gaze and obstinacy blazed in her eyes. "I've lived here for years and haven't needed one yet."

*Damned stubborn woman.*

"But someday you might."

"We'll see, Mr. Beaudry." She paused. "Are you ready to go downstairs?"

"I'm ready, but I'm doing it myself this time." He'd had enough of feeling like a damned invalid.

"And if you can't?"

Even when she was trying to help, she was the most contrary woman he'd ever met. "Then *you'll* be proven right." He donned his black wide-brimmed hat.

Without a word, Mattie led him out of the bedroom to the top of the stairs. "I'm going down ahead of you in case you start to fall."

Clint shook his head. "Stay here." He raised her chin gently with his forefinger. "If I fall, it's only going to be me I hurt, understand?"

"I'm stronger than I look."

He wasn't used to someone watching over him. Even when he was married, he hadn't been home enough to grow accustomed to another person worrying about him. To have Mattie so concerned about his welfare disconcerted him. "I'm not going to be indebted to you any more than I already am."

Finally, she nodded.

Relieved she'd given in without further debate, Clint grabbed hold of the banister and took the first step. The extreme pain and weakness he expected didn't come and he moved with more confidence. He paused halfway down, his legs and arms trembling.

A touch on his shoulder startled him and he turned to see Mattie directly behind him. "Do you need help?"

Impatience gave him a burst of energy. "You said you'd stay at the top of the stairs."

She shrugged innocently. "I only agreed not to go down ahead of you."

Damn, the woman could twist words around better than a lawyer. "Like I said, I'll do it myself," he said curtly.

"Whatever you say, Mr. Beaudry."

Continuing down, he almost managed to make it to the bottom. He stumbled on the second step and Mattie grabbed his arm, stopping his fall.

"Thanks," he muttered, his cheeks warm.

"That wasn't so difficult, now, was it?" she asked with a sugary-coated voice.

He wouldn't give her the satisfaction of an answer.

At the bottom of the stairs, Mattie released him. "Congratulations. You did it."

Clint pressed his hat back and wiped his damp brow. Though he'd passed his first test, if Mattie hadn't been there, he would have taken a bad tumble. He hated being so dependent on someone.

"The sooner I can do things for myself, the less time you have to spend playing nursemaid," he said.

"I don't mind."

Although warmth flowed through him at her honest admission, he wouldn't allow her to side-track his mission. "Maybe you don't, but I do. I'm not a good patient."

"I've had worse." Mattie walked toward the kitchen, her hips moving with innocent seduction. "You can sit outside and I'll bring you some coffee when it's ready."

"I think I'll have some water in the meantime."

He followed her into the kitchen and located a

tin cup from a cupboard, then began to work the hand pump. Despite the discomfort, he managed to fill his cup.

Clint took a sip of water as he paused to watch Mattie begin her daily routine. He indulged in admiring her slender figure and the thick mass of dark hair gathered at her nape. It amazed him that a passionate woman like Mattie had been without a man for ten years. When she finally remarried, her husband would more than likely have his hands full.

In more ways than one.

Clint's breath caught in his throat as jealousy slammed into his gut. He didn't want to imagine Mattie married to some fumble-fingered man who only made love to her under the cover of darkness. If it was him, he would turn up the lamp and undress her himself, taking his time with each button and prolonging the sweet torture. He wanted to see her pale skin and full breasts in full glory.

Hot blood raced through his veins. *Damn.*

"I'll call you when breakfast is ready," Mattie said.

Startled, Clint hoped she hadn't been able to read his lusty thoughts. He went out to the porch and glanced at his usual chair. Too restless to sit down, he placed his empty cup on the seat and walked gingerly across the yard, a hand pressed to his side.

He stopped at the corral and Dakota greeted him with a nicker. Clint carefully leaned against the top pole and his horse nuzzled his ear, making him chuckle. He rubbed Dakota's forehead affectionately. His horse was the one thing in his life that had remained constant for the past ten years.

"Did you miss me, girl?"

The sorrel tossed her head and snorted.

"Thanks a lot." Clint glanced around the pen, which also held an older mare. "If I had it as easy as you, I wouldn't have missed me, either."

"I curried and brushed her every day, like I do with Polly," Andy said.

Clint glanced down to see the boy beside him. He ruffled his hair. "Thanks, Andy. Both Dakota and I appreciate it."

"That's a funny name for a horse."

"A Frenchman sold her to me in a town called Medora, up in the Dakota Territory."

"Where's that?"

"About five hundred miles away."

Andy shook his head. "That must be near the end of the world. What were you doin' there?"

"Bringing a prisoner back to stand trial for murder," Clint replied.

"You a lawman?"

Damn—he'd slipped up. "Used to be."

"Why'd you quit?"

Clint patted Dakota's neck and shrugged. "Things happen that make you move on."

"You don't want to tell me, do you?"

Startled, Clint looked down at Andy, who was dressed in overalls and wearing a straw hat. "Why would you say that?"

"Because Ma does the same thing. When I ask

her about my pa, she never answers my questions, but says he died doing his job."

"What did he do?"

"He was the sheriff of Green Valley, just like Sheriff Atwater is now."

Clint mulled over this new piece of information.

Andy climbed up and perched on the top corral rail, then reached over to pat Dakota's neck. "He died before I was born."

Sympathy tugged at Clint's heart. He and his father didn't always see eye to eye, but Clint still loved and respected him. "Kinda tough not having a pa."

Andy took a deep breath. "I s'pose, but I don't like to tell Ma that. She works real hard trying to take care of me all by herself." The boy threaded his fingers through Dakota's mane. "But she doesn't understand what it's like."

"What what's like?"

"All the other boys know how to use a gun except me. She says that if I don't ever learn to use one, I won't end up being killed like my pa was."

Clint's gut muscles clenched. So that's why Mattie was so hell-bent against guns. "Maybe I can talk to her, get her to let me teach you how to shoot."

Andy's eyes sparkled with excitement. "You think so?"

Clint laid a hand on the boy's shoulder. "I can't promise. All I can do is try. If nothing else, maybe we can get her to let you use a rifle. A man needs to know how to hunt."

"That's what I told her, but she still said no."

Clint could understand Mattie's protectiveness, but she shouldn't smother the boy. "You let me talk to her and we'll see what happens," he said.

"All right, but I won't get my hopes up." He grinned at Clint. "Ma can be as stubborn as a cross-eyed mule."

"Yep, I've figured that out myself."

Clint and Andy's shared laughter drifted in through the open kitchen window and Mattie stopped to look out at them. Standing by the corral, Clint had his arm around Andy's shoulders. The image burned itself into Mattie's mind and her throat tightened.

When she'd married Jason, she'd dreamed of moments like this. She'd pictured him as the perfect father, playing with his children and teaching them right from wrong. The reality, however, was that Jason had been a child himself, selfish and petulant. He hadn't truly loved her—he'd only wanted her.

The smell of burning flapjacks jerked Mattie's attention back to breakfast. She quickly removed the pancakes from the griddle. Ever since Clint Beaudry had shown up, she found herself wool-gathering too often.

Ten minutes later, she called everyone in to eat.

Clint and Andy strolled to the house from the corral, talking and laughing. Herman came out of the barn and joined them. Mattie watched them approach, her son sandwiched between the two men.

An odd sense of contentment filled her and for a moment she wished this could be an everyday sight.

Herman paused on the porch and sniffed the air. "Must be Saturday. I can smell the flapjacks."

"What do flapjacks have to do with Saturday?" Clint asked.

"Ma only makes them once a week, though they're me and Herman's favorite," Andy said.

The flapjacks disappeared quickly, as did the bacon Mattie had fried up to go with it. Clint's appetite had returned as he healed from the bullet wound and Mattie noticed his lean frame was filling out. His face wasn't nearly as gaunt as it had been, and his ribs weren't so prominent anymore, either.

It wouldn't be long before he was well enough to leave them. In the short time he'd been there, she'd grown accustomed to having him around. She would miss his husky-voiced morning greeting and his damnable pride that got her dander up.

But most of all she would miss the way he made her feel when he looked at her—like she was still young and pretty.

And desirable.

The following morning, Mattie hesitated by Clint's bedroom and glanced inside. It was empty. Had he left?

Raising her skirt hem a few inches, she flew down the stairs. Clint came out of the kitchen and she stopped abruptly.

"Where's the fire?" he asked with a twinkle in his eyes.

Her heartbeat thundering in her ears, Mattie met his mischievous gaze. "I, ah, I was just wondering where you'd gone to."

"Afraid I left?" He winked rakishly and Mattie's bones suddenly turned to custard.

"No, of course not," she replied too quickly.

In two steps Clint was directly in front of her. He placed both hands against the wall on either side of her, imprisoning her between his arms. He smelled faintly of shaving soap and leather, a mixture that teased her, invited her to breathe deeply of his masculine scent. Her breasts seemed to swell, her nipples pebbling against her Sunday dress.

"When I leave, I won't sneak out like a thief in the night," he said in an intimate, low voice.

Mattie's gaze locked with his, and his penetrating eyes grew heavy-lidded and mesmerizing with temptation's promise. Her body tingled, demanding she lean forward against his hard planes and surrender to the ache in her belly.

Slowly, hypnotically, Clint lowered his head toward hers, never giving her a reprieve from the seduction in his eyes or the heat of his too-near body. Caught like a butterfly in a web, Mattie knew they shouldn't be doing this. What if Andy saw them?

She tried to summon the strength to move away from him, but then Clint cupped the back of her neck in his strong hand. Her skin tingled and heated beneath his touch, evaporating her resistance.

He splayed his fingers through her hair, which

she had left unbraided. When his warm lips feathered across hers, she lost whatever sliver of restraint remained. She placed her arms around his waist and a sane part of her remembered to be careful of his wound.

He slanted his mouth across hers, this time giving a little more, and Mattie deepened the kiss. She felt the slight pressure of his tongue against her lips and she opened herself to him, taking and giving in equal measure. She drew her body flush with his and the hard ridge of his arousal pressed against her belly.

Passion flowed fast and furious through Mattie. She only had to lead him upstairs to her room to share the pleasures she knew awaited them. It had been so long since she'd felt a man's touch that she physically ached.

But what if he got her pregnant? She'd be left to raise another child alone. And nothing was worth the pain of that again.

*Nothing.*

She flattened her palms against his broad chest and forced herself to push him away. She turned her head, breaking the kiss that had temporarily stolen her good sense. "Stop."

Clint drew back, his arms dropping to his sides and releasing Mattie from their sweet imprisonment. His face flushed and his nostrils flared in an obvious effort to regain control. "What the hell was that all about?"

Mattie froze at the anger in his voice. "You were the one who started it."

"With your permission."

Her face heated with humiliation. "You didn't give me a chance to say no."

"When a woman puts her arms around me and opens her mouth to mine, that says yes to me. What are you afraid of, Mattie?" he asked quietly.

Startled, she snapped her head up to look at him and found his anger was gone, replaced by concern. "Not a darned thing, Mr. Beaudry."

"The name's Clint."

With her back against the wall, she edged sideways. "I have to start breakfast."

"I already made coffee—should be hot and ready." The glint in his eye told Mattie the double meaning was intended.

She didn't rise to the bait. "I'll call you when breakfast is on."

Before Mattie could flee, Clint took her chin between his thumb and forefinger. "I wouldn't leave without paying for room and board," he said softly, then his mouth gentled to a smile. "I'm not that kind of man."

An hour later, Mattie and Andy strolled into the churchyard in Green Valley. She had asked Clint if he wanted to accompany them to Sunday service, but he'd declined. Mattie suspected he hadn't set foot in a church in a very long time.

She greeted people she'd known most of her life as she walked into the building. Mattie always welcomed the break in the week to visit friends and take her away from the drudgery of her day-to-day work. Today, however, as she listened to the Reverend Lister drone on about the evils of drunkenness, Mattie found her thoughts straying to her too-handsome patient. Then the sermon shifted from drunkenness to temptation in general, and she slouched a little lower in her pew, certain everyone could see the guilt in her face.

Finally, the tedious homily ended and the concluding hymn was sung. Mattie and Andy followed the crowd out into the churchyard, where Andy joined his friends Buck and Josh for a game of tag.

Sheriff Atwater joined her. "Mornin', Mattie."

She smiled fondly. "Hello, Walt. Have you been keeping out of trouble?"

"Can't get into much trouble with the gout actin' up." He chuckled. "Besides, ain't I supposed to be askin' you that?"

Mattie's face warmed. "Now, what kind of trouble could I get into out there by myself?"

"I hear Beaudry's still stayin' with you."

She wasn't surprised he knew. Walt made it his business to know everybody else's business, which Mattie supposed was his job. "He's still healing. That bullet nearly killed him."

"What about Kevin—where's he been?"

She glanced away guiltily. Kevin had only dropped by once since he'd returned, and she hadn't even missed him. "I haven't seen him much. I guess he's been busy."

"I reckon there have been a lot of babies bein' born lately." He scratched his grizzled jaw. "It's just that I been concerned about you, Mattie."

Impatience fluttered through her. "There's no need to worry about me."

"Don't get your hackles up. It's just that I seen how you looked at him and how he looked at you. You been alone a long time, maybe too long."

"I'm not alone—I have Andy."

"You know what I mean, Mattie St. Clair." Walt fingered the brim of his hat. "I'll drop by for a visit later this week."

Mattie appreciated his fatherly concern; Walt was a good friend and she did enjoy his visits. She reached out and clasped his hand. "Remember to come around suppertime."

The lawman patted his somewhat generous girth. "I ain't about to forget." He donned his hat. "Good day, Mattie."

" 'Bye."

She watched the lawman limp away, concerned that he was getting too old for the job. Her husband had been twenty-two when he'd been killed and Walt was a lot slower than Jason had been. She shook her head. When Walt came to visit, she'd have a talk with him, try to convince him to retire.

Mattie heard her name called and joined a small group of women to hear the latest gossip.

The next day after breakfast, Clint said to Mattie, "If you don't mind, I'd like Andy to help me fix the chicken coop this morning."

She eyed him critically, noting his still too-pale cheeks and the way he favored his left side. "Are you sure you're up to it?"

"With Andy's help, I'll be fine."

"Can I, Ma?" the boy pleaded.

Amusement filled Mattie—she'd never heard Andy beg to work before. "All right, but I want you to keep an eye on Mr. Beaudry and make sure he doesn't overdo it. If he starts getting tired, you make sure he sits down and rests."

"Yes, ma'am." Enthusiasm rang in his young voice.

"And who'll make sure *you* don't overdo it?" Clint asked softly.

Mattie quickly looked away, uncomfortable with the compassion in his eyes. "I wasn't the one who was shot."

"You're driving yourself so hard, you're going to drop in your tracks one of these days."

"A little hard work never hurt anyone." She stood and gathered their plates. "What about you, Herman? What're you planning to do today?"

The old man shifted uneasily in his chair. "I reckon I can give Andy and Beaudry a hand, if they need me."

Mattie turned toward the sink to hide her smile. The hopefulness in Herman's voice told her he would prefer they *didn't* need him.

"I appreciate it, Herman. This way we can probably get it all fixed today," Clint said. "Let's get to work. The sooner we finish, the sooner you can go fishing."

The scraping of the chair legs told Mattie they were leaving and she turned to watch Clint place his hat on his head. Her gaze lingered on his back-side as he left.

Though she usually did indoor tasks on Monday mornings, Mattie decided to work in the garden before it got too hot. Her decision had nothing to do with the fact that the garden was only thirty feet from the chicken coop and that Clint would be in her sight the entire time. No, of course not.

With a bonnet on her head and gloves on her hands, Mattie knelt in the rich soil, the loamy smell surrounding her with familiar comfort. Though the garden had been weeded three days ago, new weeds had already taken their place. She tugged them out, crooning to her carrot and pea plants like she would to a baby.

The sound of laughter drew her attention and she paused, watching Clint hold a board for Andy as her son hammered a nail into it. Her throat tightened at the camaraderie that was growing between her son and the puzzling gunman. As sure as she knew her vegetables would grow if they were nurtured and cared for, she knew the same could happen with the blooming friendship between Andy and Clint. But Clint wouldn't stay long enough to allow the seed to germinate.

After she completed the weeding, she pulled some carrots and picked some peas for lunch. If there was time in the afternoon, she'd check the peach trees. A peach pie would round out supper nicely.

Mattie took her bucket and sat on the porch to

ready the vegetables. She popped the pods open and skimmed her finger beneath the line of round peas so that they dropped into the pan in her lap. It would be nice to have the coop fixed up for the coming winter. She'd despaired of having it last through the violent blizzards, and if she lost her chickens, she would lose a part of her livelihood and a food source.

She noticed Clint press a hand to his side as he leaned against the coop. Setting aside her bowl, she stood, determined to make him take a break.

As she approached him, he caught her eye and shook his head stubbornly. "I'm fine."

"You need to rest."

"I'm too old to be mothered, Mattie."

She was all too aware of how grown-up he was. "I'm your nurse, remember?"

"Not anymore. Now I'm just a boarder."

"But—"

"No buts." A corner of his lips lifted in a jaunty grin. "I hope we're having those peas and carrots for lunch."

"Provided you can hobble over to the table when it's ready." Spinning around, Mattie strode across the yard. "Damn stubborn man. Why do I even waste my energy worrying about you?"

"Because you care about me," he called after her.

Mattie's face flamed and she didn't dare turn to see his amused expression. If she were a man, she'd punch him, but she wasn't.

And therein lay the heart of the matter.

# Chapter 7

**M**attie had just finished doing the lunch dishes when she heard a wagon roll into the yard. She glanced out the window and recognized the red-fringed surrey as Orville Johnson's, the owner of the Green Valley Bank. Amelia, Orville's wife, had told Mattie that she would be coming by to pick up her husband's shirts, which Mattie laundered and pressed every other week.

She removed her apron and smoothed her hair back from her brow. Although Amelia was always friendly, the woman's expensive and beautiful wardrobe always made Mattie feel like a country cousin.

She walked past Clint, who sat in a rocking chair on the porch resting before going back to work on the chicken coop. Andy and Herman, however, had returned to their task after Clint had given them directions. Recalling Herman's look of disgust, Mattie grinned.

Conscious of Clint's gaze on her back, Mattie strolled into the yard to welcome her visitor. "Good afternoon, Amelia."

The woman smiled. "Hello, Mattie." She stepped down from the surrey, careful not to step on her hem. Shading her eyes with a gloved hand, Amelia gazed toward the porch, where Clint was half hidden in the shadows. "That must be the wounded man I heard about."

"That's right," Mattie said cautiously. "He's healing quite nicely."

"He looks just fine to me," Amelia said with an inquisitive gleam in her eyes.

Though Mattie agreed with her, it didn't set well that another woman also found him appealing. "If you had changed his bandages five times a day and cared for him while he was unconscious, you might have a different opinion."

"I'm sorry, Mattie. I'm sure it was quite a burden for you to bear, along with caring for your son."

Jarred by the woman's sincere sympathy, Mattie said awkwardly, "Thank you for your concern, but I'm doing fine." She motioned toward the house. "Why don't you come in and have some coffee?"

Amelia eyed Clint again and nodded. "Thank you."

As Mattie led her to the house, she glanced at Clint, and found his attention was also on Amelia. Her hackles rose. How dare he proclaim to want her one moment, then eye Amelia like she was a piece of chocolate cake—*with* frosting? She should have known she couldn't trust a man like him.

She stopped so suddenly Amelia almost bumped into her. Pasting on a sweet smile, Mattie said, "Amelia, I'd like you to meet Clint Beaudry. Mr. Beaudry, this is *Mrs.* Amelia Johnson, the banker's *wife*."

Clint put two fingers to the brim of his hat. "Mrs. Johnson."

"Mr. Beaudry," Amelia said. As she turned away from him, Mattie spotted something akin to desperation in the woman's eyes. "On second thought, I should get right back. If Orville comes home and I'm not there, he'll have a fit." She laughed nervously.

Puzzled by her abrupt change of mind, Mattie said, "I'll get Orville's things." She went inside to retrieve the finished laundry. On her return, her arms full, she turned to use her shoulder to open the screen door. Clint's low voice made her pause, and Mattie leaned closer to listen.

"Does he know?" Clint asked Amelia.

"No, and I'd like to keep it that way," the woman said in a husky voice.

What was going on? Did Clint and Amelia know each other?

"I won't tell him. But he's bound to find out sooner or later," he said. "It'd be best coming from you."

What would be best coming from Amelia? Was there something between her and Clint? How could there be? Clint had only arrived in town the day before he was shot.

"I don't know what he'll do when he finds out," Amelia said, and Mattie detected fear in her tone.

Peeking out, Mattie saw Clint step over to stand in front of the woman. "If he loves you, he won't care."

"You don't know Orville."

Clint put his arms around Amelia and jealousy punched the air from Mattie's lungs. They obviously knew each other well. An odd sense of betrayal cut her to the bone. Yet how could she fault Clint for his attraction to Amelia? The woman was young, with nice clothes and smooth, creamy skin. Mattie glanced down at her blunt fingernails and rough, chapped skin, then ran a palm across her patched and faded dress. What man *wouldn't* choose fresh Amelia over careworn Mattie?

She stepped a few feet back into the house and called out with forced cheerfulness, "I think I have all of Orville's things."

Mattie pushed the door open and stepped onto the porch, not surprised to see Clint and Amelia standing far apart. Clearly, they didn't want her to know about their . . . acquaintance.

"Here you are." Mattie held out the stack to Amelia.

"I'll take it," Clint volunteered, taking the pile from her arms.

"Thank you," Amelia said, her face pale. She dug into her reticule and handed Mattie some money. "I'll come by next week with another load."

Mattie tucked the coins into her dress pocket and merely nodded. She crossed her arms and watched with narrowed eyes as Clint escorted Amelia to her carriage. She didn't like the churning in her stomach, any more than she liked the way Clint's hands rested on Amelia's waist as he helped her into the buggy. Why should she care that the two of them wanted their relationship kept a secret?

She tried to tell herself it was none of her business, yet she couldn't deny the ache of betrayal deep inside, any more than she could deny the hunger that Clint had awakened.

The carriage rolled down the driveway and Clint walked back to join Mattie. She waited for him to explain the relationship between him and Amelia, but the silence stretched out, broken only by the cawing of a crow and the cackling of the chickens.

Mattie's fingers curled tighter into her palms. What did she expect? Clint had been a mystery ever since he'd arrived, remaining reticent about his past.

And wasn't that the way she wanted it? The more she learned about him, the more she lowered her guard against him. It was better to remain strangers to one another.

"Hey, Mr. Beaudry. When're you comin' back to help us?" Andy called out.

Clint grinned and etched lines appeared at the corners of his eyes, showing her he was a man who had laughed and smiled often in the past.

"I'm ready right now," he hollered back.

Mattie opened her mouth to warn him to be

careful but stopped herself. Instead, she glanced at him and their gazes locked.

"I will." Clint winked.

Flustered, Mattie looked away. It was disconcerting to have someone read her mind, especially him. She hurried into the house, afraid of what else he might see.

Mattie's feet carried her to the hearth. Lifting a hand, she ran her finger lightly over the music box's smooth surface. She raised the lid and the gentle strains of the familiar waltz encircled her.

She closed her eyes, picturing her mother and father waltzing in their small cabin. The love they'd shared had been more valuable than anything money could buy.

Opening her eyes, she snapped the lid shut. That had been a long time ago—when she had still believed in love and promises.

The moment Clint rolled over to get out of bed, he knew he had overdone it with the chicken coop yesterday. It wasn't just his healing wound that ached, but muscles he'd rarely used in the past year were also stiff. He'd forgotten how strenuous manual labor could be.

He drew on his clothes, then splashed water on his face and lathered his whiskers with soap. As he shaved, he intoned quietly, "Maybe today, Em."

*But I hope not.*

The thought surprised him. He'd chased after death for so long, but now there was a stronger will to live—and he knew why.

"Breakfast is almost ready," Mattie called from downstairs.

"I'll be down in a minute." Clint finished shaving, and finger-combed his hair, then joined Mattie in the kitchen.

"Good morning," Mattie said as she spooned scrambled eggs onto four plates.

"Morning." He inhaled appreciatively and smiled. "Smells real good, Mattie."

Pink flushed her cheeks. "Thank you. Why don't you sit down before it gets cold? Andy and Herman'll be here in a minute."

As if they'd been waiting for their cue, the boy and old man came through the doorway.

"The chicken coop didn't leak at all last night," Andy said, plopping onto his chair.

"Did it rain?" Clint asked.

"Buckets. Didn't you hear it?"

Surprised he'd slept through a rainstorm, Clint shrugged. "I must've been tired."

"After all the work you did, I'm not surprised," Mattie said. She took her seat and they bowed their heads to say grace.

"Amen," Clint murmured, remembering himself as a boy surrounded by his own family. It left him feeling oddly bereft.

"Me and Herman are goin' fishing, Mr. Beaudry. You want to go with us?" Andy asked.

Clint glanced at Mattie. "Did you ask your mother first?"

Andy's expression fell as he turned to Mattie. "Can I, Ma?"

"Sure, you worked hard yesterday. Just be home by lunch."

Clint suspected Mattie would be doing Andy's tasks as well as her own this morning. When he'd been Andy's age, he'd helped his pa from sunup to sundown most every day. Once or twice a week, his father would reward him and his brothers with an afternoon of fishing. Clint had fond memories of those days, listening to the lazy buzz of the flies and the odd rattling of grasshoppers' wings. He could almost smell the hot summer days, the thick rich odor of dirt and green grass and pond water.

"Do you want to go?" Andy asked Clint again.

Startled out of his memories, he shook his head. "No, thanks. I think I'll stick around this morning and see if your ma needs some help."

Andy's expression dimmed and Clint knew he'd hit his target. "Maybe I should, too," the boy said reluctantly.

"I think that'd be a right fine idea, Andy."

Mattie glanced at Clint, then her son. "I could use some help picking peaches. I'd planned to do it yesterday."

Indecision spread across Andy's face. "Well, I suppose I could give you a hand."

"I will, too," Clint volunteered.

Herman had the look of a mouse caught in a trap and he stood, pushing away his empty plate. "With the three of ya workin', ya won't be needin' me."

"I think a fourth helper would come in handy. How about you, Mattie?"

Her eyes twinkled mischievously. "It would make the job go faster."

The old man dropped back into his chair with a heavy sigh.

"What do you say after we finish with the peaches, we all go fishing for an hour or so?" Clint suggested.

Andy and Herman brightened considerably.

"I think you just won them over," Mattie said.

Clint leveled his gaze on her. "How about you?"

Flustered, Mattie drew her napkin across her lips. "No, that's all right. I have other things to do."

"If you don't go, none of us can. You just tell us what needs to be done, and we'll give you a hand so you can go with us."

She shuddered. "I don't like worms."

"I'll bait your hook," Clint said with a crooked grin.

She met his gaze squarely and accepted his dare. "Only if I don't have to clean anything I catch."

"What do you think, Andy? Will you clean your ma's fish?" Clint asked, keeping his eyes on Mattie.

"Sure, though I bet she doesn't catch anything," Andy said.

"I wouldn't be so quick on that bet, young man," Mattie said. "When I was younger than you, I caught Fred."

"Who's Fred?" Andy asked.

"He was the biggest and oldest fish in the pond. Smartest one, too." Mattie looked at Herman. "Isn't that right?"

Herman chuckled. "Your ma's right, Andy. Everyone in Green Valley was out to get him, but she was the one who caught him when she wasn't much bigger than old Fred herself."

"My father used to take me," she said quietly. "My mother used to come sometimes, too, and we'd make a day of it." Specters of the past flitted through Mattie's eyes, and Clint could see the effort it took her to smile. "That was a long time ago."

The sadness in her face touched him. Mattie had endured more than her share of heartache.

But he had no right offering her sympathy. He had a killer to catch—a vow to keep—and he would be leaving here soon to do it. He'd already been at Mattie's too long.

She stood and gathered the dirty dishes. "I'll clean these if you three will get the pails from the barn."

"Sounds like a good deal to me," Clint said.

"I'd rather be fishin'," Herman muttered.

Clint's lips twitched, but he wasn't about to let the older man out of doing his share around here. Mattie fed him and gave him a place to live—he owed her for that. By the looks of it, he was a member of the family, and family were supposed to help each other out and take care of one another.

Guilt caught him off guard—he'd failed to do that for his own wife.

Mattie placed her old straw hat on her head, wishing she had one of Amelia's fashionable ones.

Sighing, she knew wishing for the impossible was a waste of time. She decided not to wear her gloves, preferring to feel the softness of the peaches' velvet skin as she picked the fruit.

It would be odd to have company in the small orchard. She'd worked alone most of her life, even after she'd married Jason. He'd rarely been home, leaving her to take care of their garden and house by herself. When Andy was born, she'd had Ruth, but the older woman had been bedridden and unable to help Mattie with her infant son. Though Ruth had offered advice—more than her share— the burden was on Mattie's shoulders, just as it always had been.

Then came Clint Beaudry, who insisted on helping her with her chores and getting her son and Herman to do the same. No one had been so concerned about her welfare since her parents had died. Her throat tightened, but her heart felt lighter than it had in years.

The thought of fishing for the first time in twenty years also brought a rare bubble of excitement. How had Clint known she would enjoy such a simple pleasure?

With a spring in her step, Mattie left the house and joined Andy, Clint, and Herman, who stood by the corral with pails in their hands. As she approached them, Clint lifted his head. His steady gaze seared her clear down to her pantaloons.

"Everyone ready?" she asked with a breathy voice.

"Lead on, pretty lady," Clint teased.

Mattie led the way, grateful Clint couldn't see the heat in her cheeks. As soon as they arrived at the small orchard, Clint assigned each of them two trees. There was no doubt he was a man who was accustomed to giving orders and having them followed without question.

She reached up and plucked a gold and red peach from the tree. The smell of the fruit rose around her and she inhaled deeply. She loved the scent of growing things, whether it be the sweetest flower or a patch of skunkweed. It reminded her of the eternal rhythms of life—the seed germinating, the young plant burrowing through the soil to reach for the sun, then growing healthy and strong under the warm rays.

Mattie picked another peach and glanced at her son, who was growing healthy and strong just like her peach trees. She wanted to give him so much, especially the time to laugh and enjoy life. She didn't want him to work from dawn to dusk as she'd done in the orphanage.

"It looks like you have a good crop this year, Mattie," Clint remarked.

She touched one of the tree's branches. "Nearly ten years ago, when they were barely as big as a twig, I spent a lot of time here, keeping the weeds from choking them and giving them water when they looked thirsty. After they got big enough to fend for themselves, I didn't need to do as much."

"They must feel like your children."

Mattie thought about that for a moment, and

realized Clint was the first person to understand. "Yes, they do."

Clint grinned and returned to his task.

Mattie allowed her appreciative gaze to move across his black-clad figure. The dark trousers molded to his backside and his shirt was stretched taut across his shoulders as he reached for a ripe peach. His shaggy hair beneath the black wide-brimmed hat hung past his collar, giving him a raw, untamed appearance that suited him. Although he once again looked like the man who'd first come to her door asking for a room, her fear of him had disappeared. And it wasn't simply because he wasn't wearing his holster and revolver. She'd seen the person beneath—the man who repaired chicken coops and picked peaches.

Mattie checked on Andy and spotted him in one of the trees, balancing on a limb eight feet above the ground. Her breath caught in her chest and her heart skipped one beat, then two. "Andy! Get down from there!"

"I couldn't reach them," he called back.

Mattie's knees trembled. "I don't care. Get down from there right now!"

The boy reluctantly began to climb down.

Clint laid his hand on Mattie's arm. "He's just doing what boys always do."

Anger sparked through her. "Trying to kill himself?"

He shook his head calmly—too calmly. "Finding out what he can and can't do. Every boy has to get a few cuts and bruises in order to learn his limits. That way he won't get hurt even worse when he's older."

Mattie kept her eyes on her son, willing him to move down the tree slowly and carefully. "I don't want Andy to ever get hurt."

"If you raise him to know right from wrong, he'll be fine. Just let him be a boy."

She risked a quick glance away from Andy, and put a heavy dose of sarcasm in her voice. "I suppose that includes him learning how to use guns, too."

Clint met her gaze unflinchingly. "That's right."

Bitter anger filled her—she'd been blinded by her attraction to him. "You haven't changed, have you? You're still the same gunslinger you were before you were shot."

He stared at her, no emotion in his chiseled face. "I never claimed to be anybody else."

Tears burned in Mattie's eyes, but she refused to let him see them. Andy made it safely back on the ground and relief made her light-headed. "What have I told you about climbing trees?"

The boy met her gaze, and in his eyes Mattie read defiance. "You wanted me to pick peaches."

Andy's insolence startled Mattie, then made her angry. "Don't sass me, Andrew Jason St. Clair."

"I'm sorry."

She didn't hear any repentance in his tone. With helpless frustration, she grabbed his shoulders and barely restrained herself from shaking him. "Don't you ever do that again, do you understand?"

Andy's lips thinned, but he nodded.

Mattie released him and her son moved back to his tree, his shoulders straight and his lower lip stiff.

"He'll do it again," Clint said.

Mattie yanked a peach off the tree. "Not if he knows what's good for him."

"You can't stop him. You can only be there to catch him when he falls."

Mattie whirled to face him, fury pulsing through her. "Don't you dare tell me how to raise my own son. I don't need you or anyone else telling me what to do."

She turned away from him and continued plucking peaches. Her buoyant spirits had disappeared, trampled by anger and doubts.

Clint's hand on her shoulder halted her in mid-motion. "You've done a fine job, Mattie."

She expected him to add something else. Instead, he squeezed her shoulder gently, then withdrew, leaving her feeling empty and alone.

# Chapter 8

❧

"**Y**ou gonna make a peach pie for supper tonight, Ma?" Andy asked as they ate dinner.

Mattie shook her head somberly. "No."

Both Andy and Herman stared at her as if she'd just kicked a puppy.

"I'm going to make *three* pies." She didn't bother to hide her smile.

Andy cheered and Herman grinned.

Mattie glanced at Clint, who'd been unusually quiet since their confrontation in the orchard. Maybe she had overreacted, but Andy was all she had.

"Do you like peach pie, Clint?" she asked.

He lifted his gaze and his green eyes glittered, making her stomach flutter. The man knew just how to use those devastating eyes to set her pulse racing. Did other women fall prey to him so easily?

"Almost as much as I like fishing," he said. "The deal was we'd help you pick peaches if you went fishing with us."

Mattie fingered her napkin. She wanted nothing more than to spend a carefree afternoon, but she had responsibilities. "I've got to take care of the peaches. Besides, I have to make pies for supper."

"You mean you're going back on a promise? What kind of example are you setting for Andy?" Clint asked with exaggerated disbelief.

He had her boxed in and they both knew it.

"Yeah, Ma, you did say so." Andy twisted the knife a little deeper into her conscience.

The hopefulness in his young face tipped the scales and Mattie nodded reluctantly. "All right, but if the pies aren't done tonight, it won't be my fault."

"Pies can wait, fish can't." Clint winked at her, sending her heartbeat into a flat-out gallop.

She reminded herself he was a gunman who didn't see anything wrong with teaching a little boy how to shoot, that he lived a life of violence, and most importantly, that he would be leaving soon. One brick at a time, she must build a wall around her heart that even Clint's teasing couldn't penetrate.

Mattie stood to collect the plates, but Clint beat her to the task as he piled his dish atop Andy's, then picked up Herman's.

"You go skin the peaches," he said.

"I thought you said—"

"If you don't make those pies before you go, you're going to worry about them like a dog worrying a bone and you won't be able to relax." He gave her a gentle nudge. "Go make your pies and us men will do the dishes."

Herman snorted.

"Huh?" Andy asked.

"You heard me," Clint said firmly. "Come on, let's help your mother so she can have some fun, too."

Unexpected tears stung Mattie's eyes. Nobody had ever cared if she had fun or not.

Nobody until Clint.

Make that *two* very tall, very solid brick walls around her heart.

Clint's side throbbed, but it was tolerable and he wasn't about to spoil Mattie's afternoon by canceling or complaining. Sitting under a tree in the late summer with a fishing pole in hand wouldn't be too strenuous.

He glanced at Mattie walking in front him, her arms swinging loosely at her sides and her backside swaying enough to kick his imagination into gear. Not that he needed a whole lot of incentive to start picturing her in nothing but a smile. He'd painted that portrait hundreds of times in his mind, and each time it brought the same inevitable reaction.

Lust, pure and simple.

Or *was* it that pure and simple? It wasn't just her

body that attracted him, though it was a damned good beginning.

Her tireless energy amazed and fascinated him. Before they left, she'd made three pies in less than an hour, ready to bake when they got back home.

After all the work she'd done that day, she still carried her shoulders erect and moved with the willowy grace of one of her peach trees bowing in a gentle breeze. He'd bet she brought that same energy to lovemaking, too.

Clint carried Mattie's fishing pole with his as the four of them walked down the path to the pond. She and Herman led the way, while Andy walked beside Clint. He recognized the boy's thirst for a father, and even though he wouldn't be here much longer, Clint felt a certain paternal protectiveness toward him. Before he left, he hoped to teach Andy to help out his ma and do his chores before playing. There was no doubt Mattie was a good mother to the boy, but he couldn't understand why she spoiled the kid.

"Here it is," Herman announced. "Home of Fred number two."

"Looks like I'll have to show you all how it's done," Mattie said with a saucy grin.

Her violet eyes danced with mischief and Clint marveled at the carefree change in her. He couldn't help but smile at her playfulness.

He handed her a fishing pole, then dug into the can of worms Andy had brought with him. His fingers closed around a plump juicy one and he held it up to Mattie. "Here you go."

She wrinkled her delicate nose and took a step back. "Part of our agreement was that someone had to bait my hook."

"I'll teach you how to do it," Clint offered.

"I already know *how*, it's just that I *won't*."

Andy rolled his eyes. "Aw, Ma, don't be such a baby."

"I'm not. It's just that I . . ." She shrugged awkwardly. "Feel sorry for the worm."

"A worm don't feel nothin', Mattie," Herman said.

"How do you know? Have you ever asked one?"

"If you ain't the most dang-blasted softhearted woman I ever met." There was unmistakable fondness in Herman's gruff tone.

Clint reached for her line. "Give me your hook."

She handed it to him, then turned away. Mattie's vulnerability grabbed at his heart, surprising him with the strength of the tug. He'd already seen through her disguise as a tough-as-nails widow, but he hadn't realized the extent of her compassion and sensitivity. Or his inability to steel his own heart against it.

He wrapped the worm about the hook. "You can look now."

Mattie quickly tossed the line into the water, clearly not wanting to see the sacrificial worm. She lowered herself to the ground, sitting cross-legged and keeping a close watch on the cork connected to her line.

Smiling, Clint found another worm in the dirt-filled tin can and baited his hook, then he joined

Mattie, resting his back against an oak tree's wide trunk. Herman and Andy moved to a place about fifteen feet away, whispering anxiously to one another.

Clint leaned toward Mattie and spoke close to her ear. "I'll bet they have a secret hole where they figure old Fred is hiding."

"Fred the Second," she corrected. "My mother fried up Fred number one twenty years ago."

He chuckled. "That's right. Mattie the Magnificent caught him."

She blushed, but she met his gaze without hesitation. "My father used to call me that."

"You loved him a lot, didn't you?" he asked quietly.

"Yes." She smiled sadly. "I overheard you telling Andy that fathers were for taking their sons fishing." She turned her attention to her line. "A father also takes his daughters fishing."

Her soft words made Clint's breath falter. And in that moment, he made a silent vow that if he had children, he'd take them all—sons and daughters—fishing.

Clint watched a pair of mallards at the other end of the pond, their tails pointed skyward as they nibbled on the plants beneath the water's surface. A blue heron flew in, landing with ungainly grace in the shallows not far from the ducks.

The smell of honeysuckle and pond lilies drifted to Clint's nose, and an occasional whiff of Mattie's rose scent curled through his insides. Cicadas buzzed shrilly, their voices dwindling to nothing, then starting the cacophony all over again. A red-wing blackbird, sounding like a rusty gate, warned another bird away from his stand of pussy willows.

In this peaceful setting, Clint found it hard to imagine that his wife had been killed in such a gruesome manner. But she had, and he owed her for not being there . . . for not protecting her like he had promised.

Restlessness skated up and down his spine. The killer's trail was already three weeks cold.

So why did the thought of leaving Mattie and her small family make his insides feel chilly and alone? Like something vital would wither up and die? For over a year he'd lived on grief and the taste of vengeance, but now it seemed as if that wasn't enough. He craved something of more sustenance to feed his empty soul.

In an odd way, he felt like he was waking from a nightmare—a nightmare that had begun when he'd found his wife's lifeless body.

He shifted on the hard ground, the absence of his gunbelt another reminder of how he'd changed since he'd been here. At first he'd felt as if he were partially dressed without the holster and gun, but he'd grown accustomed to not having the weight on his right hip.

"I've got a nibble," Mattie suddenly said in a low, urgent voice.

Clint peered at her cork in the pond and saw it dip beneath the surface, bob up, then go down again, this time deeper. "He's tasting your worm to see if he likes it."

She shot him a pained look. "That isn't funny."

He barely managed to hold back his laughter.

The fish kept playing with Mattie's line and she got to her feet. Wrapping her fingers around the pole more firmly, she watched the cork with rapt attention. Suddenly she jerked the line, setting the hook, and let out a little shriek. "I got him!" Mattie leaned back, slowly pulling the fish in. "He's huge! It must be Fred the Second."

Clint scrambled up, ignoring the sharp twinge in his side. If she really had Fred, she might need some help. He moved behind her, his arms coming around her to grab hold of her pole, one hand above her hands, the other below. Mattie's back fitted snugly against his chest while her soft backside pressed against his crotch.

He tried to concentrate on the struggle with Fred the Second, but his erection had an agenda all its own, and Mattie's excited movements didn't help one bit.

"I think it's coming," she exclaimed.

Clint closed his eyes—damn, he wished she hadn't said that.

Abruptly her whole weight was thrown against him. He tried to stay on his feet, but with the combination of surprise and the sharp jab of pain in his wound, Clint fell backward, managing to turn slightly so he didn't land on his bad side. He also succeeded in hanging on to Mattie, partially cushioning her fall.

He groaned, but he wasn't certain if it was from the reawakened ache of his injury or the pleasant distress in his groin. She laid on him a moment as if stunned, and her womanly curves seared every inch of his body.

Mattie scrambled up, her red face and shocked expression telling him she had no trouble discerning his rigid length through her skirt and undergarments. His gaze dropped to her breasts, which rose and fell rapidly with her breathing. Her nipples were plainly visible against her blouse.

He'd never wanted a woman as badly as he wanted Mattie St. Clair.

"You okay, Mr. Beaudry?" Andy asked, his eyes wide.

*Not even close.*

"I think so," he managed to say.

Andy helped him up while Mattie stood off to the side, much too engrossed in brushing off her skirt.

"It looks like Fred got off the hook," Clint said.

"He ain't the only one." Herman's knowing eyes and chuckle told Clint the old man knew exactly what had transpired between the two of them.

Mattie's blush went all the way down her neck, giving her pale skin a pink glow, and Clint couldn't help but wonder how much lower it went.

"C'mon, get another worm on, Ma. Fred's still down there somewhere." Thank heavens Andy was unaware of the currents traveling between the adults.

Grateful for the diversion, Clint found another worm and put it on her hook. This time, Mattie stood ten feet away from Clint. He couldn't blame her—the attraction was as tangible and electric as a bolt of lightning.

And equally as devastating.

An hour later each of them had caught one fish, except for Mattie, who'd brought in two, though none were the escaped Fred. They trudged back to the house, tired but elated to have fresh fish for supper.

A rabbit hopped across their path and Andy's eyes lit up. He handed his fish and fishing pole to Clint and took off after the bunny.

Mattie called after him, "Be careful of the old well."

"I will."

The three adults kept walking, and a few minutes later Andy rejoined them. Sweat trailed down his face and his hair was plastered to his forehead.

"He got away," Andy said, breathing heavily. "Next time I'll catch him."

They arrived back at the house and mounted the steps to the porch.

"It looks like there might be some fresh blood on your shirt," Mattie said.

When Clint tried to twist around to see, pain sliced through him and cold sweat dampened his brow.

Mattie took his arm and steered him toward a chair. "You sit here on the porch. Herman and Andy, you two clean the fish. I'll get the pies in the oven, then change that bandage for Mr. Beaudry."

"Yes, ma'am," Clint said, barely suppressing the reaction to salute her.

He lowered himself to the chair and closed his eyes. If he kept reopening his injuries, it would be a long time before he got back on the trail of the killer—his ambusher. But he couldn't just sit around, either. He had to push himself, see how much he could do. Just as Andy had to push his limits.

The problem was that Mattie didn't understand either one of them.

Mattie washed her hands and gathered her medical supplies. If she hadn't landed on Clint after the infamous Fred the Second had gotten away, his wound wouldn't have broken open. Some nurse she was.

She placed the pies in the oven and headed outside, nervous about seeing Clint shirtless. An almost healthy Clint Beaudry was temptation with a capital *T*.

Stepping onto the porch, she spotted him sleeping with his chin resting against his chest. Her heart collided with her throat. How could he look so innocent and vulnerable?

He had done too much today. She shouldn't have accepted his help in the orchard, but it was easy to forget he was hurt when he acted as if nothing were wrong. But she should have known; she'd been trained by Kevin to recognize symptoms.

Guilt warmed her face. She had spared little thought for Kevin while he'd been gone, and after he'd returned, she hadn't sought him out when she'd gone into town.

Shamefully, she remembered the kiss she and

Clint had shared. Why didn't Kevin's kisses make her dizzy with longing?

*Kevin is a good, decent man, who truly cares for me.*

Clint was a drifter who lived on the fringes of civilization. His irreverence and blunt honesty were the characteristics of a man who was accustomed to answering to no one but himself. He took what he wanted, when he wanted it, and damned the consequences.

Yet she couldn't deny she was physically drawn to him. If that's all there was between them, she could resist the fire he ignited in her blood. However, it was the memory of the anguish in Clint's eyes and voice while he'd been delirious, and his thoughtfulness for her, that drew her so powerfully toward him. Both told her that Clint Beaudry was a man of deep feelings and deeper secrets.

She sighed, not wanting to wake him, but needing to change his dressings. Leaning over him, she spoke his name quietly. "Clint."

He opened his eyes, and after a moment of confusion he smiled self-consciously. "Sorry."

"You shouldn't have done so much today," she scolded to hide her concern.

"I won't get any better lying around."

She rolled her eyes. He sounded so typically male. "Thank you for those words of wisdom, Dr. Beaudry."

He chuckled, then winced. "Don't make me laugh. That's not on the doctor's list of treatments."

"Take off your shirt."

"Gladly."

The single word slipped across Mattie like velvet over bare skin, making her fingers tremble and her belly tighten with suppressed desire.

She ignored the wicked glint in his eyes as she removed his bandage. Curiosity nibbled at her until she had to ask. "So what's on this doctor's list of treatments?"

Clint arched his brow. "For starters, a gentle hand, which has already been administered."

She nearly laughed. "I can change that. What else?"

He frowned, though his eyes twinkled. "Plenty of bedrest."

"Now, that's a sensible one."

"With a woman."

Her breath gusted through her lips as her nipples hardened. She put a few more inches between them, but the heat between their bodies still intensified. "Are you always this forward, or do I just bring out the worst in you?"

He raised his hand to brush her cheek with the back of his fingers. "Hardly the worst, Mattie."

His gentle touch brought goose bumps to her arms and her brain lost all track of coherent thought. Oh, Lord, she didn't need this. Not now.

Some perverse part of her liked the control she held over him, but another part recognized the control he held over her. If Andy and Herman hadn't been there . . .

She *had* to resist him if she was to hold on to her fragile pride.

"Save it for some woman who's willing," she managed to say with just the right amount of flippancy.

He cupped her chin and gave her a devilish wink that turned her knees to mush. "You're willing, Mattie. You just won't admit it yet."

Damn him! He was right, but thankfully her mind still managed to control her hot and willing nature.

*So far.*

As she applied a clean dressing, her fingers brushed the light smattering of hair across his chest and her thoughts skittered back to the feel of his hard body against her own.

"I can do this," she muttered.

"I sure hope so. Or maybe you haven't had enough practice yet."

*And I'll bet you're willing to teach me.* Mattie shoved the rebellious thought aside. He only meant changing his bandages. Hadn't he?

The half-smile on his lips was open to interpretation. Her fingers trembled as she knotted the bandage around his middle. She reached for his shirt and thrust it at him. "Put it on."

He made no attempt to take it from her. "What's wrong? Don't you trust yourself around me?"

The gall of the man! "That's right. I don't trust myself not to slap that smug look off your face."

She tossed his shirt at him and stalked back into the house—but not fast enough to escape the sound of his laughter.

# Chapter 9

The smell of baking pies and frying fish wafted out onto the porch, making Clint's mouth water in anticipation. He closed his eyes, imagining Mattie bustling about in the kitchen. The image was a dangerously enticing one. She was like a little whirlwind, full of energy that Clint had hoped to channel in other directions. But the woman was as stubborn as she was seductive.

*Damn.*

The sound of hoofbeats and squeaking leather brought Clint's eyes open. At the hitching rail, the sheriff dismounted and tossed the reins loosely around the pole.

Then he climbed the steps to the porch. "Howdy, Beaudry."

Clint tensed, wondering if Atwater had any news about the man who'd shot him. "Sheriff. What brings you out here?"

Atwater sniffed deeply and a wide smile creased his face. "If that ain't reason enough, then you ain't human."

Clint chuckled and relaxed.

The sheriff sat down and removed his hat, then mopped his brow with a handkerchief. "You look like you're healin' right fine."

"Thanks to Mattie."

Atwater leaned back and eyed him for a long moment. "You should be ready to move on real soon."

The hint was anything but subtle, and though Clint had come to the same conclusion himself, he didn't like another man telling him what to do. Especially when it came to Mattie. "Is that an order?" he drawled.

"Nope, just some friendly advice."

Any question that the sheriff had come visiting only for Mattie's cooking was dispelled. He was checking up on Clint, ensuring that he hadn't taken advantage of Mattie. Clint couldn't blame the lawman—the idea had certainly crossed his mind more than once. But Mattie St. Clair was a special woman, and he had no intention of using her like he would a saloon gal.

"I plan on leaving the day after tomorrow," Clint finally said.

"Does Mattie know?"

"No. I'll tell her this evening."

Atwater rocked silently and Clint listened to the muffled creak of the chair, trying not to think about how he was going to break the news to Mattie.

"It's for the best, you know," the sheriff said quietly. "You got too damn much hate and anger inside you. It's only goin' to destroy you and hurt everyone around you."

Clint couldn't deny it. "You'd feel the same way if it'd been your wife."

"You tell Mattie about her yet?"

"No."

Atwater shrugged. "Might make things easier for her to understand."

"My business is my own," Clint said coldly. He wasn't about to turn his wife's death into grist for the gossip mill in Green Valley.

"Have it your way."

"I always do."

Mattie appeared in the doorway and smiled. "I thought I heard voices. Hello, Walt. You chose a good night to come calling. Andy, Clint, and Herman helped me pick peaches this morning and we all caught enough fish for supper."

"I was just tellin' Beaudry here how good your cookin' is, but I was preachin' to the choir. He already knows, right?" Atwater gazed at Clint.

"Yep." Clint forced a smile to ease the sting of his curt tone. "Did you know she makes the best flapjacks in the world, but only on Saturday mornings?"

"You don't say."

"She says they wouldn't be as good if we had them every day."

"That's a woman for you. My Sarah was the same

way," Atwater said. "Would only make chicken 'n' dumplin's on Sundays."

"Who knows how a woman thinks?"

"Ain't that the truth."

"If you two are finished with your illuminating conversation about women, you can come in and eat," Mattie flounced back into the house.

Atwater's twinkling eyes met Clint's gaze. "You got any idea what that was all about?"

"Nope."

The two men stared at one another a moment, then chuckled, easing the tension that had sprung up between them. Clint opened the door and allowed the sheriff to enter ahead of him.

Herman and Andy, already seated at the table, didn't seem surprised to see the sheriff. Either Mattie had told them of his arrival or they were accustomed to him dropping by now and again.

"Howdy, Sheriff," Herman said. "How's your lumbago doin'?"

Atwater pressed a hand to his lower back. "Sometimes better'n other times."

"You want me to rub some of Ma's smelly stuff on it again?" Andy asked.

"Maybe later," the sheriff said, ruffling the boy's hair.

Jealousy caught Clint off guard. It was clear Atwater was a member of Mattie's extended family. For a moment, he wondered what it would be like if he gave up the hunt and settled here. Could he become part of her family, too? A very close part?

He shook aside the treasonous thought—he had a job to do and he couldn't let a raven-haired angel beguile him into forgetting his responsibility.

Clint and Atwater moved toward the same chair, and when they both tried to sit on it at the same time, Andy laughed.

"You two playing musical chairs?" the boy asked.

"Seems that way," Clint muttered. He motioned for the older man to sit down, then took the chair on the other side of Andy.

After they said grace, the food was passed around.

"Anything happen in town lately?" Mattie asked.

"Not much," the sheriff replied. "Finally caught young Tommy Kidder stealin' the tailfeathers from Old Lady Shingle's turkeys. Said he needed 'em to make a pair of wings."

Clint smiled, remembering his own days as a lawman and the stunts kids used to pull.

"And Miss Lathrop is airin' out the schoolhouse, gettin' ready to start classes in a couple weeks, soon as the harvest is in."

Andy groaned.

"You should be grateful you have a teacher. My ma taught me to read and write," Clint said.

He could recall the many evenings sitting by the table in the light of a single kerosene lamp. His mother, exhausted after caring for six children, would still find time to teach them their letters and numbers.

"Where was that?" Atwater asked.

"Down around the Texas panhandle."

"How did you end up here?" Mattie asked.

Clint saw Atwater's eyes narrow, but Clint wasn't ready to tell Mattie the truth. He shrugged. "Itchy feet, I guess."

Before she could probe further, the sheriff spoke. "You'll probably be gettin' some boarders soon," he said to Mattie. "Folks'll be lookin' for a place to hole up over the winter." He deliberately gazed at Clint. "Or they'll be headed to warmer weather."

Mattie glanced downward, obviously understanding the sheriff's pointed remark.

For the remainder of the meal, she was quieter than usual. Herman and Atwater compared their aches and pains, and Andy had to show everyone the scar under his chin he'd earned when he stumbled chasing a fox kit. Then they all laughed about the time the boy had fallen in the creek while trying to "catch" a log.

Suddenly feeling like an intruder, Clint pushed back his plate. "My side's getting a little stiff. I think I'll go take a walk."

"Don't you want some pie?" Mattie asked.

He forced a smile and patted his belly. "I'm full up right now. I'll have some later after I make some room."

Escaping the odd loneliness that had settled in his chest, he stepped outside. He didn't belong here any more than a fox belonged with the chickens. He had no right disrupting their peaceful existence with the rage and vengeance that ate away at his insides.

Where *did* he belong? Chasing down a murderer for the rest of his days, or in a place like this, with a woman like Mattie?

He slid his hands into his jeans pockets and strolled down to the corral. Dakota met him with an enthusiastic nicker and Clint patted the animal's neck. Light shone invitingly from the house's windows, and melancholy stole across him.

No, he didn't belong here any more than his Colt did.

Later, when he headed back to the house, he saw Mattie and Sheriff Atwater step onto the porch and he drew back in the shadows. Mattie's womanly curves were silhouetted in the light spilling from the doorway and Clint curled his fingers into tight fists. He knew how those curves would feel, how they would fit snugly against his hard body.

"You should retire, Walt," Mattie said.

Clint pressed his back against the side of the house and shamelessly eavesdropped.

"You worry too much."

"I have reason enough."

"Tarnation, Mattie, that was ten years ago. The town is civilized now, not like when your husband was sheriff."

"Your reflexes aren't what they used to be."

"You sayin' I'm gettin' too old for the job?" Atwater asked, a definite edge to his voice.

Clint tensed, recognizing the tone of a man who'd just had his pride injured.

"No. I'm just afraid you might get hurt one of these days."

"I ain't ready to be put out to pasture yet, Mattie St. Clair. And even if I was, there's no one around who would be willin' or able to take over for me."

"But—"

"There ain't any buts. I'm Green Valley's sheriff and plan on stayin' that way."

Atwater strode down the steps and to his horse at the hitching post. Before he turned the animal to leave, he touched the brim of his hat. "Thanks for supper, Mattie."

He reined the horse around and trotted away.

Clint remained where he was. After a few moments, he heard Mattie mutter, "Stupid fool." Her staccato footsteps told him she'd returned to the house.

He emerged from the shadows and frowned. Mattie was right: Atwater *was* getting too old for the job. Clint had seen it before—men who didn't know when to give it up. He himself had been guilty of the same, only he hadn't paid the price— his wife had.

He gazed at the porch where Mattie had stood in the silvery moonlight, and the breath left his lungs like he'd been gut-punched.

Maybe he was paying the price now.

Early the next morning, Mattie sat on the porch paring a peach as the sun rose above the eastern horizon. Normally she blanched the peaches to remove their skins, but the kitchen was warm and the porch was cool and the air fresh. As she removed the stone from the peach, she listened to the comforting sound of the sparrows as they chirped and hopped around the yard, looking for breakfast. A few pigeons cooed from the barn roof and a crow cawed in a nearby tree.

Clint's horse snorted and Mattie watched the animal trot around the enclosure. Dakota was getting restless from being penned for so long, just as her master was. Mattie had seen the barely restrained impatience in Clint's eyes last night when he'd excused himself from the table. She knew what he was thinking, and she couldn't completely blame him for wanting to go after the man who'd shot him.

But why would someone ambush Clint?

Uneasy and unwilling to think too deeply about the answer, Mattie returned to paring the fruit.

"Mornin'."

The low, gravelly voice sent a shiver down her spine. She looked up at Clint, who ran a hand through his long, tousled hair. For an insane moment, Mattie wanted to reach up and do the same. Then he set his wide-brimmed hat on his head, shading his features against the morning sun and giving him a strangely menacing appearance.

"Good morning. How're you feeling?" she asked.

Clint lowered himself to the chair beside her. "Stiff, but I expected that." He looked at the two pails brimming with skinless peaches. "You must've gotten up early."

"I planned on doing this last night, but after Walt left, I was too tired."

Even though she was exhausted, she'd slept restlessly. She didn't tell him that her dreams had been filled with images of the two of them, their limbs intertwined, their lips seeking one another, and hot skin touching hot skin. She didn't tell him that she'd awakened early in the morning, the damp blankets tangled around her body. She didn't tell him she had to get up because every time she closed her eyes, she could see his virile body in its full glory.

He chuckled, the rich sound warming her. "Mattie the Magnificent actually gets tired?"

In spite of herself, she smiled. "I want to thank you for yesterday." She stared down at the fruit in her hand. "You didn't have to help in the orchard or take me fishing, especially after how I treated you."

"You were just worried about your son."

She raised her gaze to meet his curtained eyes. "Yes. He's all I have, Clint."

He rested his elbows on his thighs and leaned forward. "I know I'm just passin' through and I have no right telling you how to raise Andy, but—"

"I don't want him to grow up the way I did," she interrupted.

"What?"

"I know what you're going to say. You're wondering why I let him play so much instead of tending to the chores." Memories of the gray, cold place where she'd been placed after her parents died sent a shiver down her spine. "When I was Andy's age, I had already been in an orphanage nearly two years. I worked from sunup to sundown six days a week. On Sundays we had to sit through a three-hour service without squirming." She smiled bitterly. "Do you know how difficult it is for a child to sit still for three hours?"

She wasn't expecting an answer, and Clint remained silent.

"After that, we were able to play for an hour, then had to do more work until we went to bed to start the week all over again. When Andy was born, I promised myself I wouldn't have him work the way I did. I want him to enjoy his childhood."

"There's a difference between working a child too hard and teaching him responsibility," Clint said quietly. "You keep giving Andy what he wants, and he's going to expect it when he's an adult, too."

"So what do *you* think I should do?"

"I don't claim to be any expert on kids, but I think if he does more chores, he'll appreciate his playtime more. His rewards have to be balanced by his labor, Mattie."

That made more sense than she wanted to admit. "Maybe I have spoiled him a little."

She continued to mull over his words even as she grew increasingly aware of his nearness. She could make out a tiny nick along his left jawline, most likely from his shave that morning. The scent of soap and his own masculinity swirled around her, making her heart beat faster and her palms grow damp.

She drew the sharp blade of her knife around and around the fruit, peeling away the skin with practiced ease. If only she could remove her attraction to Clint as easily. Out of the corner of her eye, she saw him stand and return to the house. She was relieved; it was difficult to concentrate with him watching every movement.

Five minutes later he returned and Mattie glanced up in surprise. In his hand, he carried another paring knife.

"I put a pot of coffee on." He grinned boyishly. "And I figured I could give you a hand with these while I'm waiting for my first cup."

Clint picked out a peach and expertly began to pare it. Mattie watched his long fingers curve around the fruit, gentle enough that he didn't bruise it, yet firm enough that it didn't slip from his palm.

A bolt of sensual energy shot through her, and her pulse ricocheted through her veins. Her dreams came back to tease her with the reality of the man beside her. He'd made no secret of the fact he wanted her. All she had to do was say the word. . . .

The sound of Andy clomping down the stairs brought sanity crashing back down upon Mattie and her cheeks bloomed with heat.

Andy joined them on the porch and seemed startled to see Clint helping her. "Where's breakfast?" the boy asked.

Grateful for the interruption to her lustful thoughts, Mattie dropped the peach she'd been working on into a pail and stood. "I'll start it."

Clint grasped her wrist firmly, but his gaze was on Andy. "Give us a few more minutes to finish up here, then your ma will get something ready."

"But I'm hungry."

"We all are," Clint said. "But you don't see your ma or me complaining, do you?"

Mattie could tell Andy wanted to argue, and if *she'd* told him that, he would have. She wasn't certain if she felt better or worse that he didn't debate the issue with Clint.

"I'm gonna go down and see Dakota and Polly." Andy trudged away toward the corral.

"I have a better idea," Clint said. "Go gather the eggs and feed the chickens. That way, you'll get breakfast a little faster."

For a moment, Andy stared at Clint as if trying to decide if he wanted to argue. Finally, he nodded and headed toward the repaired chicken coop.

She settled back in her chair uncomfortably. "I could've finished the peaches after I made breakfast."

"Andy has to learn that he can't have his way all the time and that people aren't going to drop everything to cater to him." He shrugged. "Besides, he's old enough to start taking over some of the chores you've been doing."

Much as Mattie hated to admit it, Clint was right. Maybe she spoiled him to make up for his not having a father.

"I'm taking Dakota out for a ride today," Clint announced.

Mattie's knife slipped. *He's getting ready to leave.*

"That might not be such a good idea, since your wound broke open yesterday," she managed to say calmly.

Clint shrugged. "Maybe not, but I can't stay here much longer, Mattie." He paused. "I'm leaving tomorrow."

Her throat closed and she stared down at the peach in her hand until it blurred. She didn't want him to leave. He had given her back the joy of fishing. He'd awakened her slumbering femininity and made her want a man for the first time since her husband's death.

"That soon?" she managed to ask.

"I've already been here longer than I should've." He paused and gazed at Andy, who was tossing grain out for the chickens. "You saved my life, Mattie."

She couldn't let Clint see how much his leaving would hurt her. "I only did what I had to." She picked up the last peach left to be peeled. "What will you do?"

"I have to find him."

Mattie didn't need to ask who "him" was. "I can't understand why he shot you."

She glanced up to see his face had gone hard and his icy eyes were filled with hatred. Her insides grew as cold as the look in his eyes.

"He's the man who killed my wife."

Mattie's stomach dipped and churned. The image of husband didn't fit with the dangerous man who sat beside her. "Your wife?"

"Emily."

Mattie's eyes widened. That was the name he'd spoken when he'd been delirious. Most of the pieces of the puzzle dropped into place. "Why didn't you tell me?"

"What? That I couldn't protect my own wife?" Clint's voice was filled with self-loathing.

"Surely you don't blame yourself."

He pinned her with a stare that made her draw back. "Who else can I blame? If I'd been home, I could've saved her."

"Or maybe you would've been killed, too," Mattie said quietly.

"Maybe it would've been better if I had," he said, equally as softly.

Her heart cried for him and his loss, as well as the guilt that was eating at him. She wanted to wrap her arms around him and comfort him, but she was afraid—afraid that he would reject her solace and afraid of her burgeoning feelings for him.

Her hands trembled as she struggled to finish paring the last peach. She stood and spoke awkwardly. "I'll start breakfast."

"Do you want the peaches in the kitchen?" he asked, his voice stiff.

"Yes, that'll be fine." Her voice didn't sound much better.

She picked up one of the full pails and carried it into the house. Clint followed with two more and set them in a corner. He made two more trips before all the peach pails were in the kitchen.

As Mattie mixed a batch of biscuits, Clint poured them each a cup of coffee.

Startled, she accepted it with a thank-you. She'd never known a man so thoughtful and considerate. She'd been so wrong about him.

Instead of taking his cup onto the porch, Clint sat by the table and watched her silently. Mattie dared to glance at him . . . once. The embers in his intense eyes rekindled the banked fire inside her, and she quickly looked away.

"I didn't tell you about my wife to scare you or get your sympathy," he said gently. "I figured you had a right to know why I'm in such a hurry to leave."

"You don't owe me an explanation." She cursed the breathiness of her voice.

"Maybe not, but I wanted to give you one."

She should have been pleased that Clint thought enough of her to tell her the truth, yet the more she learned of him, the more she weakened toward him. She couldn't take many more revelations without completely surrendering to this man who touched her so deeply. No longer could she look at Clint as a mere gunslinger, and to deny her attraction to him was ridiculously naive. Although it would be difficult to say good-bye tomorrow, it was for the best.

He'd obviously loved his wife very much to leave his home and track down her killer. Mattie wondered what it would be like to have a man love her so much he'd give up everything for her.

She took a deep, unsteady breath. No matter how much it hurt to see him leave, it would be selfish to try to dissuade him.

A frightening thought struck her and her heart skipped into her throat.

What if the killer came back to finish his job? He'd already killed a woman—he'd have no compunction about killing a little boy.

# Chapter 10

Clint stifled a grimace as he lifted the saddle onto Dakota's back, not wanting Mattie to see that the wound still pained him. She was reluctant to see him go for a ride, and she'd be even more reluctant about his next request.

"I want my gun, Mattie."

"Why?"

Clint wasn't surprised to see revulsion in her face or hear it in her voice. He had considered not wearing his gunbelt, but only for a moment. Although he was only going for a short ride, he was leaving the relative safety of Mattie's sanctuary and taking the first step on the journey back to his own violent world. To do that, he needed his weapon.

"I know you don't like guns, but that Colt is as much a part of me as an arm or leg."

She folded her arms around her waist and her eyes met his. "What's Andy going to think? He looks up to you."

Something twinged in Clint's chest. He hadn't sought the boy's admiration; it had sneaked up like a rustler in the night. Still, Andy had to learn that a gun didn't make a man, and that a man chose how he used a gun.

"Andy's fishing." Clint tightened the cinch beneath Dakota's belly. "Besides, he's seen other men with guns."

"They weren't you."

The twinge close to his heart struck even stronger. He couldn't deny that he cared for the boy more than he should. Hell, he cared for Mattie and even Herman more than he should. After all the time he'd spent in their company, they'd become like family.

Like the loving family he'd been raised with.

Like the family he'd wanted for his own someday.

But that door was closed to him until he made his peace with his guilt.

"Once I'm gone, he'll forget me soon enough." Clint tried to make his voice gruff, but it came out husky. Why was this so damned difficult?

He lowered the stirrup and turned to Mattie, resting his arm across the saddle seat. The afternoon sun glossed her thick hair with a bluish sheen, like a raven's wing, beckoning his touch. The angry flush in her cheeks and the fire in her eyes only made her more desirable. She was the first woman since Emily whom he wanted for more than just a night.

"I can't change who I am," he said in a low voice. "And with all due respect, ma'am, I was shot in the back. If he tries again, I'm going to need my gun."

She had to understand he'd lived by the gun for too long. He'd feel naked and defenseless without it.

Mattie spun around and flounced away, her pace brisk and her shoulders stiff. He sighed, knowing she wouldn't listen to anything he said, so why bother to explain himself? And why did he care what she thought, anyhow? He was leaving tomorrow at sunup.

Mattie returned a few minutes later. She held the gunbelt like it was a poisonous snake and thrust it at him. "Here."

Her lower lip was thrust out, and Clint wanted nothing more than to kiss her until her pout disappeared.

Determinedly, he wrapped the belt around his hips and fastened the buckle, then tied the rawhide thong around his thigh to hold the holster in place. Glancing up at Mattie, Clint noticed her gaze was centered right below his belt buckle. When she caught his eyes, she quickly looked away, her lips settling into a thin line.

"You shouldn't frown so hard, Mattie," he teased. "Your mouth might stay that way, and that would be a downright shame."

"I don't care what you think, *Mister* Beaudry,"

she snapped. "If you weren't leaving tomorrow morning, I'd kick you off my place right now."

Some perverse part of him made him smile and he brushed the back of his fingers along her cheek. She jerked away, but the blush that sprang to her face told him she wasn't as immune to his touch as she pretended. "We both know you don't want to do that."

She closed her hands into tight fists. "You are so . . . so impossible!"

He grinned lazily. "Gonna kiss me good-bye?"

Her gaze flickered to his lips, betraying her cool facade. Clint's breath quickened and his blood surged through his veins. It was clear she wanted to, and that was enough for him.

Damning the consequences, he swept an arm around her waist and leaned down to capture her mouth with his. Her lips remained firm and unyielding . . . for only a moment. Then she surrendered with a soft moan. She tasted sweet, like peaches, and her rose scent spiraled through him as she arched toward him, branding him at every junction of her curves against his body.

He parted her lips and she met his invasion with her own—advancing, retreating—in the battle of passion. His erection pressed into her belly and her hips moved in the oldest rhythm of time.

Then Dakota nickered, and Mattie pushed away from Clint, her breath raspy. "No," she whispered, her face flushed and eyes dark with unappeased desire. "This is wrong."

Clint breathed deeply to cool the wild fire racing

through his blood. His gaze fell to her breasts, which moved with her shallow gasps. He ached to draw her flush against him once more, ached to feel her lips against his.

Ached to bury himself within her.

Clint framed her face in his palms. "Don't deny it, Mattie. This is something we both want."

She took his hands in hers and lowered them slowly. "Just because we want it doesn't make it right." Her gaze went to his gunbelt and the weapon within the holster. "I can't love a man who lives by the gun. Not again."

She released him and walked away, her shoulders slumped and her footsteps dragging.

Clint stared after her. If he hadn't given up his gun for Emily, he wasn't about to for Mattie St. Clair, no matter how tempting she was.

His obsession with her would be his downfall if he didn't rein his lusty thoughts back under control. He'd been thinking of her when he'd been ambushed. He might not be so lucky next time. Besides, she was the kind of woman who would want a wedding ring to go along with a tumble in bed, and Clint couldn't make any promises.

Not now.

Not yet.

Taking a deep, fortifying breath, Clint hauled himself up into the saddle. It had been over three weeks since he'd ridden, the longest time in his adult life that he'd been off a horse. He touched his heels to Dakota's flanks and the horse responded eagerly. As the sorrel cantered down the road,

Clint relished the breeze on his face and the landscape moving past him in a blur of greens, browns, and blues.

It was definitely time to move on. He didn't need a woman to cloud his judgment or make him careless. Getting away from Mattie would restore his good sense and give him time to cool his lust.

Turning slightly in the saddle, Clint looked back. Mattie was standing on the porch, a hand shading her eyes as she watched him. What was she thinking?

And why did he care?


After Clint left, Mattie wandered through the silent house. Their disagreement over his Colt and their subsequent kiss had thrown her thoughts into turmoil.

She understood why he wore the gun, but violence begat violence. That's what Kevin always said, and she believed him. She'd witnessed it firsthand.

She traced her still-tingling lips with a fingertip. How could she hate something so much about a man, yet crumble when he kissed her?

Because there were more things to admire in Clint Beaudry than there were to dislike. Things like his compassion, his willingness to help, and his good-natured teasing that made her feel like a girl again.

Mattie picked up a dustcloth and absently swished it across the knickknacks and framed pictures in the parlor. Her footsteps carried her to the fireplace mantel and her gaze fell upon her mother's music box. She cradled the cool metal in her palms, and almost against her will, she raised the lid. She closed her eyes as the waltz's tinny melody washed through her.

In her mind, she saw herself held securely in Clint's powerful arms as he twirled her around. His green eyes were on her alone, filled with an adoration so strong, it made her breath quicken. Her chest ached as she indulged in the romantic daydream. No man, not even Jason, had inspired such fanciful thoughts.

Only the dangerously arousing Clint Beaudry.

Mattie opened her eyes to the emptiness of the parlor. A slight breeze rustled the curtains, making them dance. A fly buzzed against a window and Jewel mooed in the yard. The clock on the mantel struck three, its monotonous rhythm clashing with the light notes flowing from the music box.

Was Mattie's life like the clock—dull and plodding? Was she merely counting the seconds into minutes into hours? Then into days lost, never to be recaptured?

She'd turned her adult life into a mirror of her life at the orphanage—constantly working from sunup to sundown. By sparing Andy that kind of existence, she'd denied her own needs. She had convinced herself the only type of man she wanted someday was someone like Kevin Murphy. He was kind and compassionate, but he didn't make her heart skip wildly or bring wicked thoughts about their naked bodies touching, burning. . . .

Like Clint did.

Every time he looked at her or brushed her arm or kissed her, Mattie's toes curled and she throbbed. The desire was even stronger than what she'd felt for Jason, because now she knew the rewards. And Mattie knew instinctively that the pleasure of lying with Clint would be far greater than anything she'd experienced in her brief married life.

Her heartbeat pounded in her ears and her muscles trembled from the wanton pictures in her thoughts. She had enough memories of his lean body that she had no trouble envisioning him in her bed.

Jewel's moo startled her, and Mattie clapped the music box shut. She shouldn't have allowed her thoughts to run out of control. It was only giving temptation a stronger hold on her. As if Clint Beaudry's mere presence wasn't temptation enough. . . .

She set the box back in its place and climbed the stairs to finish dusting up there. At the top of the steps, Clint's door was open, inviting her to enter. With only a slight hesitation, she crossed the threshold and ran her dustcloth over the dresser, then across the nightstand. Spotting one of his shirts tossed on the bed, Mattie picked it up, intending to hang it in the armoire.

Clint's scent washed across her, and after a quick glance into the hallway, she drew the shirt close to her face. She inhaled deeply of the rich masculine scent that was Clint's alone and closed her eyes.

*It just ain't natural to be without a man for so long.*

Ruth's words, spoken so long ago, came back clearly. Maybe she'd been right.

Maybe it had been too long.

Clint paused on the outskirts of Green Valley and removed his hat to draw his forearm across his sweaty brow. The hour-and-a-half ride had given Dakota some much-needed exercise and Clint time to extinguish the flames in his blood. Without Mattie's presence to distract him, he'd been able to set things back in perspective.

His goal hadn't changed—it had only been diverted for a time. Although his wounds still ached, he felt more like himself again with the familiar gunbelt around his hips.

He spotted a saloon, placed his hat back on his head, and urged Dakota down the dusty street. Dismounting stiffly by the hitching rail, he tossed the reins loosely around the post and traipsed into Billy's Saloon. Although it was only a little after four, there were a dozen customers, including a fancy gambler and a handful of dusty cowhands. There was also a dark-haired barmaid wearing a knee-length yellow dress and black fishnet stockings.

He paused beside her as she cleaned off a table, and tipped his hat brim with two fingers. "Afternoon, ma'am."

She swept her gaze from his hair down to his boot toes, then back, pausing a moment at his gunbelt. An interested gleam entered her eyes and she placed a hand on her hip in a seductive pose. "Looks like you're in need of some company. My name's Sunny Joy"—she leaned close enough that her breasts brushed his arm—"and I can bring you lots of sunshine and happiness, cowboy."

Clint grinned, appreciating her obvious alias and feminine assets. Sunny Joy might be exactly what he needed to get his mind off Mattie. He winked at her. "I might just do that. But right now I have some drinking to do, ma'am."

"Call me Sunny or Joy." Her eyes glittered with ribald promise. "I ain't no ma'am."

She turned and sauntered away, her hips swinging.

Clint smiled in appreciation. Sure enough, a roll with Sunshine would do him a world of good.

At the bar, he propped a booted foot on the brass rail running along the bottom. He slid his hat off to rest against his back, held in place by the buckskin string at his throat.

The bartender, a heavyset bald man with an earring in his left ear, stepped over to Clint. "What'll it be?"

"Whiskey and a beer," he replied.

Clint laid two bits down as the bartender set the drinks in front of him. The bald man scooped up the coins with stubby fingers and strolled to the other end of the bar, leaving Clint to drink alone.

He downed the shot of whiskey, grimaced at the burn in his throat, then picked up the beer and took a few swallows of the lukewarm liquid to ease the whiskey's sting. Liquor was something he'd been without at Mattie's, too, though he hadn't missed it. Maybe it was because Mattie was intoxicating enough.

*Geezus, Beaudry, get a hold of yourself. Pretty soon you'll be spouting love poems.*

He resolutely turned his attention to the saloon's customers. It was second nature for him to keep an eye on everyone, and he used the mirror to surreptitiously observe the clientele. After ensuring nobody posed a threat, he allowed his gaze to follow the barmaid. She turned, caught his eye in the mirror, and winked at him, though it was Mattie's face he saw.

*Shit.*

Disgusted, Clint picked up his beer mug and moved to a table. He eased himself into a chair, heedful of his tender wounds. He'd been too sick to appreciate Mattie's gentle hands on him before, but the memory of her feathered touches now made him grow as hard as a stallion in a herd of mares.

"Get ya another beer?" Sunny Joy asked him.

Clint glanced at the empty mug and nodded. "Thanks."

"No problem, cowboy."

She leaned over to pick up his glass, her bountiful breasts in danger of spilling out of her dress. Her scent—a mixture of vanilla, tobacco, and whiskey—washed across him, reminding him of other women in saloons too numerous to recall.

"You look like you could use a little . . . relaxin'," she said.

Clint appreciated an impressive bosom as much

as the next man. But Sunny's face had the hard lines common among women in her profession, unlike Mattie's skin, which was smooth and silky. He shook his head. "Thanks for the offer, ma'—Sunny, but I'm not interested right now."

She frowned in disappointment and straightened, laying a hand on his shoulder. "When you get interested, you know where to find me, handsome."

He couldn't remember the last time he'd turned down a willing woman's invitation. What kind of magic did Mattie have that made him want only her?

The batwing doors swung open and the sheriff entered. His gaze roamed around the room until it settled on Clint, and he crossed the floor to join him. Dropping into a chair, Atwater removed his hat and ran a hand through his thinning gray hair. "Hot 'nuff to wither a fence post out there."

"Yep, it's warm." Clint eyed the lawman warily. "You stop by for a reason or just to pass the time?"

Atwater shrugged. "Thought that was your horse out there. Didn't see no travelin' gear on it, though."

"Told you I was leaving tomorrow. I just took my horse out for a ride."

"Fine-lookin' piece of horseflesh. Oughta put out some good foals if'n you ever settle down."

That was one of the main reasons Clint had bought the mare—he'd figured to use her to help start his herd. So many plans had been killed along with his wife. . . .

Sunny interrupted his melancholy thoughts as she set a beer in front of him. "The usual, Sheriff?"

" 'Fraid so, Sunny."

She smiled fondly. "Comin' right up."

"You goin' after him?" Atwater asked Clint after Sunny left.

"Yep."

"What're you gonna do when you find him?"

"Kill him," Clint replied without hesitation.

Atwater narrowed his gaze. "You're talkin' cold-blooded murder."

An icy ball of hatred settled in Clint's gut. "I'll give him as much of a chance as he gave my wife."

"That ain't your decision to make, Beaudry. Leave it to a judge and jury to hang him legal-like."

"The courts won't convict him without better evidence."

"Then how do *you* know it was the same fella who shot you?"

"I was on my way home the night it happened—the night she was killed. I saw a man on a blond horse, just like what the man who shot me was riding." Bitterness rose in Clint's throat. "That's not enough evidence to convict a man for murder."

Atwater stared at Clint silently with no expression on his face. "That's right. More'n one man rides a palomino."

Clint took a long swallow of his beer, hoping it would fill the well of anger and emptiness in his chest. It didn't. Nothing would until vengeance was satisfied. "But not many, and it's damned coincidental that I've been after the murderer for a year and just as I'm getting close, I'm bushwhacked."

Atwater studied him from beneath bushy gray eyebrows. "What if you're wrong?"

The sheriff's quiet question brought a sliver of doubt to Clint that he quickly extinguished with burning rage. "I'm not."

"I used to be just like you, Beaudry. So damned sure of myself and certain that I couldn't make a mistake. But back when I was even younger'n you, somethin' happened that nearly made me quit bein' a lawman for good." Atwater paused and his gaze turned inward. "Some men came off a trail drive, all ready to raise holy hell. They got drunk in record time and started makin' trouble. I was a deputy then, so full of myself I couldn't see nothin' but how I could be a goddamned hero."

Self-recrimination swept across the older man's face. "I met them on the street, goaded one of 'em into a gunfight. We drew. He missed, but I got him." He swallowed. "He missed *me*, but his bullet killed a woman who was crossin' the street at the other end of town."

Though Clint sympathized, he didn't see how it applied to him. "That's a risk we all take when we pin on a badge."

The sheriff slammed his fist on the table, startling Clint. "*We're* supposed to take the risk, not those we're protectin'. We make a mistake, innocent people suffer."

Clint knew that all too well. Anguish clogged

his throat, but it was anger that spoke. "Why the hell do you think I turned in my badge?"

Atwater leaned back in his chair, and his features eased as empathy replaced his anger. "Maybe you made a mistake in not bein' home with your wife, but seems to me you can't handle the choices a lawman's gotta make." Atwater paused, then said quietly, "Maybe that's the real reason you turned in your badge."

# Chapter 11

Clint wanted to be righteously angry, but the sheriff's words hit too close to home. Emily had accused him of the same thing—being irresponsible. Maybe they were both right. Even though Clint had married, he wasn't sure if he'd wanted to settle down. At the time, it just seemed the thing a man his age should do.

He used to relish the pursuit of outlaws and bringing justice to the untamed Texas frontier. Now Clint had grown tired of the chase. Maybe that's why Mattie's home and her small family had drawn him in so deeply.

Clint studied the aging sheriff and he saw himself in Atwater's creased features. The image disturbed him and made him wonder if he'd be alone, just like Atwater, twenty-five years from now. It wasn't a pleasant thought.

Sunny returned carrying a glass of milk and set it in front of Atwater. "Here ya go, Sheriff."

"Thanks, Sunny." He smiled up at her. "You decide if you're gonna marry me or not?"

She laid a hand on his shoulder and winked. "I don't think I could keep up with you."

Atwater chuckled and Clint smiled at their friendly banter. He remembered another barmaid—Arabella—from another time. He hadn't expected to see her again, especially in a town like Green Valley as Mrs. Amelia Johnson.

Sunny glanced at Clint hopefully, but he didn't give her any encouragement. She sighed and sashayed off to the next customer.

Atwater elbowed him in the side. "She likes you, Beaudry."

"I like her, too."

"Then take her up on her offer. If I was twenty years younger, I would." He paused. "On second thought, I was married twenty years ago, so I guess that wouldn't have worked, neither. Sarah woulda killed me."

Clint chuckled, and found himself warming toward the man. He pulled a cheroot from his pocket, placed it between his lips, then lit it with a lucifer. Clint enjoyed the tang of the tobacco and exhaled a lazy swirl of smoke. "Have you lived in Green Valley long?"

"Nearly fifteen years. I been sheriff ever since Mattie's husband got hisself killed. Before that, I was Jason St. Clair's deputy."

Mattie hadn't told Clint the details surrounding

her husband's death and he was curious. "What happened? Mattie doesn't talk about him."

"St. Clair was a hothead, and he could be mean-er'n a rattlesnake on a hot skillet if he was crossed." Atwater shook his head. "St. Clair was a helluva charmer when he wasn't bein' a bully. Mattie was just a girl, not even seventeen when Jason laid it on thick for her. Mattie didn't have a chance—bein' raised in the orphanage, she didn't know nothin' but work. St. Clair plumb swept her off her feet and right into his bed. Gertrude Hotzel caught them there."

Clint shifted uncomfortably in his chair. He couldn't picture the Mattie he knew crawling into bed with a man like Atwater described.

"She was just a kid," Atwater reiterated, as if reading Clint's thoughts. "All she knew was that St. Clair wanted her—nobody'd wanted her since her folks died."

Clint's throat tightened, imagining young Mattie and her happiness when a man had paid atten-tion to her. He wondered if her husband had ever taken her fishing, and quickly discarded the notion. Jason St. Clair didn't sound like the type who fished.

"The wedding was two days later," Atwater said. He took a sip of the milk and grimaced. "Damn stomach. Don't ever get old, Beaudry. Everythin' starts fallin' apart."

"The way I'm going, I doubt I'll give myself time to start falling apart," Clint said wryly.

"You don't have to go that way." He eyed Clint

shrewdly. "Fact is, I bet you could find a job here real easy if you decided to stay."

Clint had a strong hunch he knew what the older man was talking about. "You have one in mind?"

"Much as I hate to admit it, Mattie's right. I'm gettin' too damn old for this job, but there ain't been nobody I can trust to take care of the folks in this town. That is, until you showed up."

Clint held up his hands as if to push the offer away. "I'm done with being a lawman."

"Bein' a sheriff in Green Valley's a whole lot different than bein' a U.S. marshal. First off, there ain't no travelin'. You marry someone like, say"—Atwater's smile reminded Clint of a politician—"Mattie, and you can be home every night."

The thought of being with Mattie every night had its share of advantages—advantages Clint wouldn't mind exploring. But even if he gave up the hunt for his wife's murderer, he wasn't certain he was ready to take on the responsibility of a ready-made family. Besides, though he admired Mattie and lusted after her, he didn't love her.

"If I was interested—which I'm not—it would never work. Mattie's all fired up against guns and there's not a sheriff around who'd give up his weapon." Clint snorted. "Hell, he'd be crazy if he did."

"I wear a gun and it don't seem to bother her," Atwater said.

Startled, Clint realized the sheriff was right. Was it just himself that Mattie didn't like wearing a gun? And if so, why? Did he remind her too much of her dead husband? Or would she look at the situation differently if Clint agreed to become Green Valley's sheriff?

*Hold it right there, Beaudry.*

"It doesn't matter, Sheriff. I'm moving on, come morning," Clint said.

Atwater finished his milk. "All right, son, you made your point. But this fella has nearly a four-week head start on you. How do you expect to find him?"

"I'll start where you left off after you trailed him."

"That'd be about twenty miles from here, near Whitecliff. Lost the trail in some rocks."

"You have any idea where he might've been headed?"

Atwater shook his head. "You might have a better idea than me, since you been trailin' him for so long."

Clint shook his head in frustration. "This is all new territory." He glanced out the window to the waning light. "I'd best be getting back before Mattie starts worrying." He pushed himself up.

"Think about what I said, son," Atwater said. "You could do a lot worse than settlin' here and becomin' Green Valley's sheriff."

"I got a job to do before I can even think about settling down."

"Good luck to you, then, Beaudry." Atwater held out his hand and the two men exchanged a firm handshake.

"Thanks, Sheriff."

After sitting for so long, Clint's side had stiffened. Grasping the saddle horn, he clenched his teeth as he mounted his horse. He should stay at Mattie's at least another week to heal completely, but time had already gotten away from him.

It was only a quarter of a mile to Mattie's, and Clint kept Dakota to a walk. When the mare caught the scent of the familiar place, she wanted to stretch out into a canter. He held her back, though he wanted to hurry back himself. In the short time he'd been there, it had become the first home he'd truly had since leaving his ma and pa's place over fifteen years ago. As much as he tried, he couldn't call the place he'd shared with Emily for two years home.

Clint reined in Dakota at the corral and unsaddled the horse, carrying the tack into the barn. He returned to curry and brush the horse, and found Mattie, her back to him, petting the mare.

Clint paused to enjoy the view. She stroked Dakota with a gentle hand and whispered something Clint couldn't hear. Mattie was a ball of contradictions rolled into a fetching package: gun hater and tender healer of bullet wounds; hard worker and spoiler of her young son; straitlaced lady and passionate woman who'd tumbled into bed with a hotheaded charmer.

She intrigued and frustrated him.

As if sensing his presence, she turned and gave him a reprimanding look. "I thought I'd have to go looking for you."

"Worried about me?" He grinned—there was

something about her that made him want to get under her self-assured shell.

She crossed her arms and glared at him. "I was worried about Dakota—she could've stepped in a hole or gotten a rock in her hoof."

Stifling his laughter, he crossed the few yards separating them. "I like it when you worry"—he paused—"about Dakota."

She snorted and her cheeks pinkened, but her eyes danced with humor.

Clint chuckled. He admired her courage and backbone, but he especially liked her unselfconsciousness.

"You caught me. I was worried about you, too." She held her thumb and forefinger about half an inch apart. "About this much."

Clint wanted to wrap his arms around her, but it was safer to curry Dakota. "You be careful you don't worry too much—I'd hate to see you strain yourself."

She laughed lightly, the melody weaving itself inside Clint's chest and holding him captive.

"Okay, so I was afraid you'd been thrown and your wound had reopened," she admitted.

"I would've been back an hour ago, but I stopped by the saloon. Talked with the sheriff for a while."

Mattie's body tensed. "About what?"

Her defensive reaction surprised him. Was there something she didn't want him to know? "This'n that."

"Like what this'n that?"

Clint paused in his task. "Are you afraid we talked about you?"

She drew back as if affronted. "Of course not. I'm sure you and Walt had more important things to discuss than me." She paused, watching him closely. "Didn't you?"

He smiled innocently and continued grooming Dakota.

Mattie stamped her foot. "Sometimes you're impossible."

"You already called me that once today."

As Mattie built up another head of steam, Clint glanced over her shoulder to see Herman coming toward them at a staggering run, waving his arms.

"What's wrong with Herman?" Clint asked.

Mattie turned her head, puzzled. "I don't know." She raised her skirt and ran toward the old man.

Clint dropped the curry brush and followed her, apprehension ballooning in him. Something was obviously wrong.

Mattie reached him first and grabbed his arms. "Herman, are you all right?"

Panting, with sweat rolling down his face, the old man nodded weakly. "I—I'm all . . . right. It's . . . Andy."

Mattie's eyes widened. "What happened?" Herman tried to answer, but couldn't get enough air to speak. "Where's Andy?"

Clint laid his hands on her tense shoulders. "Let him catch his breath, Mattie."

"He . . . he fell . . . in . . . the well," Herman finally got out.

Mattie's face lost all color and Clint thought she was about to faint. He tightened his grip on her.

She covered her mouth. "Oh, God. Is he—?"

Herman shook his head. "On an old board. But if he . . . falls, he's gonna drown."

"Can't he swim?" Clint asked.

Mattie shook her head. "We have to get him out of there," she said in a near-hysterical voice.

Clint glanced at Dakota, but there was no time to resaddle the mare. "Where's a rope?"

"In the barn, by the door," Herman replied.

Clint dashed to the barn and time seemed to stretch into forever as he searched for the rope. His eyes adjusted to the dim light and he spotted it on a nail to the right of the door. He grabbed it and raced back to join Herman and Mattie.

They were gone.

He spotted them zigzagging through the brush and quickly followed them, his heart pounding in his chest. The taste of fear filled his mouth, just as it had when he was in a gun battle. Only this battle was much worse—Clint had no control in this situation.

Catching up to them, he clasped Mattie's elbow just as she stumbled. She glanced at him and the terror in her white face punched Clint in the belly. If something happened to the boy, Clint didn't know what Mattie would do.

"He'll be all right." Clint knew he shouldn't offer empty reassurances, but that was all he had to give. If he could have traded places with Andy, he would have gladly done it to erase the fear in Mattie's face.

They arrived in a small clearing where there was a gaping hole in the earth. Mattie tried to rush toward it, but Clint held her back. "The soil around it may give way. Call out to him."

"Andy, honey. Andy, can you hear me?" Mattie's voice trembled only slightly, though her body shuddered like a leaf in the wind.

"Ma," came his faint reply.

Mattie closed her eyes momentarily and the relief in her features made Clint's heart skip a beat. "Andy, are you all right?" she shouted with more strength.

"Yeah, but I hurt my ankle."

With an injured ankle, Andy wouldn't be able to climb out himself. That left only one other option.

"I have to get down there," Clint said. "Keep him talking, Mattie. Reassure him."

She nodded with a jerky motion.

Clint looked at Herman. "Help me tie off this rope so I can use it to climb down the shaft."

Mattie grabbed his arm. "But you're not strong enough yet."

"I'll be fine," Clint said impatiently. "Besides, we don't have time to wait for help. That board could go at any minute."

He hated to be so blunt with her, but he didn't have time to argue.

"Be careful," she said softly.

Clint gave her slender hands a gentle squeeze, but couldn't grant her any more empty promises.

Clint ran over to a tree about twelve feet from the hole and wrapped one end of the rope around it as he listened to Mattie's soothing voice reassure her son. He jerked on the rope, testing the strength of the knot. It held.

"I'm going down there to get Andy and climb back out with him. If I can't do that, you and Mattie are going to have to pull him up—can you do that?" Clint asked Herman grimly.

"I ain't that old yet, Beaudry. Get your ass down there and save that little boy," Herman said. "And don't go killin' yourself in the bargain."

"I don't plan to." Clint slapped the man's bony shoulder and quickly removed his gunbelt.

Then, carefully, he inched toward the edge of the well. "I'm going to throw a rope down there, Andy, so cover your head with your hands," he called.

"All right," he answered. Though the boy's voice was muffled, Clint could hear the fear in it.

Clint tossed the looped rope down the well. "Are you okay?"

"Yep. And I got the rope, too."

"Good. I'm going to climb down. Once I reach you, I'll tie the rope around you, then your ma and Herman will pull you up, okay?"

" 'Kay."

Clint could feel Mattie's and Herman's anxious gazes on him. He neared the well's entrance, the rope in his hands. Some soil near the lip crumbled beneath his toes. Knowing he had little time, Clint took a tighter hold on the line and squatted by the shaft.

Taking a deep breath, he eased himself down the rope until only his head was aboveground. He saw a single tear roll down Mattie's cheek as her lips moved in silent prayer.

He lowered himself deeper, trying not to use the sides of the well too much. The more he did, the more dirt would fall on Andy.

"It's dark," the boy said, his voice sounding small and anxious.

"That's just me blocking the light," Clint called down. "Don't look up or you'll get dirt in your eyes."

The muscles in Clint's arms and shoulders protested the strain. He'd been inactive for too long. Inch by exhausting inch, he traveled downward. He glanced up once and dirt spilled across his face, reminding him to follow his own advice. Sweat rolled down his brow and dripped onto his grimy shirt.

How far down was Andy?

Clint's arms trembled with fatigue and he had to brace his boots against the side for a few moments to regain his breath and strength.

"Clint? Are you all right?" Mattie yelled down.

Her concern brushed across him like an angel's wings and gave him the energy to continue. "I'm all right."

A minute later, his foot nudged something soft.

"You made it." Andy's voice was very close.

"I'm going to put my feet on the sides of the board you're on."

"You'll break it."

"No, I won't," Clint said calmly, though he wasn't nearly as certain as he sounded. "I'll keep my weight against the sides."

In the blackness, he used his boot toes to find the ends of the board and lowered himself. The wood creaked menacingly, and Andy jerked against Clint's leg.

"It's gonna break!" Andy hollered.

"Relax, Andy." Clint paused a moment. "I need you to stand up very slowly—no sudden movements. Can you do that?"

A moment of tense silence.

"Yeah."

Clint could feel the boy move against his legs. He reached down and hooked a hand beneath the boy's arm, then helped him rise. There was barely enough room for them side by side. Clint had thought he might be able to scale the rope with Andy clinging to his back, but the well was too narrow.

"Ow," Andy muttered. "My ankle."

"Your ma'll look at it once you're out of here."

He drew the rope around the boy's back and under his arms. Almost blind, Clint had to rely on his sense of touch to secure a knot at Andy's chest. Clint's legs grew shaky from bracing himself against the well's sides, but he didn't dare add any more weight to the board.

"How does that feel?" Clint asked.

"All right."

Clint placed his hands on the boy's thin shoulders. "Herman and your ma are gonna pull you up. If you can help them by climbing up the wall some, go ahead and do it. Are you ready?"

He felt more than saw Andy's nod.

Clint tilted his face upward and cupped a hand to his mouth. "Pull him up!"

The rope grew taut and Clint put his hands around the boy's waist to lift him. As the boy was drawn upward, Clint leaned back against the dirt wall so Andy could squeeze past him. He helped raise the boy, taking some of the burden off Herman and Mattie. Then Andy was out of reach.

Clint could see the boy's silhouette as Andy was hauled steadily upward. He dislodged some soil as he climbed, and Clint dropped his head so the dirt fell in his hair and down his back, mingling with the sweat.

He listened to Andy's harsh breathing and the shuffle of the kid's feet against the well to distract himself from the cramping in his own legs. Keeping his weight pressed to the sides instead of on the board was harder than he'd figured. His knees trembled from the stress and the hot, clammy air sent sweat rolling down his face in steady rivulets. His shirt grew damp and sticky.

Clint flattened his palms against the sides to try to take some pressure off his legs, but it wasn't enough. If only he could put one boot flat on the board . . .

The cramps spread from his calves to his thighs, and his muscles trembled like he had palsy. He wasn't going to make it—he had to chance some of his weight on the wooden ledge. Shifting cautiously, Clint eased his toe onto the board first. The wood protested and he paused a moment, then continued lowering his foot. Finally, he reached a point where it took some of the strain off his screaming muscles.

The board held and Clint sighed. He glanced up to see Andy drawn out of the hole and he closed his eyes, breathing a silent thank-you.

"You okay down there, Beaudry?" Herman hollered.

"Just waitin' for that rope," Clint replied with a smile.

"Heads up. It's on its way."

A moment later, Clint felt the slight sting of the rope as it struck his back. He turned to find it and the wood cracked menacingly. He froze, then the wood snapped with a sound like a rifle shot.

Clint twisted to grab the line, but his knuckles only grazed it as he floundered for a foothold that wasn't there. Pain arrowed through his side.

He plunged down the remainder of the shaft, his shoulders scraping the walls. He struck the water feet first, and the cold water stole the breath from his lungs. Then he was completely submerged, surrounded by blackness. Panic gripped him, but he forced himself to remain calm. Finally, he stopped sinking and the natural lift of the water pushed him upward. A few moments later, his head broke the surface and he gulped in air.

Fortunately, his father had taught him how to swim when he was a boy. He treaded water, keeping himself afloat even as his limbs began to complain about the frigid temperature. A few minutes earlier Clint had been sweating. Now his teeth chattered and his skin began to tingle.

"Clint! What happened?" Mattie shouted down, her worry obvious though her voice was faint.

"The board broke," he yelled. "The water's freezing."

"Can you make it up on your own?"

That was a damned good question. He shivered. His fingers and toes would be numb before long. "I'll make it," he shouted, then muttered to himself, "Yeah, sure you will, Beaudry."

He searched for the rope and spotted it above his head. Lifting a hand, he attempted to grab it. He was a few inches shy. Muttering an oath, he kicked at the water, propelling himself upward, and snatched at the line, but missed again.

"What're ya doin' down there, Beaudry? Takin' a nap?" Herman hollered.

Clint bit back a caustic reply. He needed to hold on to his strength if he was going to make it out of here.

He glared at the rope, wishing like hell he could add another few feet to its length by merely staring at it. Taking a deep breath, he impelled himself upward again and this time the fingers of one hand curled around the end of the line.

Carefully, afraid he was going to lose his tenuous grasp, Clint slowly drew himself higher. He managed to grip the rope with his other hand. With more confidence, he began to climb the rope, one hand over the other.

His damp palms abruptly slipped, and he dropped nearly two feet before catching himself once more. His heart thundered in his chest and sweat returned to his brow, even as he shivered uncontrollably.

"Clint! Are you all right?" Mattie's words echoed and reechoed down the narrow passage.

He panted, trying to regain his breath to answer her panicked question. "I'm . . . all r-right."

"We'll try to pull you up," she hollered.

"No. Stay back from the hole," Clint called back. "I can do it."

Herman's voice drifted down and Clint could make out only one or two words. It sounded like he was trying to reassure Mattie.

With his back braced against the wall and his feet wedged against the opposite side, Clint prepared himself for the long climb. He closed his eyes, listening to the harsh sound of his breathing.

The bullet's exit wound throbbed and burned. He'd be lucky if he could get out of bed tomorrow, much less mount a horse and ride for hours.

Provided he made it out of here at all.

"Maybe today, Em," he whispered. It had been a few days since he'd spoken those familiar words, and a realization struck him like a thunderbolt: He *didn't* want to die anymore. For the first time since Emily's death, he had more to live for than to die for.

"*Not* today," he said firmly. Flinching, he gripped the rope tighter and painstakingly climbed up the shaft. He worked hand over hand, shifting his feet against the wall with every advance. His muscles shuddered and sweat drenched his clothing, mixing with the dirt to cover him with mud. At one point, he paused to swipe the grime from his stinging eyes and nearly lost his hold.

He continued on as exertion began to take its toll. Although there were only about twenty feet left to scale, Clint had little confidence he'd make it. He went a few more feet, then using some of his meager strength, he lifted his head to gaze up at the well's opening. A silhouette moved across the dimness and Clint recognized Mattie.

She wasn't supposed to be so close to the hole. The edge could easily crumble beneath her, plunging her downward.

"Get back," he called hoarsely.

She didn't move. "Come on, Clint, just a little farther."

Her encouraging voice brushed across him like a physical caress, and he resumed climbing. She sounded like she actually cared about him. Could she?

After a few more feet, his movements grew clumsier and he slowed until he was only moving inch by inch. Nearly there. . . .

"Dammit, Beaudry, I didn't save you just to have you die. Get up here!"

She could make a drill sergeant sound like a sissy.

He gathered what little strength remained and hoisted himself upward. The fingers of one hand curled over the outer edge, while he clung to the rope with the other.

He'd made it!

Then the ground crumbled beneath his fingertips.

# Chapter 12

**M**attie grabbed for his hand as the dirt began to disappear beneath it. She managed to clasp his wrist, but his weight nearly took her over the edge. She cried out at the sudden jerk on her shoulder, but if she let go he would plunge to his death.

Her breath rasped in her throat and her fingers grew slippery around his wrist. Herman dropped down beside her and wrapped his bony fingers around Clint's hand.

"Pull," Mattie said through thinned lips.

"Don't drop him," Andy said frantically from behind them, far enough back that if the ground gave way, he'd remain safe.

As Mattie and Herman hauled Clint upward, she could feel him using the rope to take some of the strain off them.

Clint's head cleared the hole, his face and hair dark with reddish mud—Mattie hoped it was merely mud. Then his upper body and legs followed, and he finally dropped onto his belly between Mattie and Herman.

Panting, they all lay there.

Mattie's heart pumped like a steam engine as she rested her trembling hand on Clint's back. His warmth seeped through his wet, filthy shirt and reassured her that he had survived. He had risked his own life to save her son. If he hadn't been there, Andy would have died. Mattie knew it with a certainty that sent chills skating down her spine and into her soul.

Andy crawled up to kneel beside Clint and laid a small, dirty hand on the man's shoulder. "Are you okay, Mr. Beaudry?"

The fear in his voice gave Mattie the strength to sit up and examine Clint. "Are you hurt?"

He moaned and tried to roll over. Mattie slid her arm beneath him and helped him sit up. His green eyes appeared bright against the grime streaking his face, and his anxious gaze flitted from Mattie to Andy. His expression eased into relief, though he continued to breathe heavily. "No. Just need to . . . catch my . . . breath."

What would they have done if he hadn't come into their lives? She would have lost her son, and her heart would have been ripped out. She owed Clint more than she could ever hope to repay in a lifetime.

Mattie's throat constricted. "Thank you, Clint," she said huskily.

"I'm . . . s-sorry, Ma." Andy's lower lip trembled. "I d-didn't mean to get so close."

Tears blurred her vision and she leaned over to gather Andy in her arms. "I'm just glad you're all right." She gazed at Clint over Andy's shoulder and stretched out her hand to him. He took it tentatively, as if he weren't quite certain what to do with it. Mattie squeezed his hand.

"Thanks to Mr. Beaudry you'll be fine, Andy," she said with a husky voice.

Her son drew away from her and turned to Clint. "Thank you, Mr. Beaudry." Then he wrapped his arms around Clint's neck.

Hesitantly, Clint hugged him, then tightened his embrace and closed his eyes. "You're welcome."

Mattie heard a catch in Clint's voice and realized just how much he had come to care for her son. Who would have thought that the dangerous gunman who'd come to her door nearly a month ago would become such an important part of their lives?

She glanced past Clint to Herman, who sat quietly, his face pale and his shoulders moving in irregular gasps. Concern shot through her and she hurried over to him. "Are you all right?"

He raised his head slowly and pain filled his rheumy eyes. "Don't know. My left arm hurts some."

Mattie gingerly lifted his arm, examining it for

injuries. "I don't see anything. Maybe you strained a muscle while we were pulling Clint up."

Herman grunted. "S'pose I ain't as young as I used to be."

"None of us are," Clint said with a smile, his straight white teeth a startling contrast to the mud on his face. "Can you make it back to the house?"

"I ain't *that* old," Herman said irritably.

Mattie saw how his hands trembled and his skin remained pale and clammy. "I'm going to have Kevin check on both you and Andy." She turned to Clint. "And you, too."

"I'm fine," Clint said with a dismissive wave. "Let's get back."

With all of them injured and weak, Mattie didn't know who to help first. Clint stubbornly climbed to his feet, then lent a hand to Andy, so Mattie helped Herman.

Andy tried to take a step and grimaced, favoring his right foot. "Ow!"

"Maybe you should wait here until I can bring the wagon back for you," Mattie said.

"I'll carry him," Clint volunteered.

"You're hurt."

"I'm fine."

Though Mattie knew by the white creases around his mouth that he was lying, she bit her tongue. Clint had more stubbornness and compassion than she had ever seen in one man.

He leaned over to retrieve his hat and gunbelt, then handed Andy the holster and gun. "You have to hold this while I carry you. I don't want to get it wet."

She took a step forward.

Herman tugged on her arm. "Hush, Mattie." He paused for a breath. "The man . . . jist saved . . . your boy's life." His voice ended in a scratchy whisper.

Mattie clamped her lips together. Herman was right.

She glanced up to see Clint watching her, and she gave him a slight nod. The lines in his brow eased and he picked up Andy, holding the boy in his strong arms, while Andy kept hold of the gunbelt.

Tears pricked her eyes. She'd always been so certain she could take care of Andy herself. Yet she hadn't been able to save him from a simple accident. It had been Clint who had risked his life to go down into the well to rescue her son, and who now cradled Andy against his chest as if he were a small child instead of a ten-year-old boy.

Just as a father would do.

And a father was the one thing she hadn't been able to give her son.

Swallowing her despair, she wrapped an arm around Herman's waist, and with a shuffling gait, they followed Clint and Andy.

"You could do worse," Herman murmured.

Startled, Mattie shot him a glance. "What're you talking about?"

"Beaudry. He's a good . . . m-man. Lot better . . .

than that f-feller you . . . married," Herman said in between panting breaths.

Mattie recognized the truth in his words, but Clint wouldn't settle down until he had killed the man who murdered his wife.

Or died trying.

She stumbled slightly. She'd almost lost both Andy and Clint today.

*A man who lives by the gun usually dies by it.*

The cold words returned to haunt her. She couldn't bear the thought of him being shot down, nor did she want him to leave.

"I know," she finally said to Herman, then forced a lightness she didn't feel. "But what do I need another man for? I have you and Andy."

They followed Clint silently for a few moments.

"I g-got a bad . . . feelin'," Herman said. He drew a thin hand across his face. "I ain't . . . l-long for this earth, Mattie."

An icy ball of fear settled in her chest. "You're going to live to be a hundred," she said firmly. "You just wait. Kevin'll tell you the same thing."

She wouldn't let him die. There'd been too many changes in her life since Clint had stepped into it—she couldn't handle another one. The problem was, she had as little control over Herman's life as she had in protecting Andy from the unforeseen.

The house came into view and Clint stopped by the pump so they all could wash off most of the mud before going inside.

Five minutes later, Andy and Herman were settled at the kitchen table. Mattie knelt down in front of Andy and removed the shoe and sock from his injured ankle. It had already begun to swell, ballooning like bread dough on a hot summer day. A bluish purple bruise told her he had probably twisted it.

"I need some ice," she said. Rising, she brushed her hands across her skirts impatiently. "I don't have any here, so I'll pick up some when I get Kevin."

"Give me a minute to change into dry clothes, then I'll go so you can stay with Andy and Herman," Clint said.

He left the kitchen before Mattie could reply and she heard his footsteps on the stairs.

Mattie wet a cloth with cold water from the kitchen pump and wrapped it around Andy's swollen ankle. The boy flinched and her heart skipped a beat. She hated seeing her son in pain. "It'll be all right, Andy. Dr. Murphy will make it all better," she reassured with false cheerfulness.

"He'll do what he can, Ma." Andy sounded so grown-up, she lifted her head to make sure it was he who'd spoken.

"He's right, Mattie," Herman wheezed. "No need to be talkin' to the boy like he's still a tyke."

Troubled, she remained silent. She'd never really thought about Andy growing up, and he was doing it right before her eyes. Only she had kept her eyes closed, refusing to see what was right in front of her.

Mattie dampened another cloth and pressed it against Herman's forehead. "How're you feeling?"

"Better. Just wore out, is all."

The sound of footsteps made her turn to see Clint reenter the kitchen. He had changed into another pair of black jeans, but instead of a completely black shirt, he wore one with white vertical stripes running through the material. It clung to his chest and tapered down to his trim waist.

The sight stole Mattie's breath.

"I'm going to get Dr. Murphy and the ice now," he said.

"Thank you," she managed to say.

In spite of the pain he had to be experiencing, Clint strode away. Mattie followed, catching up to him as he stepped onto the porch.

"Clint," she said.

He stopped and turned to face her in the dusky light. His long hair brushed across his shoulders, increasing the illusion of wildness about him . . . increasing her attraction to the unattainable.

"What?" he asked.

She moistened her lips and kept her gaze above his gunbelt, away from the Colt strapped to his thigh. "Be careful."

He furrowed his brow. "I'll be fine."

"Your wounds . . ."

Clint raised his hand to cup her cheek, and she leaned into his palm. "What is it, Mattie?" he asked softly.

She lifted her gaze and found herself trapped in the depths of his unusual eyes. How had she ever believed him a murderer . . . a hired gun? Wrapping her fingers around his forearm, she welcomed the comfort of the simple contact. "I would have lost him," she whispered.

His thumb brushed her cheek in slow, sensual motions. "You would have saved him."

"No. If you hadn't been here, Andy would have drowned. And I'd be alone again." Her voice broke on the last word.

One tear spilled down her cheek to be caught by Clint's thumb. His mouth opened but he didn't speak. Instead, he gathered her in his arms and Mattie pressed her cheek against his chest. She clutched his shirt in her fists, clinging to him, to the haven he offered. His heat burned through the material and his heartbeat thudded in unison with hers.

His familiar scent eased the tension within her. She'd been so terrified for Clint when he'd gone down into the well. If something had happened to him, part of her heart would have died. A very large part.

The revelation shocked and frightened her, and she crushed his shirt tighter in her hands. She couldn't release him any more than she could have let go when the ground had crumbled beneath his fingers.

"I have to go," Clint said softly, his warm breath skimming across her neck.

"I know." She continued to hold him.

He shifted so his chin rested on her crown and he rubbed her upper arms gently. "Let go, Mattie."

Mustering every ounce of willpower, she uncurled her fingers, leaving his shirt wrinkled.

She tried to smooth the material, but nothing short of a hot iron would help. She took a step back, her throat burning.

"I'll be back soon," he promised.

Unable to trust her voice, Mattie nodded.

As he walked away, she wrapped her arms around her waist to hold the growing inner chill at bay.

Why did she suddenly feel like she was standing on a high precipice . . . completely alone?

Less than half an hour later, Clint returned with Dr. Murphy and a block of ice. Clint sat down at the table to chip pieces of ice into a bowl.

Kevin checked Andy first, removing the cloth Mattie had placed on his ankle. He probed and shifted the ankle, making Andy grimace. Mattie knew her son was hurting, but he didn't cry out. Her little boy was growing into a man and she hadn't even noticed.

"It's not broken, is it?" Mattie asked.

Kevin shook his head. "Just twisted." He squatted down so he was eye level with the boy. "You won't be able to put any weight on that ankle for a few days, which means no running around or fishing."

Andy scowled. "What *can* I do?"

Kevin's spectacles caught the lantern light, winking brightly as he turned. "What do you think, Mattie? Maybe some early school lessons?"

The boy moaned as if in agony. "Is that my punishment for gettin' too close to the well?"

"Be glad it's not any worse," Mattie said. "And when that ankle heals, we'll be having a little discussion about listening to your mother and helping out more around the house."

Clint raised his head and caught her eye. She read approval in his slight nod and smile, and warmth suffused her cheeks.

"I'll even come by and bring some of my medical books if you want to look at the pictures," Kevin said, gazing at Mattie hopefully.

Kevin hadn't been around much since he'd come back to town, but it appeared he wanted to make up for lost time. A month ago, Mattie would have eagerly welcomed his attentions, but now . . .

She looked over at Clint, then back at Kevin. One man tall and lean with the keen eyes of a predator, the other slightly built with compassion written in his pale complexion and gray eyes.

One man would leave and the other would stay.

She managed a smile for the doctor. "I think Andy would like that." She paused and forced herself to add, "And I'd like that, too."

Kevin's smile was almost puppylike. "Then I'll stop by tomorrow."

He stepped over to Herman next and pressed the stethoscope to the old man's chest.

Herman jerked away. "You keep that thing on the ice?" he demanded. "It's cold enough to make a man go into a fit."

Kevin ignored his complaints and, after a minute of listening to the man's heart, he straightened. "He needs to stay in bed for a day or two," he said to Mattie.

"What's wrong?" Herman demanded.

"Your heart is beating faster than it should."

Herman snorted. "Course it is. I pulled that big galoot from the well."

Clint glanced up from his task. "You talking about me or Andy?"

Mattie smiled at the twinkle in his eyes as relief made her almost giddy. Andy's ankle wasn't broken and Herman's color and familiar grumbling had returned. If they only needed a couple days' rest, then they'd come out of this calamity much better than she had feared.

"You should check Clint out, to make sure he didn't reopen his wounds," Mattie suggested.

Kevin nodded immediately, but something indefinable flickered in his eyes. Did he know about her attraction to Clint? It didn't matter—it wasn't as if she could ever *love* a man like him.

A man who helped her with chores no one else would. A man who risked his own life to save her son's. A man who, with a simple touch, made her feel more alive than she'd ever felt.

No. It was only gratitude, not love. She'd made that mistake before.

Herman started to push himself up and Clint helped him. "Thanks, Beaudry."

"It's me who oughta be thanking you. If you and Mattie hadn't pulled me out of that well . . ." He smiled wryly and extended his hand to the older man. "Thank you."

Herman shook hands with Clint. "You remember that next time you're wantin' me to help you fix somethin' or t'other."

He winked and Clint chuckled.

"I reckon I'll head back to my room and lie down awhile, seein' as how the doc told me to," Herman said.

Mattie smiled fondly. He was going to milk that excuse for all it was worth over the next week. "Good idea," she said. "You want me to come get you when supper's ready?"

"Naw. I think I'll jist hit the sack. I'm pretty much tuckered out."

Mattie gave his arm a quick squeeze as he shuffled past her. "Good night."

Herman only smiled and continued out.

"Could you remove your shirt, Mr. Beaudry, so I can examine you?" Kevin asked.

Clint shrugged. "Sure." He handed Mattie the bowl full of ice chips.

"Thanks," she said. She noticed the tightness around his mouth and eyes. "Are you all right?"

"Just a little sore."

As he removed his shirt and lowered himself to the chair, Mattie wrapped some ice in a cloth and placed it on Andy's ankle. She stood behind Kevin, her arms crossed and her hands fisted as she watched Kevin remove the damp bandage around Clint's middle.

After a few minutes of poking and prodding, Kevin re-covered the wounds with a fresh dressing.

"Can I travel tomorrow?" Clint asked.

Kevin glanced up, startled. "You're leaving?"

Clint curtained the expression in his eyes. "I planned on it."

"You've just put your healing body through a very traumatic experience. I wouldn't be surprised if you're unable to get out of bed in the morning. Your muscles will be stiff and sore, not to mention that bullet wound." He paused as reluctance crept into his features. "If I were you, I'd wait a day or two before leaving. I'm sure Mattie won't mind."

Her heart skipped in her chest. "No, I don't mind." She looked at her son, whose eyes were closing with exhaustion, and laid a gentle hand on his head. "I'm sure Andy won't, either."

"I don't ever want Mr. Beaudry to leave," Andy slurred.

"I'm sure he has things that need doing," Kevin said.

"That's right," Clint said tightly. "But right now, I'll carry Andy up to his room."

"Do you have any of that liniment left?" Kevin asked Mattie.

She nodded. "About half a bottle."

"Good. Give it to Mr. Beaudry so he can put some on before he goes to bed." He looked at Clint. "It'll help with the soreness."

"Thanks." Clint replaced his shirt, then lifted the nearly asleep boy in his arms. Though he managed not to groan, Mattie could tell the effort cost him. She started to follow them, but Kevin's hand on her arm stilled her.

"I have to talk to you," he said quietly.

She didn't want to talk right now, but her guilty conscience wouldn't allow her to refuse him. She'd already put Clint ahead of Kevin too many times. "What about?"

He stuffed his stethoscope in his bag. "I'm sorry I left Beaudry here with you. I thought he wasn't going to make it, so I didn't think I had to worry."

Mattie blinked, shocked. "You mean if you had thought he was going to live, you wouldn't have left him with me?"

"Essentially, yes."

"Why?"

"He's a gunslinger, Mattie, the type of man you don't want Andy around, yet I left him here."

"He's *not* a gunslinger." The certainty behind her words surprised Mattie as much as Kevin.

"Of course he is. We've both seen his type before."

"No. He's not like that, Kevin. If he was, he wouldn't have risked his own life to save Andy's."

He eyed her silently. "What is he to you, Mattie?"

Her heart leapt into her throat. "He was my patient, and now he's my friend."

"And?"

Mattie could feel the color rise in her face, but she couldn't tell Kevin what she felt for Clint Beaudry, because even she wasn't certain herself. "And nothing," she said. "He's good with Andy and this is the first day he's worn his gunbelt since he's been here. He's not a bad man, Kevin."

"I wish I could be as sure of that as you." He

dragged a hand through his thinning hair. "I should never have left him here."

"Then he would've died. Is that what you wanted?"

"No," he replied without hesitation. "I'm a doctor, Mattie. My job is to save lives."

She took his cool hands in hers and couldn't help but compare them to Clint's slender fingers and wide, strong palms. She dashed the traitorous thought aside. "Since I'm your nurse, it's my job, too. You couldn't have done anything differently."

He smiled slightly. "You're right. If I only treated people I liked, I'd have an awfully small patient list."

Mattie laughed softly, but it wasn't genuine. Before Clint had come into her life, she'd been so certain she would come to love Kevin. Now her emotions were in turmoil. She had never seen this side of Kevin before—a jealous, almost caustic side.

"You don't mind if I come by tomorrow with that book for Andy, do you?"

Mattie swallowed hard. Clint would probably be gone then. Tears burned her eyes and she blinked them back. "No, of course not. What time?"

He smiled boyishly. "I was hoping you'd say around dinnertime."

Mattie smiled. "That would be fine."

Kevin pressed his dry lips against hers. After a moment's hesitation, Mattie kissed him back. She wanted to feel what she felt when Clint kissed her. She *needed* to feel it.

She opened her mouth and swept her tongue across his lips. Kevin quickly drew back, his face as red as a ripe strawberry. "Ah, well, I'd best get back. Someone might be looking for me."

Mattie folded her hands together and held them properly in front of her. Despair filled her and she fought to keep the emotion from her voice. "Yes, you'd better. I guess I'll see you tomorrow then."

"Good night," Kevin said, then fled.

Mattie grasped the back of a chair. She wanted so badly to feel for Kevin what she felt for Clint.

Why couldn't she be attracted to the right man instead of the wrong one? It had to be that passionate nature Mrs. Hotzel had accused her of having.

Mattie took a deep breath—Clint would leave and Kevin would remain. It was the perfect solution. A woman couldn't fall in love with a man if he wasn't around, could she?

Not wanting to dwell on the answer, Mattie climbed the stairs to get Andy settled in bed, but froze in the doorway to his room. Andy was already tucked in and Clint was sitting in the chair beside the bed.

The lamp's light flickered off the handle of his revolver. Her fingernails pressed into her palms. She had told him the rules about wearing his gunbelt under her roof. How dare he?

Then Clint reached for the book on the nightstand and held it up to Andy. "This one?" he asked.

The boy nodded.

"Okay, now close your eyes and I'll read to you for a little while," Clint said softly.

Mattie drew back so she wouldn't be seen, but listened while Clint's rich voice brought the story to life. As his tone rose and fell, his wearing the gunbelt seemed unimportant. It was only one part of Clint Beaudry—and not the most vital.

Gentle, soft-spoken Kevin had never read aloud to Andy. In fact, Kevin did very little with the boy. The offer to bring the medical book over to entertain him was the first overture the doctor had made toward him. Yet in the little time Clint had been there, he'd done so much more with her son—fishing, working together, saving his life, and reading him a bedtime story.

The blood drained from her face and she flattened her palm against the wall as she realized it was too late.

She'd already fallen in love with Clint Beaudry.

# Chapter 13

～◌◌◌～

Clint read until Andy's eyes remained closed for ten minutes, then he quietly laid the book back on the nightstand. Rising, he barely managed to restrain a groan. His body ached in places he'd never ached before.

He blew out the lamp and tiptoed out of the room, but stopped to glance back at the boy, who appeared small and vulnerable. It had been so close. Instead of lying in his bed tonight, Andy could have been laid out in a pine box.

Clint shivered. Death could strike so unexpectedly.

The smell of frying meat and fresh coffee reached him and his stomach growled in response. It had been a long time since he'd eaten lunch—another lifetime ago, before he'd taken a ride and talked with the sheriff, and spent an eternity in that dark well.

He started toward the stairs, but paused when he noticed the weight of his gunbelt on his hips. He'd made Mattie a promise that he wouldn't wear it in her house. Backtracking, he entered his own room and removed the belt and holster, placing them in a dresser drawer beneath his few clothes.

He descended the stairs, his legs and back protesting every movement. How the hell was he going to mount a horse tomorrow? Maybe he *should* stay another day or two, just until he felt better.

He froze on the bottom step. Where had that come from? He couldn't waste any more time here; he had to get back on the trail of the killer.

He continued into the kitchen, not surprised to see Mattie at the stove. Her cheeks were pinkened by the heat and dark tendrils curled around her face. The fear so evident earlier was no longer there.

"Smells good," he commented awkwardly.

Startled, she turned and her gaze flickered to his waist. "You took it off," she said in surprise.

He dropped into a chair and smiled sheepishly. "I forgot earlier. Sorry."

"That's all right," she said.

Clint hadn't expected her to be so calm about it.

She speared the round steak in the iron skillet and turned it over. "I saw you reading to Andy."

Clint rubbed his sore eyes. "He was tired, but he didn't want me to leave until he'd fallen asleep." He shrugged. "Guess I'd feel the same way if I'd almost died today."

Mattie turned her whole body around to face him. "You almost did," she said with aching concern.

His throat suddenly tightened. "But I didn't."

She studied him silently for a few more moments, then gave her attention back to supper. Clint planted his elbow on the edge of the table and rested his chin in his palm. He wasn't quite sure of what to make of this Mattie. She was probably just so grateful that her boy was alive that she'd lost that starched tongue of hers—she'd be back to her usual stubborn self in the morning, after the shock wore off.

He had to admit she'd managed to remain fairly calm. While he'd been a marshal, he'd seen more than his share of hysterical mothers. None of them had possessed Mattie's levelheadedness, and he was sure no other woman would have hung on to him when the ground had given way beneath his hand. He admired her backbone, her strength, and even her stubborn pride. If only he'd met her before . . .

And then she would be the one dead, instead of Emily.

The memory of his wife's broken body caught him off guard—and this time it was Mattie's face the corpse wore. He swallowed the bile rising in his throat.

"Thanks for catching me," he said with a husky voice.

Mattie set a plate of meat on the table, then touched his arm, her fingertips scorching him through the layer of cloth. "No, thank *you*. You saved my son's life, almost at the cost of your own."

He laid his palm on her hand that rested on his sleeve. The smoothness of her skin sent heat tumbling through his veins. "I'd do it again just so I wouldn't have to see that fear in your face."

The coffee bubbled on the stove while the lamps cast flickering shadows in the corners. An owl hooted nearby, then there was the whispered hush of its wings as it swooped down from its perch. A fox yipped in the distance and another answered from farther away.

Clint barely heard the common night sounds as a backdrop to Mattie's breathing and his own heartbeat. When had this woman and her son slipped past his defenses? Why did the thought of leaving them tomorrow bring such a bitter taste to his soul?

Mattie gently drew away and returned to the stove to gather the rest of the food. Clint shifted in his chair, his nerves taut and his blood hot and thick in his veins. He desired her just as he had when he'd first laid eyes on her, but now the need was tempered with some other emotion—something more dangerous than simple lust.

*Mattie and Andy need you.*

He closed his eyes and pinched the bridge of his nose. His wife had needed him, too, and he'd let her down. He couldn't risk doing the same to Mattie and her son.

Mattie settled in the chair across the table from

him and placed her napkin in her lap. She lifted her gaze to his once, but quickly lowered it when she caught his eye.

Clint filled his plate and tried to pretend the air between them didn't sizzle like water on a hot frying pan. The absence of Andy and Herman added to the tension, allowing him no respite from his awareness of the woman.

"You really should stay until you're healed more," Mattie said, breaking the silence.

Clint couldn't tell her how tempted he was to do just that. But even one more day among this family might break his resolve completely. The drive to find Emily's killer had lost much of its force, battered away by the temptation to return to a normal life . . . with Mattie and Andy.

"It's better for everyone if I leave tomorrow." He remembered Dr. Murphy's thinly veiled dislike for him. "Especially for your doctor friend."

Mattie's face reddened. "Kevin wouldn't want you to do anything that might hinder your recovery."

Clint smiled crookedly. "Kevin doesn't like another man hanging around his woman. If you were my woman, I sure as hell wouldn't let another man near you, even if he was supposed to be healing from a bullet wound."

He could see her heartbeat fluttering in her slender neck and was tempted to press his lips to the pulse point.

"Kevin has no reason to be jealous. You'll be leaving sooner or later," Mattie said stiffly.

He studied her a moment, trying to gauge her feelings. "Which would you prefer—sooner or later?"

"From a medical standpoint, later would be better."

The tremor in her voice betrayed her and Clint pressed his advantage. "What about Mattie's standpoint? Do *you* want me to leave sooner or later?"

She set her fork on her plate and dropped her hands in her lap. "That isn't fair, Clint."

His heart skipped a beat. "What isn't fair?"

"If I ask you to stay longer, you will, but for the wrong reasons. *You* have to want to stay."

"Is that an invitation?"

Mattie met his gaze squarely. "*You* have to make the choice."

His mouth had gone as dry as a sun-baked bone. "Why can't I do both? Why can't I leave to take care of my business, then return when I'm done?"

She shook her head. "Because I won't wait for a man who's determined to get himself killed."

Clint's gaze became unfocused. His first reaction to Emily's murder had been disbelief, then rage, and finally guilt. Had his vow to catch her killer been his way to die without actually pulling the trigger himself?

"I'll do my best not to get killed," he said.

"Then give it up."

Her challenge lay between them like a brick wall.

"I can't," he finally replied in a barely audible voice.

Moisture shimmered in her eyes, but she lifted her chin proudly. "That's what I thought." She stood and gathered their dishes.

Clint remained where he was, confused and disgusted and angry, though he wasn't certain to whom his feelings were directed—Mattie for pointing out the truth, or himself for not being able to bend.

Mattie washed the dishes and Clint dried them in silence, both knowing this was the last night they'd spend under the same roof. Even if he returned, he wouldn't—couldn't—stay here again. It was even possible that if he came back, she'd be married to Dr. Murphy.

He had nothing against the doctor, but Mattie needed a man who was just as passionate as she was. A man who could satisfy her in bed as well as out.

A man like him.

The house was silent and still, but Mattie couldn't sleep. She tossed the light covers off and sprawled on her back staring at the ceiling. After the near tragedy, her restlessness shouldn't have surprised her. However, it wasn't the memory of her fear for Andy that kept her awake, but the burning fever Clint had ignited.

Just the recollection of his hand on hers that evening made her breasts swell and her loins ache. Erotic images of Clint rising above her and burying himself in her damp heat chased sleep away. The faded memories of lying with her husband paled even further beside the waking dreams of Clint. There was a barely restrained wildness about him that her body begged to release.

She closed her eyes, drawing her fingertips lightly across the gown's thin fabric, imagining Clint's hands on her bare breasts, his fingers playing with her nipples. The crests pebbled beneath Mattie's touch and she quickly dropped her hand to the mattress beside her. Embarrassment made her cheeks burn, but the feelings and images she'd evoked set the rest of her body aflame.

Abruptly, she sat up and swung her feet off the bed. She couldn't lie here any longer. She tugged on her robe and grimaced when the material slid across her sensitized breasts.

With soundless steps, she walked down the hall and looked into Andy's room. The boy slept peacefully, his soft snores punctuating the night's silence. She leaned against the doorjamb and merely watched him, thanking God that he had survived this day.

She swiped a hand across her moist eyes and descended the stairs. Halfway down, she noticed the flicker of light in the parlor. Who was in there?

Her hands trembling, she picked up the broom and gripped it like a club, ready to defend her home. Gliding across the floor, she made it to the wide doorway and paused. She caught the movement of a black shadow coming toward her and swung the broom forcefully.

"Ooomph," came the satisfying reply.

"Who's there?" she demanded. "You'd better come out or I'll shoot you."

"With what—a broom?"

It was Clint's very irate voice.

*Oh, no.*

"I'm sorry, Clint," she said, setting the broom down. "I didn't realize it was you."

He emerged from the darkness and the firelight danced across his frowning countenance. He had a hand pressed to his nose. "You should've called out," he muttered.

"That would've warned off the thief."

"There wasn't a thief, just me." The exasperation in Clint's voice was almost funny.

She put a hand to her mouth to stifle her laughter. "That isn't the point. You could've been."

"And what would I steal?"

*My heart.*

Her humor died. "I'm sorry." She reached out to pull his hand away from his cheek. "Did I hurt you?"

"It's nothing," he said.

She rolled her eyes. "Let me light a lamp so I can take a look at it."

Mattie steered him toward the sofa and sat him in the corner closest to the lamp. After she lit the wick, she took a good look at him. Wearing nothing but black jeans and socks, he was the epitome of temptation. Just what she needed.

"Oh, Lord," she murmured.

"What?" Clint asked.

"Nothing." Mattie rubbed her brow, trying to erase the images she'd conjured as she had lain in her bed. This wasn't the glass of warm milk she expected to find down here.

"Did you break my nose?" Clint's question intruded into her frenzied thoughts.

"Let me take a look." She leaned close, but her gaze kept flitting down to the crinkly blond hair sprinkled across his chest and tapering down to his bandage.

"Well?" His voice sounded strange, like he was being strangled.

She glanced down to look at him and saw where his gaze had settled. Her robe gaped open to reveal the swell of her breasts. Grabbing at the material, she tugged the sides together to hide her cleavage.

*Turnabout is fair play.*

"Shut up," she muttered.

"I didn't say anything," Clint said.

Heat flooded her cheeks. This had to be a nightmare.

Or a dream come true.

"I was talking to myself," she said. "I don't think your nose is broken and it's not bleeding. Probably just bruised. It's a good thing I didn't put any force behind my swing."

A smile lifted a corner of his sensuous lips. "Maybe you did."

She propped her hands on her hips, knowing he was teasing. "Are you saying I'm weak?"

"Never, Mattie St. Clair." His grin faded. "You're the strongest woman I've ever met."

She blinked, unprepared for the serious turn of the conversation. "Then you don't know me that well."

"Or you don't know yourself well enough."

He took hold of her wrist and gently pulled her down beside him on the sofa. Her thigh pressed against his and she could feel the hard muscle of his leg through her robe and gown. Warmth exploded along the line of contact.

*This is* not *a good idea.*

Clint rested his arm along the back of the couch as if their closeness had no effect upon him.

"What brought you down here in the middle of the night?" he asked, as if it were normal to have a conversation at two in the morning with an indecently clad woman.

She slid her gaze to his bare chest. At least they were both indecently clad.

That thought did nothing to douse her sparking nerves.

"I couldn't sleep." Why did her voice sound so breathy?

"Why?"

Mattie's heart hammered against her ribs. "It must've been the excitement of the day." She prayed he couldn't see her pebbled nipples pressing against her robe. "What about you? What're you doing down here?"

He flashed a rueful smile. "I couldn't sleep, either."

"Why?" She had to keep the conversation away from her.

Clint's eyes glittered like emeralds as his gaze

settled on her. "I kept thinking about you, knowing you were just two doors away."

Mattie shivered and forced a laugh. "I would've thought you'd be exhausted."

She felt him touch her hair, stroking it gently. "I'm tired, but I . . . had other things on my mind."

His rhythmic motions lulled her into a sensual calm. She closed her eyes and concentrated on the heat radiating from Clint's chest, and the faint scent of the liniment he'd applied earlier, and shivered again.

"Are you cold?" He wrapped his arm about her shoulders, drawing her snug against his side.

*Hardly.*

Then he passed his other arm in front of her and enclosed her within his secure embrace. God forgive her, but she didn't want to escape.

The air was thick. Expectant. Clint's warmth surrounded Mattie, his breath cascading across her cheek and his body heat radiating to her. Her breasts felt heavy and her limbs sluggish, but at the same time, something sizzled beneath her skin.

Awareness of Clint branded her with a passion she was tired of fighting. For ten years, she'd lived the life of a cloistered nun. She hadn't allowed any man but Kevin to touch her, and those caresses had been chaste at best.

Now she had a chance to grab the brass ring for one night. All she had to do was say yes and surrender her mind to what her body already demanded. Her heart hammered and her breath grew ragged. Did she have the strength to let herself go for one night? To feel totally alive with the man she loved but couldn't have?

Trembling, Mattie pulled away from Clint's arms and stood to walk to the fireplace. She had to do this, or she'd forever wonder. . . .

With shaking fingers, she raised the lid of the music box and the strains of the waltz circled around her. She turned slowly and faced Clint. For a moment, all she could do was stare at him—the muscles playing across his chest and shoulders, his blond hair shimmering in the firelight, and his eyes so rich and intense and compassionate—she could disappear in those depths and never return.

Slowly, almost as if it weren't her, she removed the sash from her robe and allowed the heavy material to slide to the floor. Clad just in her white nightgown with the fire behind her, Mattie stretched out a hand to him. "Would you like this dance?" she asked huskily.

Mattie watched the light in his eyes turn to something dark and smoldering. Her belly curled and she was shaking so badly inside, she thought she'd shatter into a million pieces.

Clint came to his feet with the stealth of a predator, but Mattie wasn't afraid. She would be his willing prey for this one night.

His hand closed around hers and quicksilver glided through her blood as she curled her fingers around his. He slid his other arm around her waist and drew her close. She raised her head to gaze into his face and was captured by the tenderness in his expression. No longer was he the predator, but the lover she'd only imagined in fevered dreams.

He began to move to the strains of the waltz, and Mattie's feet instinctively followed his footsteps. No awkwardness existed between them; only a feeling that she had danced in this man's arms in another time, another life.

Mattie concentrated on every single inch of her body that Clint touched, from their clasped hands to her breasts, which pressed intimately against his torso with only the thin gown separating their hot skin. Her legs brushed his as they waltzed across the room in slow, sensual motions, and she could feel his arousal.

She laid her cheek against his bare chest and heard Clint's heart beat strong and steady. The coarse hairs tickled her face and the faint smells of leather, sweat, and masculinity clouded her thoughts with erotic images of the two of them, wrapped in damp sheets and passion.

Clint began to massage her back with gentle deliberate circular motions. Mattie tightened her hold on his hand and arched her breasts more firmly against his chest. Her body throbbed with anxious need and her thin nightgown suddenly seemed cumbersome. She whimpered with frustration—she wanted their skin touching . . . all of it.

Clint stopped in the middle of the room and cupped Mattie's face between his palms. His thumbs brushed her eyebrows lightly.

She stared up into his heavy-lidded eyes—eyes

that burned with desire and turned her insides to molten heat. Her gaze flickered to his sensuous lips and she had to kiss him. Now. She couldn't wait.

Placing her hands on either side of his face, she lowered it and slanted her lips across his. After a moment of hesitation, Clint opened his mouth to hers as his fingers plunged into her hair, and he clutched the strands in his fists.

Lust, hot and hungry, fired Mattie's blood. Her lips were crushed by his demanding ones, but she wanted more. She met his urgent tongue with hers and they mated with an intensity she craved to imitate with their bodies.

Abruptly Clint pulled away, releasing her and taking a step back. His hands balled into fists at his sides. Her gaze fell to the hard column of flesh she'd felt while they'd danced.

Hurt and confusion swirled through her.

"I can't do this to you, Mattie."

She could barely hear his words above her pounding heart. "What?"

He grabbed her upper arms and pulled her against him. "I'm leaving tomorrow and I can't leave you with regrets."

Slowly, she lifted her hands and laid them on his cheeks. The agony in his eyes tore at her heart. "The only regret I'll have is if you don't make love to me tonight."

"You don't know what you're asking."

"I know exactly what I'm asking—just one night in your arms," she said huskily.

# Chapter 14

Clint searched for any sign of reluctance in Mattie's expression, but found only mirroring passion. A passion that had been nurtured by days and weeks spent in each other's company, keeping one another at arm's length, while nature plotted to bring them together.

He finally released his control and wrapped his arms around Mattie. He sought her lips and the weeks of restraint evaporated with the feel of her mouth, eager against his. Passion banished his body's soreness and he slid his hands down her slender back, across the thin material that did little to conceal her perfect figure. The firelight behind her had hidden nothing from his greedy gaze—her tiny waist and flaring hips, her shapely legs and the shadowy junction of her thighs.

Grabbing her gown, he swiftly pulled it upward

and then cupped her rounded backside. Her skin was smooth, soft ... just as he'd imagined. He pulled her firmly against his erection and rolled his hips. She moaned and imitated his motions, bringing him to the brink of release that quickly.

He drew back and gasped like a suffocating man—suffocating in Mattie's charms. Bunching the gown in his fist, he lifted it higher and brought his other hand around to cup a full breast. Her flesh filled his palm and blood roared through his veins. He fondled her nipple, already hard as a button.

Mattie bent her head back, offering her pale throat to him. As he kissed a trail down the slender column, her fingers threaded through his hair and her hands locked behind his head.

"Don't stop," she whispered hoarsely.

A team of oxen couldn't have dragged him away. His erection pressed painfully against his jeans—he couldn't remember ever being so aroused. He had to plunge himself into her slick heat soon or he would combust.

He drew his tongue down her breast and sucked the tip into his mouth. She tasted so good, so right.

Sweet, courageous, proud Mattie ...

He'd wanted her from the moment he had laid eyes on her, and the days he'd spent in her company had only increased his hunger. He needed her with an intensity that clouded every sane reason why he shouldn't take what she offered. Moving his hands up and down her sides, pausing on the undersides of her breasts, Clint rained kisses upon her lips, her cheeks, her neck. He couldn't get enough of touching her, feeling her, caressing her skin, more soft and velvety than his most vivid imaginings.

Mattie's hands stroked his hair and skimmed down his back, then around front between their hot bodies. Her fingers slid between his belly and jeans, and he nearly jumped when they brushed him.

"Not here," he said hoarsely.

He scooped her up in his arms, hardly noticing the slight protest of his muscles, then climbed the stairs and entered Mattie's room. He closed the door behind them with his foot and sat her on the edge of the bed, facing him.

Mattie lifted her gown over her head, throwing it away impatiently. The light in her eyes smoldered. His breath stuttered when she reached out to undo his pants.

Clint swiftly shucked his jeans, and his masculinity jutted out proudly. He lay down on the bed, drawing her close beside him. Capturing the crest of one nipple, he rolled the bud between his thumb and forefinger, and she gasped with pleasure.

Mattie wrapped her fingers around his rock-hard length, surprising the hell out of him and making him throb within her grasp.

Clint bit back the groan of intense delight that crawled up his throat. He wouldn't last much longer if Mattie continued her excruciating ecstasy. He took her wrist and drew her touch away from his too-sensitive flesh.

He rolled atop her and she clutched at his hips, her fingers frantically urging him into her.

"Yes, now," Mattie cried.

Her eagerness spurred him forward and he guided himself between her thighs. The moment he touched her dampness, he lost control and plunged into her tight heat.

Mattie moaned and arched her hips upward, accepting his length and demanding more. He rolled his pelvis back and forth, drawing in and out of her slickness. She met him stroke for stroke, with no reluctance or hesitation.

As he moved within her, he cupped her breasts, thumbing the pebble-hard nubs. Her violet eyes were cloudy with passion, with the approaching climax that he sensed in her walls clutching at his hard flesh.

For just one night, he would love Mattie and carry the memory of this time within his heart.

Mattie's breath grew faster, more frantic, and he knew she was on the edge of her release. He gripped her hips and increased his rhythm, pressing himself even farther into her depths. Her body stiffened and he covered her mouth with his, swallowing her cry of ecstasy as he, too, went over the edge, releasing his seed deep within her.

Slowly, Mattie's senses spiraled downward, bringing a lethargy to her tingling limbs. She loved the weight of Clint atop her damp body, his heartbeat thudding in time with her own. Nothing in her past had prepared her for the rapture of his lovemaking. Her entire being centered on this man who had unlocked a part of her that she'd kept hidden from even herself.

Clint shifted and Mattie tightened her arms around him.

"I'm too heavy," Clint whispered.

Reluctantly, she allowed him to roll onto his back beside her. He slid his arm beneath her and she rested her head on his shoulder. She brushed her fingers across the middle of his chest, where the blond hair was the thickest. The soft-rough sensation against her skin brought a smile of contentment.

"Any regrets?" Clint asked quietly.

Startled, Mattie propped herself up on an elbow. "None. How about you?"

His crooked smile shot straight to her heart. "Never." He raised his hand and stroked her cheek. "We still have a few hours before dawn."

Mattie's insides curled and a current of desire shot through her veins. "Then we'd best not waste them."

She kissed his lips, then his cheek, and traveled down the rough expanse of his whiskers. Giving back what Clint had given her, Mattie drew one of his nipples into her mouth and was rewarded with a soft groan.

"If you're trying to kill me, it's working," Clint said huskily.

Mattie raised her head. "But such a pleasant way to go."

Clint's shoulders shook with laughter. "Oh, yeah."

Mattie continued her exploration of his hard, lean body, which was growing harder by the moment. She felt his hands on her arms, urging her up. Complying, she straddled him, trapping his reviving manhood between her thighs.

He clutched her backside in his hands, kneading her soft flesh as he pressed his head back against the pillow. He knew he'd have a difficult time settling for only one taste of her lovemaking, but he hadn't expected her to be so passionate and ready for him again. Or to take the initiative.

Mattie's actions spoke louder than any words as she worked Clint into a feverish passion. Her caresses left a burning trail across his chest and her kisses branded him as hers alone. Coherent thought abandoned him and he wrapped his hands around Mattie's thighs, lifting her above his steel length.

He felt her hand upon his erection as she guided him into her eager slickness and she began to ride him. She was even hotter than the first time, but after his initial release, Clint could control himself better to prolong the sweet journey. He reached upward and filled his hands with her breasts. Every forward movement of her body rubbed her nipples against his palms.

She closed her eyes and her low moans filled the room. Her tongue swept across her lips in an erotic invitation to taste them once more. Clint wrapped his arms around her and drew her down atop him, then threaded his fingers through her hair and slanted his lips across hers.

Her belly rubbed against his, and her actions grew more frenzied. Then she convulsed around him and he captured her silent scream with a kiss.

Mattie felt his climax a few moments later as he arched up against her, and she welcomed his second gift. She sagged onto him, her sweat-dampened body sliding across his skin. Her senses were attuned to his rapid breathing, the heat radiating from his body, and the scent of their love-making.

Maybe she *was* bad because of her wanton passion—but at that moment, she didn't care.

All she cared about was this man who had stolen her heart, and to whom she had given her body—with no regrets.

Mattie awakened slowly, blinking in the sunlight that streamed through the windows. A heavy weight across her stomach made her turn her head to see Clint sleeping peacefully beside her. He lay on his side, his arm around her middle and his handsome, angular face inches from her own.

She brushed a strand of hair back from his face, enjoying the intimacy with almost guilty pleasure. The vulnerability and gentleness in Clint's face made her heart tighten.

"I love you," she whispered. She couldn't speak the words to him, but she needed to hear them aloud in her own voice.

Fragments of indescribable feelings and unexpected heights of pleasure tumbled back to her. They'd finally fallen asleep in each other's arms after making love yet again. Each time, she hadn't believed it could get better, but it had. Their bodies fitted together as if they'd been made for one another, and instinctively they each knew what brought the most pleasure to the other.

Mattie closed her eyes, reliving the moments in his arms, knowing she would live with those memories the rest of her life. Sadness caught her off guard, but she wouldn't let anguish bury the happiness she'd experienced.

Opening her eyes again, she slipped out of the bed, grimacing at the soreness in her shoulder. It had been a small price to pay for preventing Clint from falling back into the well.

She picked up her gown where she'd thrown it last night and folded it, then dressed quietly, knowing Clint needed his rest.

Before he left.

Silently, Mattie washed her face, then dressed and brushed her hair. She tiptoed to the door and opened it cautiously, then paused to gaze at Clint, who continued to sleep. Her chest hurt and her vision blurred. She didn't want him to leave, but the choice was out of her hands.

She slipped into the hallway and clicked the door shut behind her. Sticking her head in Andy's room, she was glad to see he was still sleeping, also. The longer he slept, the less of the day she had to force him to stay off his injured ankle.

Mattie descended the stairs and glanced in the parlor. Her robe lay on the floor and she hurried over to pick it up. She clutched it to her chest and closed her eyes, reliving the magical moments of the waltz she shared with Clint. Her heart aching, she opened her eyes and carried the robe up to her room. She kept her gaze averted from the bed, where Clint's long lean body was covered with merely a sheet from the waist down.

Going back downstairs, she started breakfast. Dakota whinnied from the corral and Mattie looked out the window. This would be the last day she'd see the mare prance around the enclosure. She pressed a hand to her mouth to hold a sob at bay.

She should be grateful her life would get back to normal after Clint left. Once he and his gun were gone, things would settle down into a familiar routine. No longer would her days be interrupted by a trip to the fishing pond or her nights disturbed by his presence under his roof. She should be pleased.

But she only felt lost and empty.

Mattie shook off her depressing thoughts and turned around. Her heart leapt at the sight of Clint lounging against the doorframe, his warm gaze on her. A collage of the night passed through her thoughts and her cheeks heated.

"Good morning," he greeted in a husky voice that would have tempted the angels.

"Morning," Mattie said. She averted her gaze from him and crossed the kitchen to the table. "I'll have breakfast ready in about fifteen minutes."

She passed him to lift the skillet off the hook on the wall and place it on the stove. Clint's hand settled on hers, his heat scorching her knuckles.

"You should have woken me when you got up," he said, his warm breath fanning across her neck.

"You needed the rest," she replied, keeping her gaze averted from his.

He cupped her chin and raised it so she had to look at him. Concern shaded his eyes and brought a lump to her throat. "You aren't—"

She shook her head. "No, it's not that." She paused and laid her palm against his freshly shaven cheek. Her breath faltered. "Never that."

Clint's brow furrowed. "Then what?"

"I'll miss you," she replied without hesitation, then forced a smile. "But I understand you can't stay."

The creases in his face deepened. "Sometimes I wish I understood."

"What do you mean?"

He sighed and his hand fell to his side. "I was a lawman, Mattie."

A shock rippled through her and she stepped back. "What?"

Clint turned away from her to stare out the window. "I was a U.S. marshal. My wife wanted me to quit since I had to travel so much, but I couldn't." He shrugged. "I cared more about my job than Emily. I was on my way home from picking up a prisoner when she was murdered."

Mattie took a step toward him, but she stopped when he turned stiffly.

"If I'd quit my job like she asked, she wouldn't

be dead," Clint said. "It was my fault, Mattie, and I don't have a choice in this. I owe her for not loving her enough."

Mattie crossed her arms to hide her trembling. She didn't know what to say. She'd believed him to be a gunslinger and he'd been a lawman, like her husband.

And he'd loved his job more than his wife, just as Jason had.

"I should've told you before, but there are some things a man has a hard time admitting," he said. He laid his hands on her shoulders. "Even if I find Emily's killer, I can't promise I'd be able to protect you and Andy, any more than I protected her."

Mattie bit her lower lip. They didn't need his promise—they just needed him. "I didn't ask for any promises."

He smiled sadly. "No, you didn't."

Mattie drew away. "I'd better get breakfast ready before Herman comes in."

She felt Clint's gaze on her back, but she didn't dare look at him for fear he'd see the lie in her eyes. Though she hadn't asked for a promise in so many words, she had with something more precious. And his actions last night had told her he had strong feelings for her, too—though they weren't powerful enough to make him break another promise.

But he wouldn't be the man she loved, if he did.

Clint finished his coffee. "I'm going to check on Dakota."

Mattie nodded, but didn't turn to watch him leave.

The back door opened as Mattie was putting the bacon and eggs on the table. She glanced up, expecting to see Clint, but it was Herman who shuffled in. Disappointment brought a frown to her lips. "Morning, Herman."

The old man frowned. "Don't look so happy to see me."

Mattie blinked, then chastised herself for being so selfish and smiled. "I'm sorry, Herman. I was thinking."

"He's still down by the barn."

She smiled self-consciously. "Am I that obvious?"

"Yep." Herman plopped himself in his regular chair. "Wearin' your heart on your sleeve ain't healthy, Mattie. Have you told him?"

"He knows." She glanced out the window toward the corral, then added quietly, "In his own way, he knows."

"Some men are fools, Mattie. And I can say that 'cause I'm one myself."

"So you're finally admitting it?" she teased.

Herman snorted. "Respect your elders, girl." He squinted at Mattie. "You ever wonder why I stuck around here?"

"You liked Andy and me?"

"No, before you come here."

Mattie sat across the table from him. "Why?"

"Ruth. I loved her since the day I saw her, forty-eight years ago. Only problem was, she was married to another man."

Mattie's mouth dropped open. A few moments later, she remembered to close it. "Did she know?"

"She belonged to another man."

"That's not what I asked."

Herman took a deep breath and his faded eyes glistened with moisture. "She knew." He rubbed his nose. "We had one night together in all the years we loved each other, and I ain't never forgot that time."

Mattie kept her expression calm. Did he suspect what had happened between herself and Clint?

"Why didn't you leave? It must've hurt terribly to see her with another man."

"It woulda hurt worse if I never saw her again. When her husband died, I asked her to marry me." Herman tried to smile but failed. "You know what she said?"

Mattie shook her head.

"She said she didn't want to burden me with an invalid wife." Herman sniffed. "Hell, it didn't matter to me if'n she was bedridden or not. I loved her, but she was a proud woman. Never gave an inch." His hunched shoulders rose and fell with a sigh. "If you love him, don't let your pride get in your way."

Mattie wanted nothing more than for Clint to stay, but she loved him too much to ask. "It's *his* pride that's in the way, and I won't ask him to stay if he doesn't want to."

Herman reached across the table and laid a blue-veined hand on hers. "Just like Ruth—too pig-headed to see what's right in front of you." He squeezed her hand. "I only wanna see you happy before I join her."

Mattie's eyes filled with tears and she laid her hand on his. "With any luck, by the time you join Ruth, Kevin and I will be happily married."

"Married, maybe. Happy?" He shook his head. "I ain't so sure about that."

Mattie didn't know how to deny his words without lying.

Clint's lean figure appeared in the doorway and Mattie's breath caught. Had he heard their conversation?

"I hoped you saved some food for me," Clint said.

"Why would we do that?" Herman asked. "Seems to me if you don't show at the table on time, you're plumb out of luck."

"We just sat down," Mattie said.

"Good." Clint slid his hat off to hang down his back, then sank into a chair. "How're you feeling this morning?" he asked Herman.

"I'd be feelin' better if the world wasn't so full of stubborn cusses," Herman replied with a scowl.

Startled, Clint glanced at Mattie in question.

"He woke up on the wrong side of bed," she said.

"At least I was in my own bed," Herman grumbled.

Mattie choked on her coffee and her face flamed. So Herman wasn't nearly as oblivious as he made out.

Clint narrowed his eyes at the old man. "Our business isn't any of yours."

"Don't go gettin' all huffy. I ain't one to blab around town and start tongues a-waggin'." Herman aimed his fork at Clint. " 'Sides, someone has to stick around to make sure Mattie's good name ain't run through the mud."

Mattie sidled a glance at Clint and a blush stained his cheeks. Herman's pointed remark struck home with blunt accuracy. But Mattie didn't need anyone defending her.

"I am perfectly capable of taking care of myself. I did it before I met either of you, so let's just eat and forget this conversation ever happened," she said.

Herman grumbled but kept his counsel to himself. Clint cast Mattie a puzzled look, but also remained quiet.

They finished breakfast in strained silence, then Mattie gathered the dirty plates.

"Ma!" Andy hollered. "Can I get up?"

Mattie's gaze caught Clint's, then she hurried to the bottom of the stairs and called up, "You stay in bed. I'll bring your breakfast up."

"I'll take it up," Clint offered when Mattie returned to the kitchen. "I have to say good-bye to him anyhow."

She nodded quickly and filled a plate with bacon, eggs, and toast, then handed the dish and a glass of milk to Clint. "Thank you."

He nodded, took the breakfast from her, and

headed to the staircase. She listened to his footsteps up the stairs, her heart squeezing with sorrow.

Clint climbed the steps, feeling as if he were ascending a gallows. He dreaded saying good-bye to the boy nearly as much as he dreaded saying farewell to Mattie.

He entered the room and Andy brightened. "Mr. Beaudry."

"Mornin', sleepyhead," Clint said, with a fond smile.

"I haven't slept this late ever," Andy admitted. "Is Ma still mad at me?"

"She was never mad at you, just worried."

Andy let out a relieved sigh. "I suppose, but she shouldn't worry so much. It's not like I'm a baby anymore."

"I don't think mothers ever stop worrying about their children. I know for a fact my ma still worries about me."

"But you're a grown-up."

Clint shrugged. "It's a woman thing. I don't think we're supposed to understand." He set Andy's plate and glass of milk on the nightstand. "Why don't you sit up so you can eat?"

He helped the boy up and arranged the pillows behind his back. "How does that feel?"

"Okay. Why can't I get up and eat downstairs?" Andy asked.

"You're supposed to stay off that ankle, remember?"

He moved his leg under the blankets. "But it feels okay."

"That's because you're not standing on it. Remember what Dr. Murphy told you—no running around or fishing for a few days."

Andy wrinkled his nose. "He's worse than Ma."

Clint balanced Andy's plate on the boy's lap. "Is that all right?"

Andy nodded and picked up his fork, then shoveled some egg into his mouth.

"Why do you think Dr. Murphy is worse than your mother?" Clint asked curiously.

Andy rolled his eyes as he took a bit of bacon. "He thinks a sliver is gonna kill me."

Clint chuckled. "He's a doctor. It's his job to worry about people."

"I s'pose." The boy paused. "Ma wants to marry him."

Jealousy sucker-punched Clint and he exhaled sharply. Though he knew the doctor would make a better husband than him, he couldn't help the possessiveness that washed through him. "He's a good man."

"I guess." Andy didn't sound convinced.

"He'll take care of you and your mother better than I could," Clint said, uncertain if he was trying to assure himself or Andy.

The boy didn't say anything, but the long face told Clint plenty. He watched the boy clean up his plate, then took the empty dish and set it back on the nightstand.

Clint laid a hand on the boy's thin shoulder. "I'm leaving today."

Andy jerked his head up, his eyes wide. "Why?"

The disappointment in the boy's expression dropped a lead ball in Clint's gut. "I have something to take care of."

"Then you'll come back?" Hope lit his face.

Clint could have lied, but to give the boy false hope would have been unfair. "I doubt it."

Andy's expression tumbled and his lower lip trembled. "I don't want you to go."

Damn, the kid made him feel like shit. "If I had a choice, I'd stay, but I don't. I have to leave."

"Why?"

"Because I have to." *You're a coward, Beaudry.* He met the boy's gaze. "I'll miss you."

Anger filled Andy's expression for a moment, then it crumbled into sadness. "I'll miss you, too."

Clint didn't know who made the first move, but he hugged the boy close to his chest. For a long moment, they remained locked in the embrace, then Andy pulled away.

A single tear tracked down the boy's face. "Be careful, Mr. Beaudry," he said solemnly.

When Clint had arrived in Green Valley four weeks ago, he never suspected he'd be leaving a large part of himself behind when he continued on.

"I will. You're big enough to help your mother around here now," Clint said, barely able to squeeze the words past the lump in his throat.

Andy nodded. "Once I'm better, I'll help her more. I promise."

Clint pushed to his feet and stared into the hazel eyes of Mattie's son, which held a maturity he'd never noticed before. Maybe it was his close brush with death yesterday, or the realization that he was becoming a man and his mother needed him.

Or maybe both.

"Good-bye, Andy," he said.

" 'Bye, Mr. Beaudry," Andy said, his voice shaky.

Clint forced his feet to carry him out of the boy's room—and out of his life forever.

# Chapter 15

Clint entered his room for the last time and paused. It suddenly felt foreign to him. He didn't belong here. Not anymore.

He pulled his saddlebags out from under the bed and jerked open the dresser drawer that contained his few belongings. He stuffed his extra underwear and socks into one side of the saddlebags, then tightened the straps and reached for his gun in the bottom of the drawer.

Instead of donning it, Clint studied the well-oiled sheen of metal and leather. He could clean the gun blindfolded and knew the heft of it instinctively, yet as he stared at it, the Colt suddenly seemed as unfamiliar as the room.

Had Mattie changed him that much? Had her dislike of guns made him reconsider his own beliefs?

No, it was merely a result of his mixed-up emotions. As soon as he strapped on the gunbelt and left this place behind, he'd be fine.

Clint donned the gunbelt and tied the rawhide laces around his thigh to hold the holster in place. Then he tossed his saddlebags over a shoulder and strode out of the room, but stopped to gaze back at it one last time.

*You're making a mistake.*

He swallowed and ignored his own inner voice.

Mattie slipped downstairs before Clint caught her eavesdropping on his farewell to Andy. She had to regain her composure before she said her own good-byes. How would she get through that if she wasn't even strong enough to witness Clint and Andy's farewell?

She picked up her broom, hoping the familiar task would calm her. Instead she recalled swinging the handle at Clint, and she pressed a hand to cover her smile as moisture filled her eyes. He had been startled, but not angry, which had surprised her. She'd apologized, but then they'd teased one another about the accident. Jason would have . . .

What would her husband have done?

Jason had been so young, so immature—he couldn't tolerate anyone laughing at him. That and his gun had led to his death. If only he could have walked away.

Hearing Clint's footsteps on the stairs, Mattie quickly brushed her sleeve across her eyes and turned to greet him, still clutching the broom in her hands.

Clint paused on the lowest step and held up his hands in surrender. "You don't plan on hitting me again, do you?"

Her heart lifted a little and she straightened, propping a hand on her hip. "It wouldn't do any good. You're too hardheaded."

He chuckled and his eyes twinkled. "I've been told that once or twice before."

She didn't doubt that. The man had more pride and stubbornness than sense, but that was part of what made him who he was. So she accepted those qualities, along with the good that she knew was within him.

Clint reached for the broom, and she released the handle reluctantly, feeling exposed and vulnerable. He leaned it in the corner and paused, resting his weight on one leg and tucking his thumbs in his jeans pockets.

Mattie's heart raced. She couldn't draw her gaze away from him—his long-legged stance, his piercing green eyes, his shoulder-length unruly hair, and the half-smile that penetrated all her defenses. Her gaze flickered to his Colt, but she felt no outrage, only sadness. The gun would always be a part of who he was, too.

"I suppose you're ready to go." She hated the fact that her voice wavered. This was something she'd been preparing herself for since the day she knew he would recover.

His gaze looked past her. "I reckon." He shifted his weight to the other foot and met her eyes. "Would you walk me down to the corral?"

"I'd like that. Wait just a moment." She hurried into the kitchen and grabbed a bag. Returning to the foyer, she handed it to him awkwardly. "I made you a lunch to eat on the way."

Clint's eyes shone with gratitude as he took the bag from her. "You didn't have to do that."

She shrugged, hoping the nonchalant gesture hid the ache beneath. "I know, but I wanted to."

"Thank you."

He laid his palm lightly against her waist to guide her out the door. She wanted to plant her heels down, to force him to stay with her and Andy, but Clint Beaudry was determined to leave, and nothing she could say would dissuade him.

They walked across the yard, passing Jewel, who glanced at them lazily, then went back to chewing her cud and swinging her tail to chase away the flies. Mattie wished she, too, could be as unconcerned about everything going on around her.

"Will you be all right here alone?" Clint asked.

"I've been all right for ten years. Why should things be any different now?"

He shrugged, his thick hair brushing across his shoulders. "I guess because now *I'll* worry about you."

Mattie's step faltered. "Don't worry about me, Clint. Just do what you have to do."

They stopped by the corral where Dakota was tied, saddled, and ready to go. Mattie leaned a shoulder against a post and crossed her arms. Clint tied his saddlebags behind the cantle and the lunch bag to the pommel, his long fingers working gracefully as he knotted the rawhide latigos.

Mattie's belly cramped with sorrow and a sob traveled up her throat. She swallowed convulsively against it. She couldn't break down—she wanted to leave Clint with the illusion that she was as strong as he believed. There would be time for tears late at night when the house was still and she was alone.

So very alone.

He turned to face her, his wide brim shading his features. "Thanks, Mattie. You saved my life." He took a deep breath. "And maybe my soul."

The lump in her throat returned. Had she saved his life only to have him lose it a day or a month down the road?

"You're welcome," she said, keeping her voice even.

Clint reached into his duster pocket and withdrew some coins. "Here's what I owe you for the time I was here."

"No, please—I couldn't take anything."

He smiled crookedly. The endearing expression battered her feeble defenses, and he took her hand. Turning her palm upward, he dropped the money in the center of it. There were six ten-dollar gold pieces.

"I can't. This is too much," she argued, trying to give them back to him.

He curled her fingers around the coins and

wrapped his hand around her fist. "It's not nearly enough, but I think this is the most you'll take without putting up too much of a fuss." He paused and brushed his fingertips across her cheek.

She wanted to close her eyes and lean her face into his palm, but that would only make his leave-taking more painful.

"I know you can use it, Mattie," Clint said. "Buy Andy some new clothes and get yourself a pretty dress and a new hat—to match your eyes."

A tear spilled down her cheek, but she didn't allow any more. "Thank you, Clint." She shook so badly she thought she'd fly into a million pieces, and only sheer force of will kept her whole. She stepped back, though every part of her yearned to stay close to him. "Good-bye."

"Don't I get a good-bye kiss?" He flashed a roguish smile, but his eyes didn't twinkle.

She wanted to kiss him, but not as a farewell. Still, this would be her last chance . . .

Mattie put her arms around his neck. He appeared surprised, and she murmured, "Kiss me, you damn stubborn fool."

Clint wrapped his arms around her and hugged her close as his lips swooped down upon hers. She opened her mouth to his and their tongues dueled in a heated contest of passion, making her throb and burn for him anew.

Just one night in his arms hadn't been enough. It would never be enough.

Someone cleared his throat behind them. Startled, Mattie drew back. She peeked around Clint to see Herman, a deceptively innocent expression on his wrinkled face.

"You young'uns about done spoonin'?" he asked.

"Not even close," Clint muttered.

Mattie ducked her head to hide her smile. It was probably a good thing Herman had shown up when he did. The way her blood was racing, she might have lured Clint into the barn to find a nice soft pile of hay.

"Wanted to catch you afore you left," Herman said, approaching them. "And looks like I done caught you good." The old man cackled.

Clint saved her from further embarrassment by extending his hand to Herman. "Thanks for everything."

The gray-haired man shook his hand. "Good luck to you, young feller. I have a feeling you're gonna need it."

Clint sent him a nod, then turned back to Mattie. He laid his warm hand on her forearm. "Take care of yourself, Mattie."

She lifted her chin and forced a smile. "You, too."

They stared at one another for a long moment. Mattie wanted nothing more than to fly back into his arms, and she could see the same reluctance in Clint's face.

She lifted a hand toward him, then let it drop back to her side. If she talked him into staying, his regrets would come to poison any affection he held for her.

He turned away and stuck his toe in the stirrup, mounting Dakota with a smooth motion that belied his wounds. Threading the reins between his fingers, he guided the mare between Herman and Mattie.

He touched the brim of his hat with two fingers and pressed his heels to Dakota's flanks. The sorrel trotted down the road, carrying away the man Mattie loved.

She curled her fingers into fists and fought the rising surge of tears. Clint was gone and he wouldn't return. Those were the facts, and she would live with them. Just as she'd lived with Jason's death.

Only Clint wasn't dead. Yet.

Herman put a thin arm around Mattie's shoulders. "It's all right, girl. You don't have to be strong now."

"Yes . . . yes, I do." She pressed lips together and shook her head. "Crying isn't going to bring him back."

"Maybe not, but it might make you feel better."

Mattie watched Clint's figure grow smaller and smaller. "The only thing that'll make me feel better is time."

Herman gave her a squeeze, then released her. He glanced back at the house and pointed to a window. "I reckon Andy ain't takin' it so good, neither."

Mattie followed Herman's finger and spotted her son in his window. From this distance she couldn't tell if he was crying or not, but it gave her something else to focus on rather than Clint's leaving. "I'd better go make sure he's all right."

She caught one last glimpse of Clint before he disappeared beyond the trees.

Folks said time mended all things, including a shattered heart.

She prayed they were right.

Clint didn't dare turn around until he was certain he could no longer see Mattie. He tightened his grip on the reins, making Dakota snort and toss her head.

"Sorry, girl," he murmured, loosening the reins.

There was a dull ache in his side, but it was nothing compared to the ache in his chest. Leaving Mattie behind was the most difficult thing he'd ever done. If she had asked him to stay, he might have done so. But she hadn't. She had given him his freedom without any recriminations.

The Mattie he'd met nearly four weeks ago had changed and softened. She had stopped denying her womanhood, but the cost to him had been higher than he could have imagined.

Mattie St. Clair had stolen his heart.

He glanced upward at the blue sky and wondered if Emily was gazing down at him. And if she was, what was she thinking? Did she think he was a fool for leaving Mattie and her son? Or did she want him to find her murderer and reap vengeance?

"I won't break my promise to you, Em. I'll find the sonuvabitch who murdered you, but I can't give you my todays anymore," he whispered. "Those belong to Mattie now."

He took a deep breath and urged Dakota into a canter. The future extended only as far as it took to find Emily's killer.

After that . . .

The sound of an approaching horse sent Mattie scurrying to the window. She swept aside the curtain and recognized Kevin's buggy coming up the road. Her heart fell, and she chastised herself. For the past month, every time Mattie heard a horse, her pulse quickened and she held her breath, hoping Clint had returned.

Her foolish anticipation refused to be squelched no matter how hard she tried to convince herself he was gone for good. The plain fact was, Mattie didn't *want* to let him go. Every night as she lay in her bed, she relived the glorious hours spent in his arms. But every day, she pasted on a smile for Andy and Kevin.

She suspected Herman knew how much she missed Clint. She would catch his rheumy eyes on her, watching her with something akin to sympathy. Her situation was too much like his unrequited love for Ruth.

Kevin hopped down from the buggy and climbed the steps to the porch. Mattie smoothed a hand across her hair, then down her skirt. Kevin had been coming by at least three days a week. At first it had been to check on Andy's ankle, then it had gradually changed to outright courting. She truly cared for Kevin, but there was no spark like there had been with Clint.

She smiled to herself—what she and Clint shared could hardly be called a mere spark. More like a wildfire.

Kevin knocked on the door and Mattie opened it wide. "Hello, Kevin," she greeted, inserting a note of pleasure.

He smiled and removed his narrow-brimmed hat. "Good afternoon, Mattie."

"Won't you come in?" She motioned for him to enter.

Ever since Clint had left, Kevin had been behaving much more like himself, relaxed and easygoing. But today, when he stepped inside, he silently turned his hat around and around in his hands.

"Is something wrong?" Mattie asked, genuinely concerned.

He flashed a too-wide smile. "No, no, of course not. What could be wrong?"

Mattie gazed at him through narrowed eyes. "I don't know. That's why I'm asking."

"Would you like to take a buggy ride?" he blurted. "It's a beautiful day and it would do you good to get out for a little while. In fact, we could go down to that pond Andy and Herman like so well."

No doubt about it, Kevin was rambling. And when Kevin rambled, he was anxious about something—usually a patient. What was bothering him now?

"That sounds like a wonderful idea. Let me get my bonnet."

He seemed relieved that she didn't press him further, but Mattie was saving that for the ride. She hurried up to her room and pulled a hatbox down from the top of her armoire. Opening it, she lifted out a wide-brimmed straw hat trimmed with lavender ribbon and deep violet blossoms. It was one of the two extravagances she'd allowed herself with Clint's money. The other was a dress the exact color of the blossoms on her hat. She'd decided to ignore practicality for the first time in years.

She placed the hat at a jaunty angle and tied the ribbons beneath her chin. Staring at her reflection, she couldn't help wondering if Clint would like it. She often imagined herself wearing the new dress and hat as Clint waltzed her across a dance floor. The only time they'd danced, she had worn her filmy nightgown and he only a pair of jeans.

Mattie shoved the memory from her thoughts. That was the past. Today, Kevin awaited her. She turned and a wave of dizziness caught her unaware. She grabbed the bedpost and steadied herself. Her stomach fluttered, threatening to lose the lunch she'd eaten an hour ago.

Folding an arm across her belly, she wondered if she was getting sick. Or perhaps her monthly had finally arrived. Mattie frowned, and counted back the weeks since her last time.

She was three weeks late.

She had only been that late one other time in her life.

"Oh, no," she whimpered, flattening a hand to her mouth. The room wavered in and out of focus. Her knees crumpled beneath her and she dropped to the edge of her bed.

The bed where *it* had happened.

Clint was finally going to be a father, but he would never know.

Tears welled in her eyes and she blinked back the moisture. What was she going to do? She couldn't stand the thought of the townsfolk whispering about her. Again.

Well, this time she wasn't an infatuated girl who would allow them to bully her into marriage. This time she'd go to a place where no one knew her, where she could pretend to be a recent widow.

Or . . . she could search for Clint.

*No.* She hadn't been a young virgin who didn't understand the consequences. She'd known them only too well. That was the risk she'd accepted in exchange for just one night.

Kevin would be wondering where she was. She should come up with an excuse to get out of the buggy ride, but he would suspect something. Mattie sucked in a deep breath and used the bedpost to pull herself to her feet. Her legs still trembled, but at least they held her upright.

She stepped over to the mirror and, except for a slight pallor, she looked the same. So why did she feel like a completely different person?

"Mattie, are you all right?" Kevin's tentative question from downstairs brought her back to reality.

"I'll be down in a minute," she called back.

She would accompany Kevin on the ride, but after she returned, she had plans to make. Serious plans involving not just her life, but her son's. She buried her face in her hands. Why had she taken the chance?

*Because I love him.*

The simple declaration came straight from her soul and gave her courage. Taking a deep breath and pinching her cheeks to give them some color, Mattie strode out of her room and descended the stairs.

Kevin's gaze flickered to her head and he smiled. "Is that a new hat?"

"Yes," she replied stiffly. "Do you like it?"

"Very much. It matches your eyes."

Mattie was surprised by the compliment. He'd never made mention of her appearance before, though he often praised her intelligence and common sense. "Thank you."

He extended his crooked arm and Mattie threaded her hand through it. Grateful for the support, she leaned slightly against him. Although not as tall or as muscular as Clint, Kevin possessed a strength that belied his smaller stature. For a moment she wanted to share her newly discovered secret with him, but quickly thrust the impulse aside. Though compassionate and open-minded, Kevin would probably be disgusted by what she had done.

Kevin assisted her into the buggy, and Mattie

adjusted her skirts while he climbed in on the other side. He snapped the reins and the horse drew the buggy down the road.

The early fall day boasted a bright blue sky, and the faint scent of autumn was already evident. Mattie rested a palm against her belly. Clint's child would be born in the spring, when the cycle of the earth was also beginning anew. When seeds would be planted, take root, and grow healthy beneath summer skies.

Where would she be then?

"You're quiet today," Kevin commented.

Mattie lifted a shoulder nonchalantly. "I've been busy getting the rooms ready for winter boarders. After sitting empty for a summer, they need a good airing out."

Kevin pressed his lips together.

"All right; I've waited long enough. Tell me what's bothering you," Mattie said.

"How long have we known each other, Mattie?" He kept his gaze directly ahead.

"About three years, ever since you moved to Green Valley."

"That seems like enough time for a man and a woman—" He cleared his throat and his Adam's apple bobbed up and down. "For a man and a woman to get to know one another . . . to find out if they would be . . . compatible."

Mattie's heart leapt into her throat and she closed her eyes a moment. *Please don't let him propose.* Though she had hoped for a proposal before, she could never marry him and trick him into thinking the babe she carried was his. That was too cruel to consider.

"What do you think?" he asked.

"Think about what?" Her voice sounded too high.

"Our, er, compatibility. Do you think that our personalities are such that we could make a home and"—he shifted to put some room between them on the seat— "raise a family?"

He made marriage sound like a business transaction. Where was the love? She almost snorted—who was she to accuse him of not loving her? A month ago, when Clint had left, she'd decided to marry Kevin if he asked, knowing she could never love *him*.

And now it was too late for any match—loveless or otherwise.

She thought about his question a moment, determined to be gentle. "We have things in common," she began carefully. "We both like to help people and we work well together. We enjoy each other's company."

"Why do I sense a but?" Kevin asked with more perception than she would have given him credit for.

Mattie's stomach churned and she couldn't concentrate. She pointed to a copse of trees. "Let's stop over there. I want to stretch my legs."

Frowning, Kevin did as she asked and soon halted the horse. He tied the reins to the brake, then hopped down and walked over to Mattie's side to help her down.

Once on the ground, Mattie crossed her arms and noticed Kevin's gaze follow her motions. He quickly looked away from her breasts, but not before Mattie spotted his guilty flush. It seemed Kevin wasn't nearly as passionless as she'd thought—but the observation brought her no comfort.

He was so different from Clint, yet they were both good men. If only she could love Kevin the way she loved Clint.

"Is it him?" Kevin suddenly asked.

Guilt made her cheeks heat and she was tempted to feign ignorance, but Kevin deserved better. "Yes," she replied.

His lips thinned. "Do you love him?"

She glanced away, at the sunlight shimmering off the babbling water. "Yes."

The doctor strode to the edge of the brook. Mattie walked over to him. She wished she could give him what he wanted. "I'm sorry, Kevin."

His hands in his trouser pockets, Kevin stared across the landscape. "He's gone, Mattie." He brought his tormented gaze back to her. "And I'm here. Do you want to live with a shadow for the rest of your life? Or do you want to share your life with a real flesh-and-blood man?"

Mattie's head ached and she rubbed her brow. Why was this so difficult? Why couldn't he just accept things for how they were?

"It wouldn't be fair to you," Mattie said.

"And watching you grow old alone when I could be with you is fair?" he demanded. "I care for you a great deal, Mattie—both you and Andy. I'd treat him like my own."

Mattie rested her palm on Kevin's arm. "I know you would, and you'd be a good father, too."

He clasped her hands in his gently. "Then marry me, Mattie. Be my wife. We would live and work side by side, and I'd treat you as an equal. You know I would."

Her throat felt raw. "Yes, I know." She had to make him see how impossible a marriage would be between them. Did she have the courage to tell him? "I can't marry you, Kevin. I—I think . . . I'm carrying Clint's child," she said, her voice trembling.

Kevin simply continued to gaze at her, his expression unchanged. "I understand."

Mattie's mouth dropped open. "How . . . ?"

"It didn't take a genius to see there was something between the two of you. I had hoped it hadn't gone that far, but . . ." He paused. "I don't blame you. I blame him and myself. I shouldn't have left him for you to care for."

She shook her head vehemently. "It's not your fault. If there's any fault, it's mine."

"It doesn't matter, Mattie. I still want to marry you, and if you agree and we marry fast enough, no one will ever suspect the child isn't mine."

Disbelief swirled through her. She had been ready to take Andy and leave her home to start over someplace, had acknowledged that as the price she must pay. Now Kevin was offering not only to care for her and Andy, but to accept the baby as his, too. But what if he changed his mind after the child was born?

"The baby will be a constant reminder," Mattie said.

"The baby is as much yours as his, and I love you." He paused, capturing her gaze with his. "So I will love your child."

He'd spoken the word. *Love.*

Weakness washed over her and Mattie lowered herself to the ground. She hadn't realized his feelings went that deeply for her. How could she marry him knowing he loved her, but that she could never reciprocate?

"Are you sick?" Kevin asked, squatting down beside her.

"I don't know." She studied his pale face and the earnest eyes that watched her with understanding and compassion.

*Why can't I love him?*

Life was so damned unfair.

"If I agreed, I'd feel as if I were taking advantage of you," she said softly. "And I can't do that."

He smiled gently and his eyes glittered behind his glasses. "That's one of the reasons I love you, Mattie. You have integrity."

She smiled wryly. "So why am I sitting here considering your offer, when I'm carrying another man's child?"

"At least you're considering it." His expression grew solemn and he clasped his hands. "I only have one stipulation."

Alarm bells clanged in Mattie's head. "What is it?"

"If Beaudry ever shows up again, you can't tell him the child is his."

# Chapter 16

Clint was dusty, exhausted, and hungry when he stumbled across a tiny town in the middle of nowhere. He steered Dakota to the livery and left instructions for the hostler to give her an extra nose bag of grain and a good rubdown. With his saddlebags in one hand and his bedroll in the other, Clint crossed the street to the hotel and registered for a room.

An hour later, after a hot bath, a fresh shave, and a change of clothes, Clint found the nearest saloon. He bought a bottle of whiskey and retired to a corner table to do some serious drinking. He downed the first and second shots without pause, but allowed the third to sit untouched in the middle of the table.

For four weeks he'd scoured the area, searching for a sign of the man who rode the palomino. Some folks remembered the horse, but they weren't certain what the man looked like. Clint had gotten so close to the bastard, then the killer had escaped. Again.

He lifted the glass to his lips and swallowed the third shot. Glancing around, he saw the same people he came across in every other saloon. Only the faces changed.

He was so damned tired of this existence, of the frustration and the loneliness. Ever since leaving Mattie, he'd become little more than a husk of a man, his insides shriveled and dead. Only the promise of vengeance kept him going, and that was fraying with the growing hopelessness of his quest.

He dreamed of holding Mattie, then woke to find his arms as empty as his soul. How much longer could he continue, not living, but not dead, either?

"Buy me a drink, stranger?"

Clint glanced up to see a redhead wearing a knee-length green dress standing beside him. He hadn't even noticed her approach. That kind of sloppiness could make a man dead. He smiled only with his mouth. "As long as you don't mind sharing."

She arched a penciled eyebrow. "I'm good at sharing."

As she lowered herself to a chair, Clint filled the shot glass and pushed it across the table's scarred surface.

She picked it up. "To new friends."

Clint tapped her glass with the neck of the brown bottle. "And old."

He tipped the whiskey to his lips and took a long swallow. The liquor was starting to work its magic, relaxing his limbs and filling the emptiness within him.

"What's your name?" he asked.

"Sally."

Clint eyed the woman. Her red hair was obviously from a bottle, but at least she was clean. She looked young, maybe eighteen or nineteen, but her eyes were twenty years older. "You been here long?"

"Long enough to know what a man like you likes." She dragged the tip of her tongue across her lips. The erotic invitation would have sent his blood straight to his groin two months ago, before he met Mattie. Now he only felt pity that a girl so young knew what men like him liked.

"Then you should know that all I want right now is whiskey," he said.

Disappointment slipped across her features, but the more familiar cynicism quickly replaced it. "Sure. But if you get a hankerin' for more than liquor, just let me know."

She stood, but Clint didn't watch her leave. He had a decision to make, and for that, he only needed whiskey.

Mattie paused on the boardwalk outside the Green Valley Mercantile and glanced at her list. Her gaze flitted across the diamond ring on her left hand. Ever since Kevin had given it to her four days ago, she couldn't keep her eyes from straying to it. The ring was more than she deserved, and every time her gaze fell upon it a tiny sliver of guilt stabbed her.

They'd set the wedding for the last Sunday in September, two weeks and one day away. The baby would arrive seven months after they were married, but Kevin reassured her no one would question his word that the birth had been early. After all, he was the doctor.

"We going in or not?" Andy asked, a whine in his tone.

Mattie paused to give him a scolding look. "Not if you're going to act like that, young man." Ever since she'd announced that she and Kevin were getting married, Andy had become sullen and hostile. She'd tried to find out what was bothering him, but her son remained tight-lipped.

Andy scowled but held his tongue.

She knew Andy missed Clint, but that still didn't explain or excuse his behavior. He was old enough to understand.

To understand what? That his mother was marrying a man she didn't love because the man she did love was gone forever? That his mother was carrying another man's baby and had sold her soul to give the child a name?

That his mother was worse than a liar?

Mattie's fingers crumpled the list in her hand. She hated this feeling of dread that accompanied her thoughts of this pending marriage. But she'd given Kevin her word, and she had never gone back on a promise before. She wasn't about to start now.

She walked through the open door into the general store, with Andy trailing behind her. He had healed completely from the ankle injury and had no lasting effects. True to form, he made a beeline for the front of the store where the jars of candy and rows of jackknives resided behind a glass counter.

"Good morning, Mattie. I hear congratulations are in order for you and Dr. Murphy," Jane Swanson said with a genuine smile.

Mattie's cheeks heated. "That's right. We're getting married two weeks from tomorrow."

Jane came around from behind the counter. Nearly as big as a rain barrel, the woman was as friendly as she was round, and Mattie had always liked her. "I heard. Reverend Lister was in here earlier. I guess Dr. Murphy talked to him yesterday about the ceremony."

Mattie's smile froze on her lips. Kevin had discussed their wedding with the minister without her?

The older woman patted Mattie's hand. "I'm so happy for you. I was beginning to despair—nearly ten years as a widow, when you could've caught a man whenever you wanted."

Mattie laughed. "I didn't want a man before C—Kevin." Her heart skipped a beat. Less than a week since the engagement, and she'd almost spilled the beans. She'd have to watch herself much closer.

Jane winked. "You caught yourself a good one. Dr. Murphy is the salt of the earth. Did I ever tell you about the time he saved Oscar's life?"

"Once or twice." It was closer to ten or twenty times, but Mattie didn't want to hurt Jane's feelings.

"Oh, that's right, I have," Jane said with a wave of her pudgy hand. "Now, what can I get for you today?"

Mattie rattled off the items on her list, and they had the counter covered in less than five minutes.

Andy pointed to a jar of cinnamon sticks. "Can I have one of those, Ma?"

"I'm sorry, Andy, but we can't afford it."

Jane smiled and dug into the jar, pulled a stick out, and handed it to the boy. "Here you go."

Andy took it eagerly and thrust one end into his mouth.

"What do you say?" Mattie reminded.

"Thank you," he said around the candy.

Mattie rolled her eyes. "Some days I just don't know about him."

"Don't worry. They grow out of it," Jane said. "Let me get William to carry this out for you." She turned to the back and bellowed, "William!"

Mattie's ears rang, but she managed a smile for the lanky boy who joined them. "Thank you. I appreciate your help. Andy, give William a hand, please."

Andy picked up the smaller box and followed the older boy out of the store.

"He's growing so fast," Jane commented.

"William?"

"Your Andy. He looks more and more like Jason, too."

Mattie nodded, but her thoughts were on the babe she carried. Would the infant look more like Clint or herself? She hoped the child took after her, to spare Kevin the embarrassment of a son or daughter who didn't resemble him at all.

"I'll see you in church on Sunday," Jane said as she took the money for the goods.

Mattie smiled. "See you then."

She walked outside and glanced up and down the main street. Seeing the same people she'd seen for the past twenty years should have soothed her, but her breath faltered. She didn't like herself for the deception she had to live. History was repeating itself, but this time the townsfolk didn't know about her impropriety. Mattie herself had made the choice to marry.

Thinking of Kevin reminded her that she had to speak to him about his meeting with the reverend. Annoyance flared, but she quickly doused it. Kevin was only trying to make things easier for her by taking care of the details. She just wished he had told her his plans.

"Andy," she called.

He looked over from where he sat on the end of the wagon, swinging his feet back and forth as he ate his candy. "Yeah?"

"I have to go talk to Kevin. Would you like to come with me?"

Andy shook his head, his nose wrinkling. "Can I

stay around town for a little while? I wanna see Buck and Josh."

"Are all the chores done?"

"I'll go on home and do them."

Her son had kept his promise to Clint about helping her more around the house, and Mattie was grateful for that. She eyed her son a moment. "How would you like to drive the wagon back?"

Andy's face lit up. "Can I?"

"You've been practicing a lot and I think it's time I start letting the man of the house take over some of the responsibilities."

"I'll be careful, Ma. And when I get home, I'll carry the stuff inside, then I'll get Herman to help me unhitch Polly."

The mature words coming out of a mouth stuffed with a candy stick brought a bittersweet smile to Mattie's face. Andy was at an awkward age—caught between boyhood and manhood—without a father to lead him down the correct path. That would change soon.

She patted Andy's shoulder. "I know you will. I'll be home after I talk to Kevin."

Andy's enthusiasm dimmed. If Mattie had been marrying Clint, she suspected Andy would be delighted.

And how would *she* feel? She quickly erased the thought.

*I'm not being fair to Kevin.*

She watched her son clamber up into the wagon seat and pick up the reins. Trepidation flared in Mattie, but she quickly doused it. Clint had been right—she had been treating Andy like a baby instead of a boy taking the first step into adulthood. She had to allow him to make his own mistakes and learn his own lessons.

Andy kept a firm grip on the reins, sending Mattie a nod instead of a wave as he cautiously headed the wagon back home.

She smiled proudly, then continued across the street to Kevin's office.

One problem at a time.

Clint noticed the color changes of the leaves as he neared the outskirts of Green Valley. The town appeared the same as it had when he'd left nearly five weeks ago. The familiar buildings came into view and he swallowed the odd lump in his throat.

A bottle of whiskey in a nameless town had given him the courage to return. He wasn't giving up his search for Emily's killer as much as he was wanting to see Mattie again. In fact, he hadn't thought much beyond telling Mattie how much he cared for her. Her reaction to his confession would determine his next move.

He swept his gaze across the dusty street, noting the wagons and horses lining the street. It must be Saturday. He'd lost track of the days since he'd left Mattie's.

He spotted a familiar figure coming out of the doctor's office and his heart leapt into his throat. Mattie. Reining Dakota, he drank in the sight of her—from her hair, which caught and spun the sunshine into bluish threads, to her pointy-toed boots. Her footsteps were firm and decisive, and her shoulders proudly erect.

He'd made the right decision by coming back.

A horse's shrill neigh made him glance up sharply to see two men running out of the bank, scarves around the lower part of their faces.

"Shit," Clint muttered.

Sheriff Atwater barreled down the boardwalk, drawing his gun as he ran. Clint's attention switched to Mattie, who had stopped to see what was going on.

His heart stumbled. She was directly across the street from the bank—where she could easily be hit by a stray bullet if this turned into a gun battle.

As if reading his thoughts, one of the robbers fired the first shot at Atwater. The next moment the air was filled with screams and gunshots. Clint kicked Dakota's belly and the horse leapt into motion, heading down the street toward Mattie. Out of the corner of his eye, Clint saw Atwater stagger. Had he been hit?

Ten feet from Mattie, Clint jerked back hard on the reins. He jumped out of the saddle and hurtled himself at her, his right arm snagging her waist and drawing her into the building behind them.

Vaguely aware of her pale face and huge violet eyes, Clint said, "Stay here."

She nodded wordlessly.

Clint drew his Colt and charged back onto the boardwalk. The two thieves had managed to mount their horses, though one of them looked like he'd been shot. Atwater slumped behind a water trough; Clint couldn't tell if the man was dead or alive.

Clint raised his weapon and fired a couple of quick rounds at the escaping bandits. Their returning fire forced him to dive behind a barrel. They thundered past him and Clint sat up, took careful aim, and squeezed the trigger. One of the men jerked, then tumbled from his horse. Startled, the other robber looked back, giving Clint the moment he needed to squeeze off another shot. The second man slumped over his horse's neck, then slid to the ground.

The abrupt silence seemed even more ominous than the explosion of the gun battle moments before. The stillness was broken by the appearance of the townsfolk, coming out from behind closed doors to stare at the two outlaws lying in the middle of their usually peaceful street.

"A few of you men check on the robbers," Clint hollered. He didn't wait to see if anyone followed his order, but loped across the street to where Atwater lay motionless and quiet. He squatted down beside the gray-haired man and eased him back away from the trough to lie on the ground.

Wet crimson soaked the upper right side of Atwater's shirt and Clint licked his suddenly dry lips. He laid his palm on the left side of Atwater's chest and was rewarded with a strong beat.

"Is he . . . ?"

Clint lifted his head to see Mattie peering down at him. Even pale and frightened, she was the most beautiful sight he'd ever seen. "No, he's alive, but he needs medical attention."

"Kevin isn't here," Mattie said, then added firmly, "Bring him over to the doctor's office and I'll see what I can do."

Clint called two men over to help him carry the unconscious sheriff across the street. Mattie led the way and opened the office as if she'd done it many times before. She motioned toward a tall bed in the center of one of the rooms.

"I'm going to need hot water," she commanded.

Clint nodded and found the kitchen. There was a huge pot on the stove already filled with water, and Clint quickly stoked up the fire to heat it. While it warmed, he returned to the examination room.

Mattie's concentration was centered on the sheriff. One of her hands was stained red by the man's blood, yet she didn't seem to notice. Clint's heart swelled at her strength and grit.

"Do you need some help?" he asked softly.

Mattie nodded without looking at him. "We need to get his vest and shirt off so I can examine the wound."

Stepping over to the other side of the bed, Clint eased Atwater's left arm from his vest, then rolled his limp body toward him carefully. Mattie pulled off the vest from his right side.

"I thought you weren't coming back," Mattie said, her voice breathy. Her gaze remained on Atwater as she and Clint worked in tandem to remove his shirt.

"I thought so, too," he said.

Mattie eased Walt's shirt off the rest of the way. Only Atwater's undershirt remained and she took a pair of scissors and cut a large circle out of it.

"It's still bleeding," she said. She grabbed a cloth from a shelf of supplies and pressed it against the bullet hole high on Atwater's right shoulder. Then she reached across and clasped Clint's hand, drawing it over to the cloth. "Press down firmly. We need to stop the bleeding."

Clint did as she said as he watched her work. Her calmness shouldn't have surprised him, but it did. She had almost been shot, yet she was acting as if it were a common occurrence.

"How's Andy?" he asked.

"Fine. Thank God he had already gone home when this happened."

"How's his ankle?"

"Fine."

"Is he helping around the house more?" Clint knew he shouldn't be bothering her as she worked, but he wanted to hear her voice and learn what she'd done while he'd been gone.

Mattie nodded but didn't speak.

He heard the outer door open and footsteps sounded as someone neared. Clint tensed, his body still taut from the gunfight. A man dressed in a smithy apron stood in the doorway.

"What is it, Frank?" Mattie asked.

"One of them outlaws is dead. The other needs a doc," he replied.

"Take the dead one to the undertaker's and put

the other one in jail," Clint said, taking charge as naturally as he breathed. "Mattie will look at him after she's taken care of the sheriff."

"How bad is the man's wound?" she asked.

"Looks like he caught one in the leg, above the knee," Frank replied.

"Wrap a scarf around it tightly. That'll take care of him until Kevin or I can examine him," she said.

Frank nodded and left.

"A person would think you do this every day," Clint said softly.

Mattie glanced up at him for the first time since they'd brought Atwater to the office. "Don't be fooled. I'm shaking so hard on the inside, I'm afraid I'm going to rattle apart."

Clint's throat tightened and he laid his free hand on her shoulder, giving it a gentle squeeze. "You're doing just fine, Mattie."

She quickly turned her attention back to the wounded sheriff, but Clint caught the blush that colored her cheeks. How had he been able to leave her?

"Did you find the man you were after?" Mattie suddenly asked.

Clint shook his head. "I lost his trail about a hundred miles northeast of here."

"So why did you come back?"

His heartbeat kicked up a notch. "I had some unfinished business."

She glanced up at him, a question in her eyes, but Clint merely shook his head. "Not now."

"I'm going to get some water and clean the wound," she said. "Hopefully by the time I'm done, Kevin will be back so he can take care of him."

"Is there an exit wound?"

She shook her head. "The bullet's still inside."

Clint heard the door open again and more than one set of footsteps neared them. A middle-aged man wearing an expensive suit and too much pomade appeared in the doorway. Behind him, Arabella—no, Amelia—stood anxious and fearful. The man had to be her husband, Orville, the owner of the bank.

"How's Walt doing?" the man asked.

"I'm not sure," Mattie replied. "He's been shot in the shoulder and the bullet's still inside him."

"Where's Dr. Murphy?"

"I found a note saying he went to deliver the Hudsons' baby. He should be back anytime now."

Orville bobbed his head up and down, his double chin moving in time with the gesture. "Good, good. Walt did a damned fine job of stopping those two thieves." He glanced at Clint. "And I noticed how well you handled yourself, sir."

Clint bit back a retort. Men like Orville existed in every town. They weren't bad men, just self-important ones—a big fish in a little pond. "Thank you, Mr.—"

"The name's Orville Johnson and I'm the owner of the establishment those two men tried to rob." He motioned to Amelia. "And this is my wife, Amelia Johnson."

"We've met," Clint said smoothly.

Amelia's eyes widened behind her husband.

"She stopped by Mattie's while I was recovering from my gunshot wounds about six weeks back," Clint finished.

Amelia closed her eyes briefly and when she reopened them, Clint saw gratitude written there.

"So you're the gunman everyone was talking about," Johnson said.

Mattie paused in her task of cleaning the blood from Atwater's chest. She glanced at Clint, her brows furrowed and her lips set in a grim line.

"I was a U.S. marshal," Clint said coolly.

Mattie blinked, as if surprised he'd admitted it.

Johnson appeared duly impressed. "So what brought you here?"

"Excuse me, Mr. Johnson, but could you save your questions until a later time?" Mattie asked. "We need to get the bleeding stopped or Walt could die."

"Oh, yes, certainly. I'm sorry, Mrs. St. Clair," Johnson apologized. He looked at Clint. "After you're done here, would you mind stopping by the bank? I have an offer for you."

Clint wondered what kind of offer that could be, and shrugged. "Sure."

Johnson turned, but paused. "Thank you again for your help."

"I'm just glad I showed up when I did."

Johnson ushered Amelia out ahead of him.

"Puffed-up little pigeon, isn't he?" Clint commented.

Mattie lifted a shoulder in a half shrug. "He's the mayor of Green Valley."

Clint withdrew the cloth from Atwater's shoulder, and there was only a small trickle of blood oozing from the wound. "Looks like the bleeding has slowed."

"Now if only Kevin would get here," Mattie said plaintively.

The door opened for a third time and Kevin rushed in. He caught sight of Clint and came to an abrupt halt. "What're you doing here?" he demanded.

Though taken aback by the man's curt question, Clint kept his features impassive. "I got back just in time to help stop a robbery."

As Kevin and Mattie exchanged a look, Clint narrowed his eyes.

"Go on over and talk to Mr. Johnson," Mattie said. "Kevin and I can handle it from here."

She didn't meet his eyes again.

Foreboding whispered across Clint as he strode to the doorway where the doctor stood. Clint tossed him the bloody cloth and he caught it without flinching.

"I'll see you later, Mattie," Clint said in farewell.

He headed back outside to find that the two outlaws had been carried off the street. The only sign that the town had erupted in violence half an hour earlier was the drying blood in the dirt.

Clint glanced back at the doctor's office and wondered what was going on. Dr. Murphy acted as if Clint were trespassing. Had the doctor staked a claim to Mattie already?

If so, it was nobody's fault but Clint's.

He'd left Mattie with no promises.

# Chapter 17

**C**lint strolled across the street to the bank and into a crowd of milling people. He wasn't surprised to see them gathered around, gossiping about the unsuccessful robbery.

The conversations faltered and wary gazes followed him when he entered, as if they expected him to be another thief intruding in their midst. Or maybe they had seen him help bring down the two outlaws.

"Over here, sir," Orville Johnson called from a doorway at the back of the bank.

A smile tugged at Clint's lips when people started talking again, but this time he knew they were speculating on why the bank owner would be calling a virtual stranger over to join him. Clint wondered the same thing. The crowd parted to allow him through and he joined Johnson, who ushered him into his office.

"Sit down, Mr. . . . ?" Johnson began.

"Beaudry. Clint Beaudry."

"Nice to meet you, Mr. Beaudry." Johnson stuck out his hand and shook Clint's like a politician a day before election. "Have a seat."

Clint lowered himself to the chair in front of Johnson's desk. He removed his hat and dragged his hand through his unruly hair. He hoped this meeting wouldn't take long—he needed a bath and a shave. "What is it you wanted to talk to me about, Mr. Johnson?"

The bank owner sat back in his plush chair and clasped his hands, steepling his fingers. He looked like a snake eyeing a mouse. "What brought you to our town, Mr. Beaudry?"

"I was shot by the sonuvabitch who murdered my wife," Clint said bluntly.

Johnson's mouth gaped and his face paled.

"Mrs. St. Clair nursed me until I was healed enough to leave," Clint added. "I came back again after I lost the trail of the murderer." He had no intention of telling him his real reason for returning.

"You're the one who saved her son's life?"

Clint lifted his right ankle to rest on his left knee. "I helped him out of a well."

"Mrs. St. Clair told my Amelia the whole story. She said her son would've died if not for you."

Uncomfortable with the praise, Clint remained silent. He hadn't done it alone—Mattie and Herman had done their share, too.

"What's your line of work?" Johnson asked.

"I told you I used to be a lawman. Now I'm only a drifter."

Johnson nodded, as if he were a teacher and his favorite student had just answered a question correctly. "I have a feeling you were a good lawman." He paused, one hand squeezing the other nervously. "I realize this just happened, but we have to find someone to take over for Sheriff Atwater."

Anger blazed through Clint. "He's not going to die."

"No, no, you misunderstand me. I'm not asking you to take over permanently, only until Walt is back on his feet."

Clint's anger retreated. "I'm not interested."

"But—"

Clint stood and the bank president scrambled to his feet.

"I gave up being a lawman over a year ago," Clint said. "I'm not ready to pin on a badge again. I don't know if I ever will be."

"I'm only asking you to do the job for a few weeks, while Walt heals."

Clint recalled the conversation Mattie and Atwater had had the evening the sheriff came for supper. "Atwater's getting old. He may not want the badge back."

"If that happens, we'll find someone else. But since you're here and we need somebody right now, I thought—"

"You thought wrong." Clint turned and opened the door, then strode out.

Outside on the boardwalk, he heard his name

called and turned to see Amelia peeking out from around the corner of the bank. He joined her in the shadows and gazed down into her wide eyes.

"You didn't tell him, did you?" she asked, desperation clearly etched in her face.

"No. Your secret's safe with me."

She closed her eyes briefly. "Thank you."

"I'm glad you got out of the business, Amelia. Most girls never do."

She shivered. "I know. I saw a friend of mine die—beaten to death by a customer. That's when I decided I wasn't going to end up like her." She paused. "What did my husband want?"

"He asked me if I would fill in as sheriff while Atwater is healing."

"What'd you say?"

"No."

Amelia's brow furrowed. "Why not? You were a good lawman."

"My wife was killed because I was a 'good lawman.'" He couldn't keep the bitterness from bleeding into his words.

"I understand," Amelia said softly. She lent him a smile. "I'll bet Orville wasn't very happy you turned him down."

Clint chuckled. "He wasn't too bad."

"He's a good man, Clint. He may seem a little overbearing, but he's always been real good to me." He could see a blush stain her cheeks. "In fact, we're going to have a baby next spring."

Clint smiled and squeezed her hands gently.

"Congratulations, Amelia. You'll make a fine mother."

"And Orville will be a good father. I'll make certain of that."

Clint laughed lightly. "I don't doubt that at all." He glanced around, ensuring no one was around. "I'll be staying in Green Valley for a little while. Will that bother you?"

She shook her head. "You're more than welcome." Amelia glanced around nervously. "I'd better get back to the house before someone sees us."

Amelia gave him a quick wave and slipped away. Clint waited a minute before following her in case someone had seen her come out of the alley.

He glanced across the street at the doctor's office. Though he wanted to see Mattie and check on Atwater, Clint figured he'd better stop by and see the prisoner first. It wasn't his job, but he felt a certain obligation to Atwater.

After he did that, he would have a conversation with Mattie.

The one he should have had with her before he left.

Mattie stepped away from the window as a cold fist tightened around her heart. She suspected Clint and Amelia had known each other before, but she hadn't realized how well until she saw them both come out of the alley across the street.

When Clint had come riding out of nowhere to haul her to safety during the attempted robbery, shock, happiness, fear, disbelief, desire, helplessness—all of them whirled through her like a twister, leaving a carnage of doubts and suspicion in its wake. The reason he'd left still lay between them, so why had he returned?

Had it been Amelia he'd come back for?

"Mattie?"

Startled and a little dazed, she turned to face Kevin. "Yes?"

His expression turned to one of concern. "Are you all right? You look pale. Is it the baby?"

She smiled past the hurt that gripped her insides. "We're both fine." Mattie bent her head toward Walt. "How is he?"

Kevin wiped his hands on a towel. "He'll be fit as a fiddle in no time. In fact, I think the most difficult task now will be to keep him in bed for a few days."

"You're probably right," she said faintly.

Her thoughts returned to Clint and Amelia. Together. Like she and Clint the night before he left. Amelia was a married woman, which in Mattie's mind made the deception even worse.

Mattie's fingernails dug into her damp palms. How had she been such a fool?

Kevin stared at her a long moment. "It's him, isn't it?"

Mattie folded her arms across her stomach to conceal their trembling. "I never expected to see him again, especially this soon."

"It doesn't change anything, Mattie. He'll leave you again."

She closed her eyes against the pain, knowing he

was right. Even if she hadn't seen Clint with Amelia, she had pledged herself to Kevin. "I know that."

Kevin cleaned his medical instruments and Mattie dried them, her motions mechanical and her mind numbed.

"Are you going to tell him about the baby?" Kevin asked, his thin features pinched.

"I promised I wouldn't," Mattie said, sharper than she'd intended. She looked away guiltily— she *had* considered telling him. It didn't seem right not to tell Clint about his own child, especially since she knew he had wanted children. Her conscience had fought a battle, and her promise to Kevin had come out the victor.

Besides, Kevin would make a much better father than Clint. He was a doctor, a man to look up to and admire. Clint lived in a world where violence was the norm rather than the exception.

Mattie shivered—she didn't want her children growing up in that kind of world.

No, she wouldn't tell Clint about the baby. The future of her unborn child, as well as Andy's, depended on her remaining silent. She'd succumbed to temptation once with Clint—she couldn't afford to do it again.

The front door opened and a few moments later Clint stepped into the examination room. His presence sucked the air from Mattie's lungs and she lowered her gaze to the surgical tool she was drying.

"How is he?" Clint asked, gesturing toward the sheriff.

"He'll be fine," Kevin replied formally. "He will have some stiffness in that arm, however, for an extended length of time."

Mattie knew Kevin was barely holding his dislike for Clint in check, but she couldn't blame him.

"How long?"

"Weeks, maybe months, depending on how fast his body can adjust," Kevin replied. "He's not a young man anymore."

Mattie's gaze skipped over to Walt's grizzled face. The older man had been like a father to her ever since Jason's death. It was scary to see him so still, so pale. Why hadn't he retired when she asked him?

She inhaled a shaky breath. She was going to have a serious talk with Walt once he was feeling better. And this time he *would* listen to her.

A tingling at the base of her neck made her glance up to see Clint studying her. "Could I talk with you, Mattie?"

"About what?" Kevin demanded.

Clint scowled, clearly not appreciating Kevin's interference. "That's between Mattie and me."

"Anything you want to tell her, you can tell me, too." He wiped his hands on a cloth, then placed a proprietary arm around Mattie's shoulders.

For a moment, she wanted to push him away, but realized Kevin was perfectly within his rights. Besides, Clint had to understand she was no longer available. He would have to make do with Amelia.

"She's going to be my wife," Kevin announced.

Clint shifted his gaze to her, his eyes narrowed and his lips thinned. "Is that true?"

Mattie lifted her chin and met Clint's eyes. "Yes."

She forced herself to hold his gaze. Why couldn't she stop caring? Why did her belly still flutter with anticipation at his presence?

Clint took a step toward her. "Are you certain about this, Mattie?" he asked, his voice low and intense.

Damn him for coming back and filling her with indecision, after she'd spent hours convincing herself to marry Kevin. She shifted her gaze to her fiancé, to the hesitancy and concern in his eyes. There was no doubt Kevin cared for her, and she owed him her loyalty, if not her love.

Swallowing hard, she reached for Kevin's hand and grasped it firmly. "I'm sure, Clint. Kevin and I will be getting married in two weeks. You're welcome to attend the wedding, if you're still in town."

Clint flinched at her last words. She hadn't meant to say them, but at least she'd made her point crystal clear. She couldn't count on him to stay around.

His gaze darted to their joined hands and resignation stole across his handsome features. "All right," he said softly. "If that's your decision, I have to respect that." He fingered the brim of his hat. "And I think I will stay around for the wedding. I haven't been to one in years." Clint offered Kevin his hand. "Congratulations, Dr. Murphy."

After a moment's hesitation, Kevin shook his outstretched hand. "Thank you, Beaudry."

Mattie's heart climbed into her throat. She hadn't expected Clint to take the news so well, but then what *had* she expected? That Clint would declare his undying love for her?

That wasn't his way. That much, she knew.

"Are you going to check on the prisoner?" Clint asked. "He's got a bullet wound in the leg. It looks like it went clear through and bled a lot. He's going to need some stitches."

Kevin nodded. "We'll go over there."

"What about Walt?" Mattie asked. "We can't leave him alone."

"I'll sit with him," Clint volunteered.

Kevin blinked in surprise. "Are you sure?"

"I've sat with wounded men before." He smiled crookedly, endearingly. "I've even done my share of patching up bullet holes."

Mattie's heart tripped. His boyish smile still turned her bones to jelly and her brain to mush. How was she to endure knowing he was in town these next two weeks, without throwing herself into his arms again?

She would hide in her home and not come out until the day of the wedding. Yes, that was the only solution.

"If he wakes up, make sure he doesn't try to move around. He needs to lie still for at least a day so the wound can begin healing. If he's in pain, you can give him some laudanum." Kevin handed Clint a brown bottle. "But only a teaspoon or two."

Clint set the bottle aside. "I can handle it."

Mattie watched him draw up a chair beside Walt's bed. Moisture clouded her vision, and she recognized the maudlin tears as a symptom of her condition. While she'd been carrying Andy, even a butterfly's flight could make her cry. However, knowing the reason for her tears didn't give her any more control over them.

"Let's go, Mattie," Kevin said softly.

She moved as if her body were someone else's, allowing Kevin to guide her out the door. Once on the boardwalk, she felt her control returning.

The worst was over. She'd done the right thing. She'd spoken the words to Clint that dismissed him and tied her to Kevin.

So why did she feel so bereft?

Clint listened until Mattie's and the doctor's footsteps faded away. He took a deep breath and clasped his shaking hands, then dragged them across his forehead and over his head, resting them at the base of his neck.

He'd arrived too late. She had told him that Dr. Murphy was seeing her, but he hadn't expected the man to move in so quickly after he'd left. He admired the doctor, though he'd be hard-pressed to say he liked him. How could he, knowing Mattie would be in Murphy's arms every night after they were married?

And why had he told them he'd stay for the wedding?

"You're a glutton for punishment, Beaudry," Clint muttered.

He sat back in his chair, his shoulders slumped. Now what? He doubted he could sit around for two weeks without going crazy, especially knowing Mattie's place was just up the road. He wouldn't—couldn't—stay there. The physical temptation would be too great, and she'd end up hating him.

Maybe she did already.

Atwater's hand moved and Clint straightened. The sheriff opened his eyes, closed them, then blinked in the subdued light.

"Just relax, Sheriff," Clint said softly, laying a hand on his arm.

Atwater turned his head and focused on Clint. "Wh-what the hell . . . happened?"

"The bank was robbed," Clint replied. "Do you remember?"

Atwater's gaze traveled inward and after a few moments he nodded. "Two men. One of them . . . shot me."

"Don't worry, we got them."

Atwater's lips turned upward. "Thanks, Beaudry." He tried to move, but stopped abruptly and groaned. "Is it bad?"

Clint shook his head. "Doc says you'll be fine. Hit the right shoulder. Nothing that won't heal with a little time." He glanced around. "Want some water?"

"Yeah."

Clint stood and went into the kitchen. He filled a glass with cold water from the pump. When he returned, he slid his hand behind the old man's head to raise it slightly and lifted the cup to Atwater's lips. The sheriff drank most of it.

"Thanks," Atwater said.

Clint set the glass on a counter that held shiny medical tools, then returned to his chair.

"Didn't you leave?" Atwater asked, his voice stronger.

Clint grinned. "I came back."

Atwater continued to stare at him.

Clint planted his elbows on his thighs and clasped his hands. "I had to see her again."

"Mattie?"

"Yeah." He attempted a smile that fell short. "Guess I'm too late."

Atwater remained silent for a long moment, then asked the same question Clint had asked himself. "Now what?"

"I don't know. I said I'd stay around for the wedding, but it's still two weeks away." Clint met Atwater's gaze. "Orville Johnson asked me to fill in for you while you're laid up."

Atwater's chuckle quickly changed to a grimace. "Didn't waste no time, did he?" He coughed raggedly.

Clint grasped the other man's arm firmly. "Take it easy. Just relax."

Atwater's cough abated, though his face remained flushed.

"I told him no," Clint said quietly, drawing back from the sheriff.

"What?"

"You heard me. I still have to track down a murderer. Besides, I don't want the responsibility again. I guess it was like you said—I just couldn't handle it."

"Bullshit."

Startled by the sheriff's outburst, Clint shook his head in confusion. "Make up your mind, Atwater."

The older man reached out and gripped Clint's sleeve. "You were a damn good lawman, Beaudry." He panted to regain his breath. "You just . . . got to realize you're only human . . . like the rest of us." He released Clint and closed his eyes.

Clint turned Atwater's words over in his mind. He *had* been a good marshal until Emily's murder. He'd protected a lot of people; how many others would be dead if he hadn't done his job?

How many might have died today if he hadn't returned? Mattie could have been one of them. What hand had steered him back to Green Valley to arrive in the nick of time? His feelings for Mattie had triggered his return, but the timing was something fate or whatever controlled.

Just like Emily's death. The same hand of fate that had enabled him to save Mattie had not allowed Emily to live. Perhaps it *wasn't* his fault she'd died.

"Take my badge, Beaudry." Atwater's low voice startled Clint. "You're the only one . . . I trust with it."

"Why are you so sure you can trust me?"

Atwater opened his eyes and smiled. "Lawman's instincts."

Clint chuckled. Reluctantly, he stood and walked

over to the pile of Atwater's clothes. Picking up the vest, he stared at the badge. He'd vowed never to wear one again, yet here he was, considering pinning another badge onto his shirt. He glanced down at the Colt on his hip. Badge and gun went hand in hand.

What would Mattie think? Hell, what did it matter? She was marrying another man.

With trembling fingers, Clint unclasped the pin and removed the badge from Atwater's vest. He closed his fingers around it, and the star's points gouged into his palm.

His gaze flickered over to Atwater, who watched him silently, his shrewd eyes narrowed.

"You know what that badge stands for," Atwater said softly.

Yes, he did. He understood the risks, but he also knew the good he could accomplish. Opening his hand, he pinned the badge to his black bib shirt, above his heart. His breath caught in his throat, but the badge felt . . . right.

It was all he'd had before, and it was all he had now.

"You can stay . . . at my place. Big enough," Atwater said quietly. He dragged in a noisy breath and said, "She doesn't . . . love him."

Clint walked back to the man's bedside. "Who?"

"Mattie and the doc."

"She's marrying him."

"Ain't the same thing." Atwater stared up at Clint, his expression paternal. "If you love her . . . you can't let her . . . marry him."

Clint pictured the stubbornness in Mattie's eyes and the pride that stiffened her spine when she'd told him she was certain about her decision to wed the doctor. Had there been love in her tone? Her eyes? He couldn't remember seeing it.

Yet she hadn't told Clint she loved him, either.

He sat back down in his chair and noticed Atwater's even breathing. The man had fallen asleep.

Clint crossed his arms and rested them against his chest. He had some pondering to do and some decisions to make. On one hand, he had the promise and his gun, and now a badge.

On the other was Mattie.

He heard the doctor's voice a few moments before the door opened. Without looking, he knew Mattie was with him. He could feel her presence like a ray of sunshine across his shoulders.

"How is he?" Clint asked when they entered the room.

"I sewed up the entrance and exit wounds. He'll be ready to stand trial," Dr. Murphy assured him.

Clint stood and turned to face them, preparing himself for Mattie's reaction. Her gaze fell immediately to the badge and her eyes widened.

"You told Mr. Johnson you wouldn't do it," Mattie said.

Clint shrugged. "The sheriff talked me into it."

The doctor crossed over to Atwater's side. "How did he seem? Was he in a lot of pain?"

"Some, but he's a tough old coot," Clint said fondly.

Mattie eyed him warily, as if she were looking at a stranger. "How long will you be sheriff?"

"As long as I need to be."

Her violet eyes remained suspicious.

"Unless you want me to leave." He offered her the challenge, prepared to go if she asked him to.

"It's a free country. You can do what you want," she said coolly.

Clint squelched his smile. Same old Mattie— filled with enough pride to choke a horse. He had time to learn the truth, and he would, too.

"Since you're both back, I think I'll head on over to the bathhouse and scrub the trail dust off." He sidled a glance at Mattie and noticed a pink flush in her cheeks. So he could still make her blush— that was a good sign. "By the way, where's Atwater's place?"

"Why?" Murphy asked.

"He said I could stay there. I figure it probably wouldn't be a good idea to stay at Mattie's, seeing as how she's engaged to you."

Her pink cheeks bloomed to red.

Murphy scowled. "About a block down from the jail. The house needs painting, but it's in good shape."

"It's the one with the rosebushes in front," Mattie volunteered. "His wife used to raise them. She gave me some to plant at my place." She glanced away, her eyes glistening suspiciously.

Clint resisted the urge to sweep her into his arms and kiss away her sadness. He wanted to take her fishing, and tease her about not baiting her own hook and allowing Fred the Second to get away. But more than that, he wanted to waltz with her in the middle of the night, then carry her to bed and make love until dawn.

"Didn't you say you were leaving, Beaudry?" Murphy's curt question broke into his pleasant musings.

Clint smiled lazily. "I'll stop by later this evening, see how he's doing."

"*I'll* be here," Murphy said.

His meaning was as clear as day. He didn't want Clint hanging around Mattie.

"Nice to see you again, Mattie," Clint said, allowing his gaze to roam from her head down to her toes and back up.

He turned and sauntered out of the office, pausing on the boardwalk to listen to Mattie's and the doctor's low voices.

Clint knew he was playing with fire, but for Mattie, he'd risk getting burned.

# Chapter 18

The kitchen door opened and Mattie looked up to see Herman enter as he removed his slouch hat.

"I hear Beaudry's back," he commented, sliding into his chair.

He'd been back five days now and she hadn't returned to Green Valley since the day of the attempted bank robbery, not even to attend church service on Sunday. Between the guilt of not telling him about his child and her seesawing emotions, she couldn't take the chance of seeing him alone.

"Good for him," she muttered. She speared a piece of side pork in the frying pan and placed the meat on a platter, realizing she sounded like a petulant child. She stabbed another chunk of well-done meat, taking out her anger on the defenseless pork.

Herman cackled. "That hog's already dead, Mattie. Don't need to kill it twice."

She rolled her eyes heavenward, praying for patience to get through another day. "Have you seen Andy?"

"He was milkin' Jewel."

Mattie pivoted and planted one hand on her hip. "That's supposed to be your job. Andy's is to gather the eggs and feed the chickens."

"The boy already done his, so I jist let him do mine, too. He asked me if he could, and I didn't want to make him feel bad."

In spite of herself, Mattie's lips tugged upward at the corners. "He's changed a lot in the last two months, hasn't he?"

"S'pose so. Beaudry got him started right." Herman studied Mattie. "He ain't come callin' since he come back."

His tone was almost accusatory. She turned back to the stove to hide a new batch of tears. Brushing at her eyes, she damned the weepiness her pregnancy caused. "Why should he? I'm betrothed." The last word almost stuck in her throat.

"Y'know, you got a say in this, girl. I like the doc and all, but any fool can see you don't love him."

"I don't think that's any of your concern," she said curtly. Afraid to see if she'd hurt Herman's feelings, Mattie removed the rest of the meat from the pan, then cracked five eggs into it. She didn't want to think about the upcoming wedding or the fact that Clint would be sitting in the church witnessing her lie in front of God and everyone. Her stomach lurched, and she wasn't sure if it was her condition or nervousness.

"Talk to Beaudry," Herman continued a few minutes later, his voice gentle. "Let him know how you feel."

Using a slotted spoon to retrieve the fried eggs, Mattie divided them between the three plates, then carried two to the table. "That's just the problem. How I feel doesn't matter."

Herman reached up and patted her arm awkwardly. "My joints are tellin' me it's gonna be a fine day for fishin'. Why don't you come with me and Andy? Maybe it'll help you clear your mind some."

Mattie glanced around the kitchen, ticking off the chores that needed to be done. But what did it matter? Less than two weeks from now, the house would be empty or maybe sold to someone else. She and Andy would move into town to live with Kevin.

Her stomach knotted again. She hated to leave this place. It had been the first thing that had been hers alone. There had been good times under this roof as well as sad times, but it was home for her, Andy, Herman, and Ruth before she died.

Mattie smiled at Herman. "All right. Seems a waste to spend the last nice days of the year inside."

He gave her arm a fond squeeze. "Atta girl, Mattie." He winked at her. "I might even be bribed into baitin' your hook."

"And how much would this bribe cost me?"

Herman's blue eyes twinkled. "Maybe if you

brought along some of them sugar cookies you made yesterday . . ."

She laughed. "I might be able to find a few."

She crossed to the door and called, "Andy, breakfast is ready."

A few moments later Andy came inside carrying a pail a quarter full of milk. He set it on the floor and washed up at the pump before sitting down. "Sorry I'm late, Ma, but Jewel didn't like getting milked this morning."

"That's all right. Thank you for doing Herman's job." She arched a brow at the old man, who had the grace to look abashed.

Andy shrugged. "I didn't mind. Mr. Beaudry told me that a little work never hurt anyone."

Mattie glanced sharply at her son. "When did he tell you that?"

"When we were working on the chicken coop."

"Oh." Her heart took a few moments to return to its normal rate. "You haven't seen him since he's come back, have you?" she asked Andy warily.

"I seen him, but I haven't talked to him," he admitted, his tone almost accusatory. He gazed at her, as if trying to read her thoughts. "Why don't you like him anymore, Ma?"

Mattie chose her words carefully. "It's not that I don't like him, Andy. It's just that I'm an engaged woman now, and it wouldn't be proper for me to visit with him."

Herman snorted and she shot him a glare, but he only continued to eat as if he had done nothing wrong.

Andy picked up his fork and shoveled some food into his mouth as he kept his gaze on his plate. Mattie could tell he didn't like her answer, but she could give him no other that would make sense to a ten-year-old.

"Your ma's goin' fishin' with us today, Andy," Herman announced. "You figger she'll catch Fred?"

Andy glanced up in surprised pleasure. "Nah. I'm going to catch him," he said with boyish boasting.

Mattie smiled and some of the concern over her son's recent odd behavior melted away. He was becoming a man and that road wasn't a smooth one. She only hoped she'd be there to catch him when he stumbled.

Either herself or his stepfather.

Mattie blinked at the unexpected image in her mind—why had she pictured Clint and not Kevin beside her son?

"Don't overdo it like you did yesterday," Clint warned Atwater as he settled him in a chair on the sheriff's porch.

"I was fine yesterday. You just got it in that thick skull of yours that I'm some kind of invalid," Atwater growled.

Clint leaned against the porch rail and crossed his arms, holding his impatience in check by sheer force of will. Walt had come home two days after he'd been shot. As Clint had tried to steer him into the larger bedroom, he'd learned Walt slept in the smaller one where Clint had thrown his gear. After losing an argument to get him to sleep in the bigger bed, a puzzled Clint had moved his own stuff into the other bedroom.

Trying to keep Walt in bed for three days was impossible—he'd barely managed two. Finally, Clint had thrown up his hands and declared Walt a stubborn jackass.

Clint glanced at the sheriff. He was pale, but he didn't seem to be in too much pain. However, if Dr. Murphy caught Walt outside, the older man was going to get an earful. And Clint would probably end up on the receiving end of some of that reprimand. The doc had insisted that Walt remain in bed for at least three days.

*Yeah, when hell freezes over.*

"Watch out for Willie Larson," Walt warned. "He likes to take things from the general store without payin' for 'em. And keep an eye on Luther at the livery. He'll cheat a stranger without a second thought."

"Does he cheat the townsfolk?" Clint asked. Since breakfast, Walt had been filling him in on some of the more colorful characters in Green Valley.

"Nope." Walt chuckled. "Knows he's gotta live here with 'em and he don't want a necktie party with him as guest of honor."

Clint shook his head in tolerant amusement. "Sounds like you know your town pretty well."

Walt laid his left hand against his sling and leaned back in his chair, rocking it gently. "I should. Been livin' here long enough." He motioned with his chin toward a copse of trees a hundred yards away. "Just over there is where my Sarah is buried. Not a day goes by that I don't miss her. I usually stop by and say hello, tell her about my day."

Clint gazed at the trees that blocked the view of the cemetery, and his thoughts took him to Emily's final resting place. She had been laid to rest in her parents' private family cemetery. He hadn't even considered arguing with them. He hadn't cared enough. All he'd wanted to do was get away and track down her killer.

He swallowed hard and scrubbed his damp palms across his thighs. "I guess that's what it's like to really love someone."

Walt settled his narrowed eyes on Clint. "You were married."

"Not as long as you." Clint knew he was only making excuses for his inability to love his wife like he should have.

Like he loved Mattie.

"I'll come by at lunch and throw something together for us," Clint volunteered.

"There you go again, treatin' me like some damn cripple." He nodded at his wounded arm. "This is nothin'. Why, I remember the time—"

Clint dropped a hand on Walt's uninjured shoulder and grinned. "Save it for later. I have to go see how your town is holding together without you."

Ignoring Walt's grumbling, Clint hopped off the porch and headed toward the jail. He walked briskly, his long black duster trailing behind him in the cool autumn morning.

Breathing deeply of the scents of fall—leaves, damp soil, and crisp air—Clint realized how little time he had left to win Mattie over.

He'd figured Mattie would stop by to see Walt since they were good friends, but she knew Clint was staying there. He had no doubt she was intentionally keeping her distance from him—which was another piece of evidence to support the sheriff's claim that Mattie didn't love the doctor.

Clint's first stop was the bank, to make sure Orville was there and not at home. He entered the quiet bank, noting that only one clerk—Norbert Loomis—was working at the counter. The door to Johnson's office was closed.

"Morning, Sheriff," Loomis greeted him brightly. "What can I do for you?"

"Morning, Norbert. I was just checking to make sure everything was all right," Clint said with an easy smile. "Mr. Johnson must be hard at work, huh?"

The little man nodded and pressed his wire spectacles up on his nose. "Oh, yes. He told me he's not to be disturbed unless it's an emergency." Norbert leaned forward and whispered conspiratorially, "An audit coming up, you know."

Clint smiled and nodded with exaggerated sympathy. "I don't want to bother him, then. Just tell him I dropped by and said hello."

"I most certainly will, Sheriff Beaudry."

Norbert's eyes gleamed behind his glasses and

Clint smiled to himself at the man's eagerness to please. He was afraid to look back as he walked out, half expecting Norbert to toss him a little wave.

Back outside, Clint surveyed Green Valley, noting how peaceful the town appeared after Saturday's excitement. He glanced at the place on the boardwalk where he'd pulled Mattie to safety.

He had every intention of fighting for Mattie, any way he could. Especially if she didn't love Murphy.

Spotting Luther outside his livery, Clint crossed the street. He might as well have a little talk with him now rather than later. "Morning, Luther."

The burly man turned and his expression soured when he saw who it was. "Mornin', Sheriff," he said with as much resentment as Norbert had enthusiasm.

Clint planted a boot on the lower corral rail. "Looks like you're keeping busy. Must be some visitors passing through."

"A few."

"Glad to hear it—visitors are good for a town. They could settle down here, become fellow citizens," Clint said casually. "You'd get to know them and they'd get to know you. I always say new blood is good for a town, don't you?"

Luther's blush started at his neck and worked all the way up across his bald head. "I s'pose."

Clint slapped the man's broad back. "I knew I could count on you to give them a nice welcome and treat 'em right. See you later, Luther."

Clint spun on his heel and strolled away, whistling a nameless tune. Luther should have understood his message loud and clear. If he hadn't, he was dumber than he looked.

Sighing, Clint headed toward the pillared house on the outskirts of town. He glanced about to see if anyone was around, but it was quiet and still, with only a light breeze tickling the leaves.

Moving quickly, he went to the front door and knocked. A few moments later, the door opened and Amelia stood staring at him. "Cl—Sheriff, what are you doing here?"

"I need your help, Amelia," he said quietly, in case there were servants with big ears around.

After a moment of surprised hesitation, she grabbed his arm and pulled him inside, closing the door behind him. "You shouldn't be here."

Clint pressed his hat back off his head so it rested between his shoulder blades. "There's a favor I need to ask you."

Amelia's brows furrowed and she crossed her arms. "What?"

"Are we alone?"

Her eyes narrowed. "Yes. I have a housekeeper who comes in three times a week, but she's off today."

Clint relaxed. "Could we sit down?"

Amelia remained where she stood, silently studying him.

"It has nothing to do with you or Orville." He paused. "This is my problem, but I need your help."

After a moment, she led him across the expansive foyer and into a spacious, high-ceilinged kitchen. She poured him a cup of coffee, then one for herself, and joined him at the table.

Clint took a sip of the hot brew to fortify his courage. "It's about Mattie St. Clair."

"She's getting married."

"That's why I need your help. I have to stop that wedding."

Amelia stared at him a moment, then comprehension widened her eyes and her mouth dropped open. "You're in love with her."

Damn, was he that transparent?

He shifted in his chair, like a schoolboy caught dipping a girl's braid in the inkwell. "Look, will you help me or not?"

Amelia settled back in her chair and grinned. "What's there to do? Just tell her how you feel."

"She won't even talk to me."

Amelia sniffed. "I don't blame her, running off like you did."

Heat climbed up his neck. "I had a good reason."

"No woman likes to have a man leave her, whether he has a good reason or not."

"You're not helping," Clint muttered.

Amelia smiled, then sobered. "After everything you did for me, I owe you. Go on, Clint."

He took a deep breath. "I want you to find out if Mattie really loves Dr. Murphy."

Her eyebrows hiked up in surprise, then she traced her cup's handle with slender fingers. "Why do you think she'd tell me?"

Clint was beginning to wonder if maybe his plan had a few drawbacks—one of them being making him look like an idiot. "Because you're a woman, just like her."

"That's like saying you can talk to Norbert at the bank because he's a man, just like you."

He tried to picture talking with the effeminate Norbert over a beer. "All right, maybe this wasn't such a good idea," Clint admitted as he stood.

Amelia laid her hand on his arm, stopping him from leaving. "Sit down, Clint. I didn't say I wouldn't help. I just need to know more."

He dropped back into his chair and asked cautiously, "Like what?"

"Tell me why you left."

He took a deep breath and told her about his wife and the promise he'd made.

"I'm sorry. I didn't know," Amelia said softly after he explained. She thought for a moment, then nodded. "All right. I'll do it, but Mattie's smart— she's going to suspect something. She and I aren't what you'd call close friends."

"I know, but I don't think she's very close to anyone besides her son and Herman." Clint balled his hands into fists. "And Murphy."

"I'll go over there tomorrow with the excuse that Orville needs one of his suits pressed for a special meeting. Come by tomorrow afternoon around three-thirty. I'll be back by then and the housekeeper will have gone."

"What about your husband?"

"He won't be home until at least six," Amelia said with fond tolerance.

Clint rose. "Thanks, Amelia. I really appreciate this."

She stood and smiled. "You're welcome." She led him to the back door. "When you come by tomorrow, use this door. There's less chance of someone seeing you."

Clint slipped out with a quick good-bye and headed back to town, his steps lighter than when he'd arrived. The only catch in his whole plan was Mattie herself. She would have to swallow a considerable chunk of pride and admit she'd made a mistake with Murphy.

And sometimes Mattie could make a mule look reasonable.

# Chapter 19

⌒⌒◯◯⌒⌒

**M**attie smoothed back the wild tendrils of hair from her face, then went out to greet her unexpected visitor. She forced her voice to sound cordial. "Good afternoon, Amelia. What brings you out here?"

The woman climbed down from the surrey, then adjusted her fashionable floral overskirt across the cream-colored skirt beneath it. A small-brimmed hat that matched the floral design was perched on her head.

*How could any man resist someone like her?* Mattie thought with a touch of bitter envy.

"I'm sorry to bother you, Mattie, but Orville has an important meeting on Tuesday and needs his good suit pressed. Would it be too much trouble for you?" Amelia asked kindly.

Mattie wanted to dislike the woman, but even

suspecting her of adultery, she couldn't. "No trouble at all, Amelia."

"Thank you so much." Amelia handed her the black suit.

Mattie pasted on a smile. "Would you like to come in for a cup of coffee? I just baked some cookies."

"That sounds wonderful," Amelia said, and headed toward the house.

"Just wonderful," Mattie muttered as she followed her guest. She reminded herself she had to remain hospitable to the woman if she wanted to learn what was going on between her and Clint.

*Be tactful, Mattie,* she told herself, walking up the steps to the porch.

After setting the suit on the pile of items that needed pressing, Mattie led Amelia into the kitchen. As she poured them each a cup of coffee, she noticed that Amelia had removed her hat. That meant this wouldn't be a short visit.

"Tell me all about your wedding plans," Amelia said. "It's just so exciting. I hadn't even realized Dr. Murphy was courting you."

Mattie set a plate of cookies on the table between them and sat down, wrapping her cold hands around the coffee mug. "There isn't much to tell, really. Kevin and I have been friends ever since he moved here and when he asked me to marry him, I accepted."

Amelia tilted her head quizzically. "But you *do* love him, don't you?"

Mattie stared down at the steam rising from her

cup. "Of course I do." She hoped God understood and forgave her falsehood, but she wasn't about to tell *this* woman her secrets.

"You don't sound convinced."

Mattie snapped her head up to gaze at Amelia. "He's kind, compassionate, a wonderful friend. What more could a woman want?"

Amelia glanced down, her forehead puckered as if she were thinking hard about something. Then she raised her head and her eyes twinkled. "Passion."

Mattie choked on her coffee. She hadn't expected *that* from Mrs. Orville Johnson. Of course, if she was carrying on with Clint . . . Mattie swiped at her watering eyes after regaining her breath.

"Are you all right?" Amelia asked, leaning forward.

"I think so," Mattie said hoarsely. "You just surprised me, is all."

A little smile lifted the corners of Amelia's lips. "Because I'm married to a man nearly twice my age?" She paused. "You think I married him for his money, don't you?"

Mattie's cheeks heated, giving away her answer.

"That's all right." Amelia shrugged. "Most people in town believe the same thing. But it's not true. I married him because I love him."

If she loved him so much, why were she and Clint . . . ? Mattie pressed her lips together, courage abandoning her.

"People see him as arrogant and demanding,

but Orville's not like that," Amelia said. "He treats me like I'm made of fine bone china, and when we're in bed together, he makes sure I'm satisfied, too."

Mattie blinked in shock. She'd never spoken to another woman about such intimacies, not even Ruth. Mrs. Hotzel had told her that what went on between a husband and wife wasn't anyone else's business, only that the woman must submit to her husband. She'd also said that a woman must not enjoy "the act," either.

That was one rule Mattie hadn't been able to follow.

Especially in Clint's arms.

"Why are you telling me these things, Amelia?" Mattie asked bluntly. "I've been married before."

"From what I understand, you were forced to marry and then you were a wife for less than two weeks." She eyed Mattie. "Have you slept with him yet?"

"Kevin?"

"Who else?" Amelia asked with an arched brow.

Mattie didn't want to answer that one. "No. He's an honorable man and believes in marriage first," she replied stiffly.

Amelia laughed. "An old fogy, huh? Take my advice, Mattie—find out if he's any good first. Pretend he's a horse that you need to take for a ride before deciding to buy him or not."

The picture the woman drew in her mind was so amusing that an unladylike snort escaped Mattie; the giggles followed closely after.

Amelia joined in and the kitchen echoed with their shared laughter.

"I'm sorry," Mattie finally managed to say. She took a deep breath to gather her composure. "I understand what you're saying, but there's more to marriage than what happens in bed." If Amelia could speak so openly without embarrassment, so could she.

"Oh, I agree completely. But one without the other makes for a boring marriage. What you have to do is find a man who excites you both in bed and out. A man who can make you feel all squishy on the inside with just one look. A man who understands you better than you understand yourself."

Mattie's breath quickened. Amelia had just described Clint Beaudry.

Amelia reached across the table and laid her hand on Mattie's forearm, startling her. "Love isn't something you choose, Mattie. It chooses you. Do you love Kevin the way a woman should love a man? If not, you're going to be sentencing yourself to a mediocre life. And when love does choose you, you won't be able to do a damn thing about it because you'll already be married to the wrong man."

The swear word on the elegant woman's lips surprised Mattie. She was finding there was a lot she didn't know about Amelia Johnson.

*Ask her about Clint.*

"Would you like some more coffee?" Mattie asked.

Amelia nodded and Mattie refilled their cups, then sat down again. She drew courage from her curiosity. "Tell me one thing, Amelia. How can you say you love your husband, then secretly meet with another man?"

Amelia's face lost all color. "What?"

Mattie's heart sank. Amelia's guilty reaction confirmed her suspicions. "I saw you and Clint in the alley together on Saturday, after those two men tried to rob the bank."

Amelia stood and Mattie thought she would bolt for the door. Instead, she crossed her arms and paced to the stove and back. She gripped the back of the chair, her knuckles whitening. "It's not what you're thinking, Mattie. I've never cheated on my husband. I love him."

Mattie eyed her suspiciously. "Then why did I see you with Clint?"

Amelia closed her eyes and took a deep breath, then looked down at Mattie. "I knew him when he was a marshal down in Texas. I—I was a different woman then."

"What do you mean?"

Amelia rubbed her palms together, then gripped her shoulders as if she were cold. "I, ah, used to work in a saloon."

Mattie's mouth gaped. "You were a whor—?" Her face heated.

"I was alone and broke. What was I to do?" the younger woman demanded. "Starve?"

Mattie's mind spun. Hadn't she been alone and broke when her husband had died? If Ruth hadn't hired her, would Mattie have done the same as Amelia?

"Clint would come by once in a while for a beer and we'd talk. Nothing more."

Mattie found herself wanting to believe her, yet she had seen the two of them in the alley together. But what had she actually seen?

Amelia dropped back into her chair and grasped Mattie's hands. "Orville doesn't know. If he finds out, he'll hate me, and I couldn't live with that." The woman's eyes filled with tears. "Please, Mattie, don't tell him."

Dazed, Mattie shook her head. This was all so unexpected. She had hoped to get a tearful confession from Amelia, but not this one. "I won't. I—I never even suspected . . ."

Amelia smiled weakly. "You weren't supposed to. Nobody was supposed to. Clint said he wouldn't tell anyone, and I believe him. I've never known him to break his word."

Mattie's throat clogged with self-pity. No, he was too honorable.

"I'm sure I've overstayed my welcome," Amelia said with false cheer. She jumped to her feet and placed her hat on her head.

Mattie stood. "No, not at all. I'm sorry for the things I thought about you and Clint."

Amelia gazed at her intently. "His heart is already taken."

*Emily.*

"Thank you for stopping by," Mattie said past

the lump in her throat. "It's nice to have a woman to talk to."

Amelia paused and smiled. "It is, isn't it?" She finished tying the ribbons beneath her chin. "Will you be attending the dance tomorrow night?"

Mattie had almost forgotten—she'd agreed to accompany Kevin. Maybe she could claim a headache. He would understand.

*That I'd rather lie to him than see Clint?*

She nodded, trying to put some enthusiasm into the gesture. "Kevin and I will be there."

Mattie accompanied Amelia to her surrey.

Before she climbed into the buggy, Amelia turned to Mattie and asked, "Do you love him?"

Mattie turned her eyes to the land, which was becoming lifeless and barren with the coming of winter. Just like her heart.

She had resigned herself to the loss of Clint and the impending marriage to Kevin. Amelia's words only confirmed her decision. Clint's heart still belonged to his wife.

She brought her attention back to Amelia and forced herself to smile. "I love him."

As she spoke the words, her mind's eye pictured Clint, but that was a secret only she and her unborn child shared.

"Are you certain?" Clint demanded.

Amelia nodded. "She *said* she loved him."

Clint stood and paced the length of Amelia's parlor, then stopped to gaze down at the thoughtful expression on her face and his jaw clenched. "So, I guess that's it."

Amelia rose to her feet, stroking her chin. "Maybe not."

"But you said—" Clint began.

"I know, but there was something odd about her when she said it." She stopped in front of Clint. "Mattie's going to the dance tomorrow night with Dr. Murphy. That's where you'll have to make your move."

Completely baffled, Clint frowned. "He'll be watching her like a hawk. He won't let me anywhere near her."

Amelia smiled coyly. "He won't be able to stop you if he's dancing with me."

"And what's Orville going to be doing during all this?"

She waved a hand. "What he always does at these kind of things—politicking. I'll even get his permission before I ask Dr. Murphy to dance."

Clint stared at her a moment, then began to laugh. "You sound like you're enjoying this."

Amelia shrugged, but a little smile played on her lips. "I always did like to play matchmaker. Besides, I have a feeling Mattie wasn't completely honest with me. Call it woman's intuition."

Clint's heart skipped a beat. "You really think she doesn't love him?"

"That's right, but it's up to you to find out for sure." She glanced down, but not before Clint caught the crease in her brow.

"What is it?" he asked.

"She saw us come out of the alley Saturday. She thought we were secretly meeting. I had to tell her—about me and how I knew you."

"I'm sorry, Amelia. You shouldn't have done that."

"And let her believe we were carrying on?" She met his gaze squarely. "No, I couldn't do that. I don't think she'll tell anyone."

"Mattie's not one to spread gossip," Clint said. If nothing else, he knew Mattie well enough to know what he said was true. "I'd best get going." He retrieved his hat from a chair. "Thanks."

As he strode down the boardwalk five minutes later, he heard someone call his name. He stopped and turned to see Andy St. Clair running to catch up to him. Pleasure filled him at the sight of the boy, and Clint leaned over to hug him.

"It's good to see you again, Andy," Clint said, his voice surprisingly husky. He rested his hands on Andy's shoulders as he looked him over. "You've grown a foot since I saw you."

Andy's face flushed. "Ma says I'm growing so fast that by the time she gets new clothes home from the store, they're already too small."

Clint chuckled. He wrapped an arm around the boy's shoulders and steered him into the jailhouse. "Looks like your ankle's all healed."

Andy glanced down. "It was all right a few days after you left, but Dr. Murphy wouldn't let me get out of bed." He wrinkled his nose. "He brought these stupid books over for me to look at."

Clint squelched a smile as he settled one hip on the corner of his desk. "He was just trying to help."

Andy scuffed his toe against the floor. "That's what Ma said, but *she* didn't have to stay in bed and look at them."

"Look at it this way, partner: You're all better now."

"Yeah, but now Ma's marrying him." Andy sighed. "He doesn't even like to fish."

It was obvious the boy didn't like the idea of Murphy being his stepfather, which Clint could use in his favor. But his conscience balked at using Mattie's son to get to her. "I can take you fishing."

Andy grinned. "Are you staying here for good?"

More than anything, he wanted to, but there was still a murderer to catch. Even if he could talk Mattie into calling off her marriage to Murphy, he wasn't certain she would accept his proposal. Especially since he couldn't have the wedding until he had completed his obligation to his first wife.

"I'm not sure. We'll have to see what happens," Clint said.

Andy's smile faded. "I wish you wouldn't have left before. Then Ma wouldn't be marrying Dr. Murphy."

Clint's muscles tensed. "Why do you say that?"

"She was real sad when you left, then the doctor came calling almost every day. He made Ma smile."

Clint's breath hitched in his throat. What he wouldn't give to see Mattie's smile again. "So he made her smile, huh?"

Andy hopped onto the desk to sit beside Clint. "Yeah, but if you look close enough, her eyes are still sad. I think she was hoping you would come back and when you didn't, she decided to marry the doctor."

Elation filled Clint and he crossed his arms deliberately. *So Amelia was right, Mattie. You weren't being honest with her.* He'd learn the truth one way or another at the dance. "How's Herman?"

Andy shrugged. "Okay, I guess. He sleeps even more than he used to. Ma says he's getting old."

Clint had grown fond of the crusty codger, just as he'd come to like Walt Atwater. The two men had looked after Mattie, cared for her like they were related by blood, and for that alone, Clint respected each of them.

"I'll stop by and see him one of these days. Maybe we can all go fishing again." He paused, smiling. "Maybe we can even talk your ma into going."

"She went fishing with me and Herman yesterday."

Clint was surprised, but glad—the stubborn woman worked too damned hard. "Did she catch Fred the Second?"

Andy laughed. "She said she had him and he got away. Herman and me didn't believe her."

Clint chuckled, imagining Mattie's mock indignation. He could picture her with one hand planted on a curved hip, her lips tipped up at the corners and her eyes dancing with mischief. His heart stumbled, reminding him how much he had to lose if she married the doctor. "Sounds like you had fun."

The boy sobered. "She didn't have as much fun as when you came with us."

"Why do you say that?"

"I could just tell." Andy turned and gazed into Clint's eyes. "She cried."

Clint's fingers curled into fists as his breath faltered. "Why? Was she hurt?"

"No. She said it was a woman's per—" He frowned, obviously unable to remember the exact word.

"Prerogative?"

Andy nodded vehemently. "Yeah, that's it. What does it mean?"

"That it's a woman's right. Kind of like being a mother, I guess," Clint replied. She'd only cried once while he'd been there, after Andy had fallen in the well. It just wasn't like the Mattie he knew to be crying over something trivial. Hell, she'd even remained dry-eyed when he'd left—something Clint himself had barely managed to do.

Was Mattie that upset about marrying the doctor? Or was something else bothering her?

He had too many questions without answers, but he'd have to curb his impatience until the dance Saturday.

"Come on, let's go over to the bakery and get some bear claws," Clint said.

Andy grinned and hopped off the desk.

Smiling, Clint followed the boy out of the office and down the boardwalk.

"Did I tell you Ma lets me drive the wagon now all by myself?" Andy asked as they walked.

Clint rested a hand on the boy's shoulder. "That's real good. Are you helping her more around the house?"

"Yep. I'm even doing Herman's chores—he lets me."

Amusement filled Clint, but he kept his humor hidden. "I'll bet he does."

Clint opened the door to the bakery and the warm scents of yeast, cinnamon, and sugar surrounded him. Andy ducked under his arm and slipped in ahead of him.

"Hello, Ellen," Clint said to the red-cheeked woman behind the counter.

"Good afternoon, Sheriff," she replied with a smile that transformed her plain face to pretty. "I see you brought a friend with you today."

"This is Andy St. Clair," Clint introduced. "Andy, say hello to Miss Willoughby."

"Hello," Andy said with a shy smile.

"You're Mattie's son? Goodness, you've grown," Ellen said. "I'll bet you'd like something to eat."

Andy nodded eagerly as he eyed the baked goods on the counters. He pointed to the largest bear claw on the tray. "I'll take that one."

"You're just like my brother. He would always pick the biggest one, too," Ellen said, then turned to Clint, her eyes twinkling. "And what about you, Sheriff? The usual?"

Clint laughed. He'd been in her place twice and had bought a bear claw each time. "Yep. I always did have a weakness for them."

He gave her a couple of coins and took the bag from her outstretched hand. "Thanks."

"You come again, and bring Andy with you," Ellen said. "Say hello to your mother for me, Andy." She paused, her expression slipping. "And give her my good wishes for the upcoming wedding."

"I will," Andy said after a moment of hesitation.

" 'Bye, Ellen," Clint said, then ushered Andy out of her place ahead of him. He was puzzled by the woman's seeming reluctance to have Andy pass on her well-wishes.

He shrugged the odd feeling aside and sat down on the edge of the boardwalk, his feet planted on the ground below. Andy joined him and Clint opened the bag, giving the boy the largest roll, then took the other one himself. Grinning at one other, they each took a monstrous bite of their bear claws.

His mouth full, Clint glanced around and spotted Dr. Murphy crossing the street, headed their way. The man had a sour look on his face, like he'd just bitten into a rotten peach.

"Afternoon, Beaudry," Murphy greeted with as much friendliness as a skunk-sprayed porcupine. He turned to the boy. "Does your mother know you're here, Andy?"

The kid's face tightened and his eyes narrowed. "She knows I'm in town."

Andy definitely didn't like Dr. Murphy.

"Maybe you should head on home," Murphy

said. "I'm sure your mother will be looking for you soon."

"Let him finish his bear claw first," Clint said, irritated by the man's dictatorial tone. "Mattie won't mind."

Dr. Murphy's eyes flashed with impatience. "It seems to me you're not in any position to presume what Mattie will or will not mind."

Andy's lips thinned and he opened his mouth, but Clint dropped a hand on his shoulder.

"Mattie trusts her son, and Andy's old enough to come visiting by himself," Clint said.

The doctor's jaw muscle clenched. "Perhaps, but I know she worries about the boy, and Mattie has enough on her mind without having to be concerned about Andy's whereabouts."

Clint frowned. Was the wedding that much of a burden on Mattie? What was the doctor hiding? Was he worried that Clint might steal her away from him?

He had every reason to, because Clint intended to do just that. But only if Mattie didn't love Murphy.

*What if she doesn't love me, either?*

Mattie had given herself freely to him, and she wasn't a loose woman. There had been more than a physical joining of their bodies—much more. He shifted uncomfortably on the boardwalk. The memory of that one night never failed to make him grow as hard as the wood he sat on. *Damn.*

He looked up at the doctor, hoping his thoughts

weren't reflected in his face. "As soon as Andy is finished, he'll head on home, right?" He glanced at the boy.

"Yeah," Andy replied reluctantly.

"All right, then." Dr. Murphy's expression softened and genuine fondness crept into it. "I'll see you later, Andy. I'm coming over for supper tonight."

He patted the boy's head and gave Clint a terse nod, then climbed the steps and entered the bakery. Clint heard Ellen's friendly greeting, then Murphy said something to her and she giggled.

He turned his attention back to Andy.

"I suppose Ma will want me to go to bed early," the boy said, rolling his eyes. "She always does when Dr. Murphy comes over."

Jealousy sucked the breath from Clint's lungs and he didn't have a comment for the boy. He pictured Murphy and Mattie in the parlor, listening to the waltz from her music box. He imagined Murphy holding her hand, moving closer to her . . .

He closed his eyes tightly as a wave of anger and possessiveness surged through him. They were betrothed—Murphy was perfectly within his rights to kiss her and . . .

*At least Murphy is marrying her. I didn't give her any promises.*

Clint forced the painful pictures from his thoughts and managed a smile. "I suppose I'll catch it from your ma for ruining your appetite."

A grin slipped across the boy's face. "Naw. I'm bottomless."

Clint chuckled and ruffled Andy's dark hair—hair the same color and texture as Mattie's.

What if Clint couldn't stop the wedding? What if he lost Mattie because he had been too damn stubborn to see what was right in front of him?

Across the street, Pete Layton stood hidden in the shadows between two buildings as he watched Beaudry and the boy. Layton narrowed his eyes. Beaudry was supposed to be dead. He'd shot him himself and seen the bullet hole.

But there Beaudry sat, big as life, his shiny silver badge winking in the sunlight. The bastard had been following him for so long that Layton had finally decided he had to take care of the problem. Though Layton had killed for money many times, no one had paid him to take care of Beaudry.

This was personal.

How could he have known that woman had been a marshal's wife? A year ago, when Layton had been looking, she'd been handy. He'd taken what he wanted and ensured he would never be identified. The problem was the marshal had caught a glimpse of him as he'd ridden away and the bastard hadn't let up, so Layton had stopped him.

Or so he had believed.

He shifted his scrutiny to the boy, whom Beaudry seemed to have feelings for. Who was he?

Layton dropped his cigarette and ground the butt into the alley with his heel. Keeping to the shadows, he walked over to the livery where he'd left his horse.

He spotted the livery owner by one of the corrals and joined him. "Howdy, Luther."

The big man turned, surprised. "You back already?"

"I got a question for you." He motioned toward Beaudry and the boy. "Who's the kid with the sheriff?"

Luther squinted. "Mattie St. Clair's boy."

"Who's Mattie St. Clair?"

"A widow woman. She runs a boardinghouse about a quarter of a mile south of town. Her husband was the sheriff—got hisself killed before the boy was even born." Luther spat on the ground. "She's marryin' again next week."

"The sheriff?" That would be fitting—Layton could have his fun with Beaudry's new wife, then kill both of them.

Luther shook his head. "Doc Murphy." He glared at the sheriff across the street, like he had a personal grudge against him. "Beaudry's just fillin' in for Sheriff Atwater. He was shot when a coupla men tried to rob the bank. Beaudry helped out and got talked into takin' the badge until Atwater healed. I hear tell Beaudry's lookin' for someone."

Layton wondered what Beaudry would think if he knew his quarry was less than a hundred yards away. He smiled. "You say the widow woman has a boardinghouse?"

Luther nodded. "Last I heard, she ain't got no boarders, though. Not since Beaudry. He was shot and she nursed him back to health." He smiled lecherously. "I wouldn't mind bein' nursed by her."

So *she* was the reason Beaudry was still alive. And she was a good-looking woman.

This was getting better and better.

"Saddle my horse. I've decided not to stay around town."

"You still gotta pay for a day's boarding and feed," Luther said.

Layton flipped him a gold dollar. "That should more than cover it."

Luther caught the small coin with one hand, then grinned widely when he recognized its value. "Give me a few minutes."

Layton kept his back to Beaudry, but lowered his head so he could watch him surreptitiously. If he had known Beaudry would be so tenacious, he might not have used the woman.

Remembering that night over a year ago, Layton smiled. No, it had been worth it.

He wondered if Mattie St. Clair would be, too.

# Chapter 20

⟨⟨◦◦◦⟩⟩

**M**attie breathed a sigh of relief when Kevin finally left at eight that evening. Amelia's visit earlier that day had tired her out more than she cared to admit. Or it could have been all the cleaning she'd done.

The fact that she carried a new life within her probably had something to do with her exhaustion, too.

After Kevin's buggy disappeared into the twilight, Mattie turned back toward the house. The sound of an approaching horse made her pause. Frowning, she watched a rider appear out of the growing darkness. Her eyes widened at the sight of the golden horse. She'd never seen one that color before.

"Hello, the house," a man called out as he drew his horse to a stop twenty feet from Mattie. "I'm looking for a place to stay for two or three nights and was told you take boarders."

A lodger was the last thing Mattie wanted, but she couldn't very well turn someone away when her rooms lay empty. "You heard right. You can put your horse in the corral and your tack in the barn, then come on up to the house."

"Thank you, ma'am," the man said, touching the brim of his hat courteously.

The few dollars would be put toward the wedding—she hated that Kevin was paying for everything. Shivering, she scurried back inside and up the stairs. She decided to give him the room at the far end of the hallway, even though she usually used Ruth's old room as the main boarding one.

Mattie did a quick check to ensure the linens were clean and no dust littered the furniture. Satisfied, she returned to the main floor just as a knock sounded. She opened the door and took her first good look at the man. He was Clint's height, but narrower through the shoulders and chest, and his hair and eyes were dark. He wore trousers and a suit coat with a white shirt beneath it. The man could have been a traveling preacher or a banker—it was hard to tell. At least he didn't wear a gunbelt.

"Come in, Mr. . . ." Mattie began.

"Layton. Pete Layton. And you must be Mattie St. Clair," he said, doffing his hat. "I'm pleased to meet you."

She shook his offered hand, but when she tried to draw away, he clung to it a few moments longer. Mattie tugged a little more forcefully and he released her. He studied her silently, leaving Mattie with a decidedly uncomfortable feeling.

"Have you eaten?" she asked to fill the awkward silence.

"No, I haven't," Layton replied.

Mattie resigned herself to another hour of work. "I'll make you something." She pointed up the stairs. "Your room is at the end of the hall, on the left. If there's anything you need that's not in there, just let me know."

"Thank you, Mrs. St. Clair. I'll just go stow my saddlebags."

"Come on down to eat afterward."

"I wouldn't want to put you through any bother," Layton said.

Mattie forced the corners of her lips upward. "No bother at all. From now on, though, breakfast is at seven, dinner at noon, and supper at five-thirty."

"That'll be fine, ma'am."

He climbed the stairs and Mattie shuddered with an odd sensation, as if someone had walked across her grave. She shoved the feeling aside. Mr. Layton seemed like a gentleman in spite of his tendency to hold her hand a little longer than necessary.

Squaring her shoulders, she walked into the kitchen and set about preparing a meal. Fortunately she had leftovers she could use, so it wouldn't take long.

Ten minutes later, she heard Mr. Layton coming back down the stairs. When he entered the kitchen, she could smell lye soap. At least he was clean—that was definitely in his favor.

"Have a seat. It's almost ready," Mattie called over her shoulder.

She filled a plate from the pots on the stove and carried it to the table.

"This looks real good, ma'am," he said.

His words were polite, but his tone sent a shiver down Mattie's spine. She didn't notice anything threatening in his expression, though.

"It's not much." She set a cup of coffee by his plate, then crossed her arms. "Could you please put out the lamps when you're finished?"

"Are you going somewhere, Mrs. St. Clair?" He studied her closely.

"It's been a long day and I'm very tired," she said firmly to cover her sudden nervousness.

A smile slid into place. "I understand. I would have been here earlier, but my horse threw a shoe a few miles from town."

"Are you just passing through?" Mattie asked, curious in spite of her unease.

"That's right. I'm a businessman."

She breathed a silent sigh of relief. It was only the long day that had set her nerves on edge. "I thought so. You'd better eat before it gets cold. Good night, Mr. Layton."

"Good night, Mrs. St. Clair."

As she walked upstairs, Mattie couldn't help but laugh at her own suspicions. She'd thought Clint was a hired gun and he'd turned out to be a lawman—some judge of character she was.

She slipped into her room and closed the door. After a moment, she slid the bolt into place.

Better to be safe than sorry.

"Whose horse is in the corral?" Herman asked the next morning as he entered the back door.

Mattie smiled. "Good morning to you, too, Herman."

"Mornin'. Whose horse is that?"

"Mr. Layton's. He came in last night after Kevin left. He was looking for a room."

Herman scowled. "You shoulda fetched me. I don't like you receivin' men so late."

"He's a businessman," Mattie said with a laugh. "And a boarder."

"A man's a man. Believe me, I know. I'm one myself and I know what goes through our—their minds when they see a pretty woman alone."

"Calm down, Herman. I'm fine and Andy's fine."

Herman dropped into a chair, his face flushed and perspiration dotting his forehead.

Concerned, Mattie stepped over to his side and laid the back of her hand against his forehead. "Are you sick?"

The old man batted Mattie's hand away and pulled a well-worn handkerchief from his pocket to mop his brow. "Don't be frettin' about me, Mattie. I'm just tired, is all." He paused. "I ain't as young as I used to be. I can't protect you and Andy anymore like I used to."

A thread of apprehension twisted through her. "Don't be silly. You still have a lot of years left."

"I'm just glad you're gettin' hitched now, even though it's to the wrong man," Herman said.

Impatience made Mattie move away. "We've been through this already. Kevin will make a much better husband and father than Clint."

"Says you," Herman muttered.

Mattie's boarder entered the kitchen. "Good morning, Mrs. St. Clair."

She smiled. "Good morning, Mr. Layton. I trust you slept well?"

"Very well, thank you. I didn't realize how tired I was until I laid down."

"Have a seat. Breakfast is almost ready." She noticed the two men measuring one another. "Mr. Layton, this is Herman. He's my handyman."

Layton stuck out his hand, and after a moment Herman shook it.

"Whereabouts you hail from, Layton?" Herman asked.

Mattie sent her friend an admonishing look, but she could tell he was going to ignore her. Herman had stepped into his mother-hen role.

The stranger lowered himself to the chair across from Herman and leaned back, crossing his legs. "Denver. I'm on my way back from a business meeting in Reno."

"Why didn't you take the train? Seems to me that'd be more to your likin'."

Mattie poured each of the men a cup of coffee

and set the cups on the table in front of them. As much as she disliked Herman giving her customers an interrogation, she was curious herself about Layton.

The visitor laughed. "I spend most of my time behind a desk. Sometimes I prefer to ride a horse instead of a train just so I can get outside."

Mattie's gaze caught Herman's and she tipped her head slightly in an I-told-you-he-was-all-right angle. "Breakfast is almost ready. As soon as my son gets in here, I'll serve it," Mattie announced.

But the older man wasn't deterred. "What's your business?"

Layton's expression lost some of its amiability. "Accounting. I make sure everything balances out."

His cool tone brought a shiver to Mattie, but when she looked at him, there was nothing in his face except friendliness.

Andy pushed through the back door carrying the milk pail. He stopped and looked at Layton. "That must be your horse down in the corral."

"That's right. And you must be Mrs. St. Clair's son," Layton said gregariously. "I'm Pete Layton." He stuck out his hand.

"Andy St. Clair." He shook Layton's hand.

Mattie watched in awe, uncertain if she'd ever grow accustomed to her son's newfound maturity.

"Nice to meet you, Andy," Layton said.

Mattie filled everyone's plates and joined the men around the table. At first the conversation was stilted, but Layton put them at ease as he told them about the places he'd traveled. Andy listened with wide-eyed fascination.

"There's a dance in town tonight," Mattie said after they'd finished eating. "You might want to attend if you have nothing else to do. Folks in Green Valley are friendly and I'm sure you won't be hurting for dance partners."

"Thank you, Mrs. St. Clair, but I think I'll just stay here and do some work," Layton said. "There's always debts to be paid and accounts to balance." His voice was almost too smooth, reminding Mattie of a snake-oil salesman.

"I'm sure it's a demanding job," she said politely.

"Can I curry your horse, Mr. Layton?" Andy asked.

The man smiled at the boy. "Sure. I'll even go along and introduce you to him." He glanced at Mattie. "As long as your mother says it's all right."

She nodded. "That's fine. But don't forget you have other chores to do."

Andy nodded and led their boarder out of the house.

"Does he pass your inspection?" Mattie asked Herman.

The old man narrowed his eyes. "He seems all right, but that don't mean much. I seen too many wolves wearin' sheepskins."

Mattie reached across the table and clasped Herman's cool, bony hand. "Thank you."

He blushed. "Ain't nothin'. 'Sides, I promised Ruth I'd keep an eye on you. I don't want her to be mad at me when I finally join her." He shuddered visibly. "A mad Ruth ain't somethin' I'd wish on my worst enemy."

"I doubt she'll be mad at you," Mattie said with a fond smile. She stood, gathered the dishes, and placed them in the washbasin.

Herman shuffled up behind her and laid his hand on her back. "I, uh, I just want to tell you that you always made me proud, Mattie. Even when you was actin' like a stubborn mule."

Though knowing Herman hated such maudlin emotions, Mattie turned and hugged him close. "I love you, too, you old coot."

His arms crept around her tentatively, but he hugged her back. Then, as quickly as it had happened, the moment was over.

"I'd best get out there and make sure Andy's doin' them chores right," Herman muttered, and slipped out the back door.

Mattie swiped at her eyes. Although she had often been irritated with the old man for his lack of ambition, she couldn't fault his loyalty. A soft heart beat under that crusty exterior.

She straightened her spine. She had a busy day ahead of her, culminating in the dance that evening, which would take much of her energy. There was no doubt in her mind Clint would be there.

She recalled the night they'd waltzed in the parlor and what had followed in her bedroom. Her heart somersaulted and she rested her palms across her stomach protectively.

Would Clint ask her to dance tonight? Would she refuse him?

Or would her heart betray her?

Clint entered the front room of Walt Atwater's home and spotted the sheriff dozing lightly on the sofa. He smiled and covered him with the blanket lying on a nearby chair.

"Your tie's crooked," Walt said.

Clint stepped back. "I thought you were asleep."

"How can a man sleep with you tromping around?" Walt groused. He pushed himself up to a sitting position. "Come here, let me fix your tie."

Feeling like a young boy going to his first dance, Clint leaned close and allowed the older man to straighten his string tie.

"There," Walt said. He glanced down at Clint's waist. "Why ain't you wearing your gun?"

Clint straightened, half wondering the same thing himself. "Mattie doesn't like it and I figured I could handle things without it. I'm not expecting any bank robbers tonight."

"That's when they show up—when you ain't expecting them."

"It'll be all right for one night."

Walt sighed in resignation. "I hope you're right." He eyed Clint. "You got your work cut out for you. Mattie's not going to be easy to persuade." Walt rolled his eyes. "Believe me, I know."

Clint rested an arm on the fireplace mantel, trying to give the impression he was more relaxed than he felt. "Any suggestions?"

Walt snorted. "A lot, but none you'll listen to."

Clint tensed. "Try me."

The older man leaned back on the couch, his good arm wrapped around the injured one. "Walk up to her, tell her you love her, ask her to marry you, then get it done before she can change her mind."

Clint wished it was that easy. He wasn't certain what her feelings were for him, and he wasn't ready to spill his guts and be totally humiliated. Besides, he couldn't marry Mattie until his unfinished business was completed.

He shook his head and pushed away from the fireplace. "It's not that simple."

Walt studied him with a perceptive gaze. "It's as simple as you make it. Good luck, son."

Clint sent him a nod and strode out of the house, closing the door behind him. The autumn air was cool but fresh, and it cleared his mind. As he walked toward the town hall, the lively strains of a fiddle became more distinct. Horses and buggies lined both sides of the street and he spotted Dr. Murphy's wagon among them. That meant Mattie was already inside.

His step faltered as doubts plagued him. Why couldn't he just accept Mattie's decision to marry Kevin?

*Because I love her.*

By habit, he reached down to rest his fingers in his gunbelt and encountered only his trouser pockets. Maybe he should have worn the holster and gun—after all, he was the sheriff.

No, he needed all the help he could get persuading Mattie that it was a mistake to marry the doctor. If he showed up wearing his Colt, he'd lose the argument before he could even state his case.

He continued to the brightly lit building with resolute steps, nodding to the folks he met on the way in. Once inside, he drew off to the side to get his bearings. A fiddle, banjo, and mouth organ played a lively tune with more enthusiasm than skill, but none of the whirling dancers seemed to mind. The air was permeated with the scents of hair pomade, bay rum, and ladies' toilet water. He sneezed.

"Bless you, Sheriff," Amelia said as she, on the arm of her husband, joined him. "You look quite handsome tonight."

"And you look lovely, Mrs. Johnson," Clint said formally.

"Glad to see you could make it, Beaudry," Orville said, shaking Clint's hand. "How's Walt doing?"

Clint had to strain to hear him above the voices and music. "His arm is healing slowly, but Dr. Murphy said he should be able to start using it in another week or two."

Orville's head bobbed up and down. "That's good news, Beaudry."

Clint nodded, but he was already searching the crowd for Mattie. Children dashed in and out of the twirling men and women, creating controlled chaos. There were nearly a hundred people crammed into the town hall, but nobody seemed to care. He spotted Ellen from the bakery, Norbert the bank teller, Luther, and many others he recognized but whose names he couldn't remember.

"Well, look over there," Amelia said, pointing to the opposite corner of the room. "Isn't that Dr. Murphy and Mattie?"

Clint's heart leapt into his throat. Mattie, dressed in a deep violet gown and with her long hair flowing down her back, was easily the most beautiful woman in the room. Her arm was held possessively in Murphy's crooked elbow.

Startled to find he'd stopped breathing for a moment, Clint sucked in a deep breath. Why the hell had he ridden away from her?

"It's about time Kevin found himself a wife," Orville commented.

"You wouldn't mind if I danced with Dr. Murphy later, would you, Orville?" Amelia asked her husband. "I'd like to congratulate him on his engagement."

Orville patted Amelia's hand. "You go right ahead, my dear. He is, after all, one of Green Valley's finest citizens."

Clint bit back a caustic remark. Murphy was a good doctor and probably a decent man, but the jealousy that ate at Clint tainted his feelings for him.

"We should go over and greet them, Amelia. Beaudry, care to accompany us?" Orville asked.

Clint nodded, unable to trust his voice.

He followed Orville and Amelia through the kaleidoscope of color and motion of the dancers and uncurbed children. People greeted him and he responded, but he had no idea what he said. His attention was focused on the woman he'd come to claim.

Finally, they made it across the room and Clint found himself face-to-face with Mattie. Her wide violet eyes matched her dress, which hugged her curves like a snug glove.

"Good evening, Orville, Amelia," Murphy said, then added with less enthusiasm, "Sheriff."

Orville gripped Kevin's hand. "I haven't congratulated you on your fine fortune in marrying one of Green Valley's own." The banker gave Mattie a fond smile.

Mattie's own smile was tremulous at best. Clint had heard how the fine citizens had forced Mattie to marry Jason St. Clair, and he wondered if she was thinking the same thing. Clint had no doubt Orville Johnson had been one of those who had done what they thought best for Mattie.

"Thank you, Orville," Murphy said. "From both of us."

Clint managed a civil nod. "I've already congratulated"—he glanced at Mattie deliberately—"both of you."

Clint was barely aware of the idle conversation between the doctor and the banker. His attention was stolen by Mattie, who kept her gaze divided between Murphy and the floor. Clint stared at her, willing her to look at him. He caught a whiff of her rose scent, and it teased him with memories of her moon-bathed skin above him. . . .

"Isn't that right, Sheriff?" Orville asked.

Startled, Clint dragged his gaze away from Mattie. Damn, he was acting like a horny kid. Again. He focused on the banker. "I'm sorry. What was that?"

"I was just saying to Dr. Murphy how we might be able to convince you to stay if Walt decides it's time to retire."

Clint forced a smile. "That'll depend on a few things." He purposely looked at Mattie, whose cheeks reddened.

Murphy's eyes narrowed. "I'm sure Mr. Beaudry is already getting restless. From what I understand, he rarely stays in one place for any length of time. That's the way it is with men who live by the gun."

Mattie flinched and Clint's muscles tensed. He took a step toward the doctor as he smiled coolly. "If you haven't noticed, I'm not wearing my gunbelt this evening."

Out of the corner of his sight, he saw Mattie's gaze flick to his hips, then back up to settle on his face. She appeared puzzled.

Murphy pressed his glasses up on his nose, a gesture Clint recognized as nervousness. "I'm surprised."

Amelia whispered something in Orville's ear, and he looked toward a group of men standing in the corner and nodded to Amelia. "I'll be back in a moment." The banker looked at Murphy and Clint. "Excuse me."

As Orville wended his way through the crowd, the band began to play a waltz.

"Would you like to dance, Mattie?" Murphy asked.

Her face paled and she shook her head. "No, thank you."

"Well, I would like to," Amelia spoke up, batting her eyes at the doctor.

Murphy blinked in consternation and looked at Mattie. "Do you mind?"

For a moment, Clint thought she would, then she shook her head. She managed a thin smile. "No, of course not. Go ahead."

As Amelia dragged Murphy out among the other dancers, Clint shifted to stand beside Mattie. He listened to the waltz, recognizing it as the same tune that Mattie's music box played. He leaned close and whispered in her ear, "They're playing our song."

Mattie tried to edge away from him, but a wall blocked her escape.

"What are you doing here?" she demanded, anger sparking her eyes.

Clint grinned. *This* was the Mattie he remembered. "I wanted to see you."

She licked her lips and he couldn't help but follow the trail of her pink tongue with a hungry gaze.

Mattie glared at him. "Stop that."

"Stop what?" he asked innocently.

She narrowed her eyes and her nostrils flared. "You know darn good and well what I'm talking about." She paused. "You weren't supposed to come back."

"It's a free country. I can go wherever I please."

He touched the sleeve of her dress. "At least you listened to one thing I said. It matches your eyes perfectly, especially when you're spitting mad. Like now."

"I. Am. Not. Mad," Mattie stated through clenched teeth. "You need to leave."

"Not until you dance with me."

"No."

He shrugged. "Then I stay."

Clint could feel her exasperation, but beneath it was the hum of awareness that flowed through his own veins. Mattie was definitely not going to marry Dr. Murphy, even if he had to kidnap her from the church.

"Want to dance?" he asked again. He winked. "At least we're dressed right for it this time."

Mattie's face turned as red as a ripe apple, but her chin lifted stubbornly. "If that's the only way I can get you to leave, all right. We'll dance." She glared at him. "But I'm not going to enjoy it."

He grinned. "Wanna bet?"

Before she could offer a retort, Clint swept her out onto the dance floor. She seemed to float, feeling as natural within his arms as she had that night they'd waltzed in her home.

"Do you feel this way when you dance with the doc?" Clint asked. He was so close to her that her breath warmed his neck.

"I've never waltzed with him," she admitted in a voice so low Clint almost missed it.

"Why?"

She remained silent, her feet gliding with his in

light easy steps and her head bowed. Clint leaned forward, intending to press his lips to her bare neck, but caught himself at the last moment. This wasn't Mattie's parlor.

"Why haven't you waltzed with him?" Clint pressed.

She took a deep shuddering breath and Clint instinctively tightened his hold on her.

"I swore I'd never waltz with a man again after my husband was killed." She finally lifted her head to meet his gaze. "He promised he'd waltz with me until we were old and gray." Her eyes glistened. "He lied."

Clint's mind struggled to put sense to her words. "But you asked me to waltz that night."

"It was for just one night and I knew that." She paused, then added quietly, "At least that's what I believed."

"No promises," he whispered, his heart thundering in his chest.

She nodded, her dark hair tickling his nose. "If a promise isn't made, it can't be broken."

That's why she understood his promise to his late wife so well, and that's why she hadn't asked him to stay with her. It wasn't because she didn't love him—of that he was certain.

His breath faltered and his heart threatened to leap from his chest. He suddenly knew what he had to do.

He tightened his arms around her. "I love you, Mattie St. Clair."

# Chapter 21

**M**attie stumbled and Clint's strong arms caught her, pulling her flush against his body. She could feel his arousal pressing into her belly, just as she had that night. . . . Her throat tightened and she searched for the courage to look into his face.

Her gaze latched on to his string tie and she valiantly moved her scrutiny upward, to his firm chin and angular jaw, his sensuous lips, his straight aquiline nose, and finally his startling green eyes.

The truth blazed from the depths of his soul— she could read it in those eyes that had captured her from the moment she'd met him. Clint Beaudry loved her.

The air was suddenly too hot, too heavy. "Outside," she gasped.

His expression concerned, Clint took her arm and guided her through the crowd to a side door. The cool, fresh air stung her face and chased away the swirling nausea. She leaned against the building, tilting her head back to drink in deep draughts of the night air. Her dizziness receded, but she remained staring upward at the stars.

Now what? Clint loved her and she believed him. So why did her own declaration stick in her throat?

"Mattie," Clint said quietly. "Are you all right?"

His warm breath fanned across her cooling cheek, but it was the concern in his voice that sent a shiver of desire through her. "I'm fine," she replied. She finally lowered her gaze to meet his anxious features. "The air just got a little close in there."

His creased brow smoothed and he smiled boyishly. "That probably wasn't the best place to tell you, but I knew I wouldn't get another chance." He grew somber once more. "Do you love him, Mattie?"

His steady gaze unsettled her. If she told him the truth, she'd be breaking her word to Kevin. Startled, she realized that although Clint had said he loved her, he hadn't mentioned the vow that had taken him away from her.

"What about your wife's murderer?" she asked, keeping her voice steady as her insides trembled.

The flash of guilt across his face betrayed him. He had no intention of abandoning his quest. Tears burned, but she held them back. Though they loved one another, they couldn't be together until Clint had erased his debt.

Nothing had changed.

"I'm marrying him," Mattie said. "I gave him *my* word."

Clint clasped her upper arms as desperation clouded his eyes. "You don't love him. You love me."

She wished she could lie and deny his words, but it didn't matter. He knew. "Love isn't enough this time."

"The hell it isn't," Clint said through thinned lips. "Marry me, Mattie."

"When?"

"As soon as I track down Emily's killer, I'll come back and we'll have the biggest wedding Green Valley ever saw," Clint said.

She wanted nothing more than to say yes, but there were too many obligations and uncertainties. Mainly the possibility of his death.

Mattie shook her head, misery clutching her heart with sharp talons. "I won't wait for a man who may never return, always wondering if you were dead or alive. I can't do that. Kevin is safe, dependable."

"You sound like you're buying a damned horse," Clint said disgustedly. He released her and held out his hands. "I'd be a good father to Andy, and a damned good husband to you. I promise I'll come back to you."

"No," she shouted, panic clawing up her throat. "Don't you dare make a promise you can't keep."

He drew back, startled by her outburst. "What if I do everything in my power to stay alive and come back?"

Mattie shook her head, which had begun to pound. "Don't, Clint. It doesn't change anything."

He studied her a long moment and Mattie wondered if he could see the wild flutter of her heart. "You promised Kevin you'd marry him," he said softly. "And Mattie St. Clair would rather die than break a promise."

That was only part of it, but Clint couldn't know the rest—the most important part. She'd given her word so her child could have a father and a name. "That's right."

He shrugged tiredly, as if exhaustion abruptly took hold of him. Mattie had never seen him look so . . . so helpless, and she lifted a trembling hand to rest on his sleeve. Her body hummed with awareness. No man had ever made her feel so alive.

"I'm sorry, Clint. It's just that . . ." How did she explain something that had been with her since she'd been Andy's age? The fear and the betrayal. . . . "My parents promised they'd never leave me, then they died when I was eight years old and I was placed in the children's home. When I was sixteen, Jason St. Clair promised he'd waltz with me until we were old and gray, then he got himself killed." Tears burned her eyes as unexpected rage surged through her veins and her hands fisted at her sides. "I am sick to death of people I love breaking their word. I won't make the same mistake with you."

His eyes widened at the same moment she realized she'd inadvertently told him she loved him. She pushed away from the wall to dash back into the hall, but Clint caught her shoulders. Realizing it was fruitless to try to escape, she stood motionless, staring down at his boots.

"Dammit, Mattie, you can't marry him if you love me," he said.

His voice trembled and Mattie could feel the waves of frustration rolling off his powerful body. His fingers clutched her arms, holding her so close that the tips of her breasts brushed his shirt, a reminder of something else—something infinitely bittersweet.

She hated this inability to curb her body's reaction to him, the subtle shift of the air between them to something alive and vibrant. She would always have a part of him in the child she carried, but that, too, would be a poignant reminder of the gunslinger who had given her a taste of love—the true love her parents had shared.

Guilt preyed upon her conscience—and soul—as she desperately wished she could tell him of his child. But she had her own promise to keep, even it meant losing the only man she'd ever truly loved.

Raising her head, she met Clint's despairing eyes. Her resolve wavered, then steadied. "Kevin will be a good husband and I'll be able to work at his side, helping him with his practice. You have your own life." She smiled, her lips quivering. "I'm only glad we had what time we did together.

Remember"—she paused, her vision blurring—"no regrets."

For a moment, Mattie thought he'd continue the fight, but then his eyes shuttered and he nodded in resignation. Releasing her, he took a step back.

He laughed bitterly. "When I first met you, I figured you for a woman who would demand a wedding for what we did. Instead, *I'm* the one trying to talk you into getting married. Who would've figured?"

Mattie flattened her hand on Clint's chest and she could feel the thudding of his heart beneath her palm. "You know I'm right," she whispered.

He stared into her eyes intently, as if trying to memorize what lay within them. Then he wrapped his fingers around her wrist and lifted her hand from his chest to press his lips to the center of her palm. The soft brush of his mouth against her sensitive skin wobbled her knees.

Mattie's throat grew thick and tight as she struggled against a new onslaught of those damn tears. It was time to leave.

Without another word, Mattie spun around and plunged back into the dance hall, bumping into a body as she came through the doorway.

"I—I'm sorry." Mattie glanced up to see Kevin's worried countenance.

"Are you all right?" he asked tenderly.

Unable to trust her voice, she nodded.

"Maybe I should take you home. You look pale," he said.

"That's a good idea," Mattie said too eagerly. "My stomach is queasy."

Kevin gathered their coats, then helped Mattie into hers. After a whirl of good-nights, Kevin led her to his buggy and helped her up. She clasped her hands tightly in her lap as he climbed up on the other side.

Kevin slapped the reins lightly against the horse's rump, then glanced at Mattie. "Did you enjoy yourself?"

"Yes." She couldn't manage more than a one-word answer.

"I noticed Beaudry was gone the same time you were."

Indignation sparked her temper. "Why don't you just ask me straight out?"

"Ask what?"

"If I let Clint kiss me? If I told him about the baby?" The words came out sharp and cutting, and she wished she could retract them, but the evening had frayed her already tattered nerves.

Kevin stiffened beside her and his lips pressed together. He remained ominously silent.

Mattie's apology stuck in her throat. It wasn't that she wanted to hurt Kevin, but the unfairness of everything made being polite difficult.

The night was clear, the stars crisp, and the air rich with the tang of autumn. A perfect evening, except Mattie couldn't enjoy it. The *clop-clop* of the horse's hooves punctuated the pounding in her temples.

"I know you wouldn't do those things, Mattie,"

Kevin finally said. He smiled, but it was oddly bleak. "You have integrity, more than even I had suspected."

She blinked and turned to look at his profile, cast in the quarter moon's pale shadows. Something was bothering him. Was he having second thoughts about marrying her?

He guided the horse into Mattie's yard, pulled the hand brake, and tied the leather reins to it. "I want to thank you for a nice evening, Mattie."

His awkward, formal tone didn't bode well.

"What's wrong?" she asked.

"I'll come by tomorrow and we'll talk."

"But—"

"Tomorrow. We're both tired tonight."

Kevin hopped down from the buggy, then assisted Mattie to the ground. He walked her to the porch and stopped in front of the door. "I had a good time tonight, Mattie."

She swallowed hard. They'd only spent an hour together, then she'd disappeared with Clint. "I did, too." Her palms dampened from the lie.

He leaned over and brushed a kiss across her forehead, like a father would do with a daughter, rather than a man would do with his fiancée. His lips were dry and stiff.

"Good night, Mattie."

"Good night."

She watched him leave, a heavy anvil across her chest. So much had happened tonight, more than she had hoped for, but more than she could ever realize. Her mind foggy, she entered the house and hung her coat on a hook. She half expected Herman and Andy to be playing checkers in the parlor.

Instead, she spotted a strange man sitting in a wing chair and her hand flew to her mouth. It took a second to recognize Pete Layton.

"You frightened me," Mattie said breathlessly.

He smiled, the firelight giving his complexion an orangish cast, and stood. "I'm sorry. I was just enjoying the warmth of the fire."

His shadow cast from the fireplace appeared distorted against the opposite wall—looking like a grotesque phantom. Unease slithered through Mattie, and she gave herself a mental shake. He was merely a businessman, a boarder.

"How was the dance?" he asked, stepping closer.

"Fine."

"Did you see the sheriff there?"

Mattie frowned, puzzled by the unexpected question. "As a matter of fact, I did. Do you know him?"

Layton shrugged. "In a manner of speaking. I'd heard you saved his life after he was ambushed."

"That's right," she said cautiously. "How did you learn that?"

"The liveryman told me. He also said you were a fine-looking woman." Layton's gaze flicked up and down her body, pausing on her breasts. "As good-looking as Beaudry's woman was."

Dread stabbed Mattie and her heart leapt into her throat. She took a step back, her knees quivering, and asked hoarsely, "Who are you?"

He narrowed his eyes and said matter-of-factly,

"I'm the man who shot Beaudry and killed his wife."

Mattie gasped and tried to run, but Layton struck like a rattler, grabbing her before she could even scream. Standing behind her, he wrapped his arm around her neck, threatening her supply of air, and whispered in her ear. "It's just you and me, Mattie. Let's enjoy it."

Mattie's heart thundered in her chest. Tiny circles of changing colors danced before her eyes. She had to try fighting him before she was too weak to do anything. Feeling his legs directly behind hers, she lifted her foot and slammed her heel down on his instep.

The choking arm dropped away and she fell to her knees, gasping. Through her fear, Mattie saw Layton was smiling—a smile filled with the promise of pain and death.

"Oh, God, no!" She tried to scramble to her feet. The hem of her violet gown caught beneath her toe and she nearly stumbled to the floor again, but caught herself. "Stay away from me," she said, her voice shaking.

"Or what?" Layton taunted, taking a step closer.

Mattie spotted the woodbox a few feet away. If she could just reach a piece of wood . . .

"Uh-oh, Ma's home early," Andy said quietly.

"Uh-oh, is right," Herman muttered. He hadn't expected Mattie to be home so soon. Maybe she'd finally come to her senses and called off her engagement with the doc. That would make Herman as happy as a flea on a hound dog. "I'll talk to her."

Andy's young face appeared doubtful. "She's going to throw a fit that I was out after dark."

Herman's step faltered on the porch. When it came to a woman's temper, Herman usually stayed far out of the line of fire, but he'd been the one to talk the boy into fishing. He had a feeling they'd be biting this evening and he'd been right—five fish dangled from the stringer in his hand.

"Maybe we could just wait until all the lights are off and you can sneak in," Herman suggested.

Andy shook his head. "Ma always checks on me before she goes to bed. She'll know."

Herman rubbed his grizzled chin. "How 'bout if you slip in the back door? Maybe you can get past her that way."

"Maybe." The boy didn't sound real sure.

A woman's cry sounded from within.

"What the—" Herman began.

He dropped the fish and grabbed Andy's arm as the boy dived for the door. It took all of Herman's strength to draw Andy over to the window. They peeked in and spotted Layton, the look of the devil on his face as he trapped Mattie in a corner of the parlor. A piece of firewood lay on the floor between them.

"Go get Beaudry and the doc," Herman ordered.

"But—"

Herman gave him a shove toward the porch steps. "Go!"

After one more terrified glance, Andy raced off toward town.

Herman turned to the scene inside once more and he cursed the frailty of his old body. By God, though, he'd do what he could to protect Mattie.

Mattie cried out again. Herman shoved the door open and marched inside, willing his strength to be enough to help the woman he loved like a daughter.

Layton wrapped his fingers tightly in Mattie's hair, and tears of pain ran down her cheeks. He jerked her head back so far she was afraid her neck would snap.

"Let her go, you sonuvabitch."

Herman's voice cut through Mattie's cries and Layton shoved her aside. She stumbled to the floor, bruising her knees on the hearth. Through tear-filled eyes, she saw Herman's enraged expression.

"Get out of here, old man," Layton said, as if Herman were nothing more than a pesky fly.

"Leave her alone," Herman ordered, deadly serious.

Layton laughed. Mattie had never heard anything so evil.

"*You're* going to stop me?" Layton taunted.

"The sheriff is on his way here, so if you got anything in that head o' yours but shit, you'd best get the hell outta here," Herman said.

Layton's smile was almost painful to observe. He'd killed a woman and probably many men—he wouldn't hesitate to murder Herman.

"Beaudry's on his way here?" Satisfaction gleamed in Layton's dark eyes. "That's even better than I could've planned."

"He's the one who shot Clint," Mattie said hoarsely to Herman.

Her old friend's face paled even further and Mattie grew frightened for him. She watched in horror as he clutched at his left arm with his right hand and swayed slightly.

"All . . . the more . . . reason t-to leave," Herman stammered between painful gasps.

Layton shook his head. "I don't think so. In fact, it works out perfectly this way."

Herman tried to take a step closer, but he stumbled against the side of the doorway. He closed his eyes tightly and his complexion took on a grayish cast.

"He's sick," Mattie shouted, and scrambled to her feet.

Layton grabbed Mattie's arm as she tried to make it to Herman's side. She kicked and flailed at him as she fought to escape, but he held her tight. She struggled to breathe through her fear. Through hazy vision, she saw Herman slide to the floor as if his bones had turned to liquid. She heard a soft sigh.

Frantically, she stared at his chest, willing it to move up and down. But it remained still.

"No!"

Mattie's body caved in upon itself and Layton released her. She collapsed to the floor and managed to crawl over to Herman's unmoving body.

She laid her ear against his gaunt chest, but heard nothing.

Turning to look at Layton, Mattie understood the hatred that had motivated Clint to make the promise to his wife. Her own loathing became a living, breathing beast, slithering through her veins. "You killed him!"

"He saved me the trouble," Layton said with a shrug. "Too bad he had to show up before we had some fun. Oh, well, this way I won't have to chase Beaudry down. He'll come to me."

Mattie's blood froze. Layton was going to use her as bait to lure Clint here and murder him.

"Well?"

Clint glanced up at the doorway of the dance hall and recognized Amelia. How long had he been standing outside? He'd watched Murphy escort Mattie to his buggy, then take her home.

"She doesn't love him," he said quietly.

Amelia stepped out to join him, a joyous smile on her face. "That's wonderful." She studied him a moment and her happiness faded. "What's wrong?"

Clint flushed his lungs with the cool air. "She's still going to marry him."

"Why?"

"It has to do with promises," he replied quietly. How did he explain that was the only thing Mattie believed in?

"I don't understand."

His whole body sagged, as if he'd just been involved in a gunfight. Only this time the ammunition hadn't been bullets, but words. "It doesn't matter." He gave her a gentle shove toward the door. "Orville's probably looking for you."

Amelia shook her head stubbornly. "When he's talking about the town's future, he doesn't even miss me." She frowned. "I can't believe you're giving up this easily. I thought you loved her."

He stiffened. "I do, and she loves me. But it's not enough."

Amelia huffed. "If you aren't the most pig-headed, stubborn man. Stop feeling so damned sorry for yourself, Beaudry. Your first wife was murdered because you weren't home. Have you ever stopped to think it could've happened even if you'd been a rancher or a pig farmer? You couldn't spend every minute of every day with her. Then you made a stupid promise to get revenge." She paused, her eyes hard. "Men do strange things when they're mad or feeling guilty—believe me, I know. I know all about men." She shuddered. "Ask yourself this, Beaudry. What the hell do you think Emily would want you to do?"

Clint stared at Amelia, but he saw and heard Arabella instead. She'd learned her lessons the hard way and she'd survived, and become the wiser for it.

Could he let go of the past? All he had to show for his year-long chase were two new scars and a hole in his heart that would never heal.

Had it all been for Emily? Or had it been for

himself? Perhaps his vow *was* his attempt to purge the guilt that had nearly destroyed him the night she'd been killed. It was time to release the past and get on with his life.

He glanced up into the starry night. Was that what Emily wanted? The answer came as gently as an angel's caress.

"Thank you," he whispered into the darkness.

A boy's frantic voice brought his attention back to the street and he stepped away from the dance hall. Watching the boy draw closer, he recognized Andy St. Clair.

His heart kicked his ribs and he ran out to meet him in the middle of the street. Catching the boy by the shoulders, he squatted down to eye level. "What's wrong?"

"Ma . . . Ma and . . . that m-man," Andy struggled to say, panting.

"What man?" Clint demanded.

A hand settled on Clint's shoulder. "Go easy," Amelia said softly. "He's scared."

"M-Mr. Layton . . . he rented a room," Andy said.

His body trembled so much Clint wondered how he stayed on his feet.

"What about him?" Clint pressed, though consciously keeping his voice low and calm.

"He was going after . . . Ma. Herman sent m-me . . . to get you."

Clint shot to his feet. "Amelia, watch Andy."

She wrapped an arm around the boy's shoulders.

"Herman said to get Dr. Murphy, too," Andy said.

Clint nodded. "You two get him. I'm going to Mattie."

He ran to the nearest saddled horse, panic flashing through him. Would he succeed this time or fail again?

Clint jumped onto the horse's back, then jerked the reins around and urged the mare into a gallop. Fear and rage pounded in his breast, keeping time with the horse's hooves on the hard-packed earth.

A few minutes later, he drew back the reins sharply and the horse dug its hooves into the ground. A flash of color in the corral caught his attention and he focused on the light-colored horse.

A palomino.

Fear balled in his gut. The man who'd killed Emily now had Mattie. Hatred hazed his mind. The bastard wasn't going to win this time.

Clint slid off the horse, then gave its flank a swat to send it back to town. Clint clawed at his hip for his Colt—and his fingers brushed only his trousers. Frustration and rage coursed through him.

Mattie's dislike of guns might be her death sentence.

Keeping to the shadows, Clint ran in a half crouch toward the house. He made it to the porch and pressed his back against the wall next to the door. He cocked his head to the side, listening, but no sound came from within.

His heart hammered in his chest. What if she was already dead? Used like Emily had been—battered and broken? Nausea crawled up his throat.

Was he too late?

Again?

# Chapter 22

From the chair Layton had forced her into, Mattie stared down at Herman's lifeless body. A tear trailed down her cheek and she wiped at it impatiently. There would be time later to mourn. Clint would be coming and Layton planned to shoot him in cold blood. Just as he'd done two months ago.

She swallowed the terrible fear and focused on the killer. He stood by the fireplace, listening and watching like a snake plotting its next meal. He hadn't bothered to tie her up, but the gun in his hand was reason enough not to try anything. Yet.

A creak sounded from the porch and Mattie's entire body tensed. Layton, who'd obviously heard it also, crossed the short distance to her. Resting one hand on her shoulder, he used the other to hold the gun close to her head. "Come on in and join the party, Beaudry," he called out.

Mattie's breath caught in her throat and icy fear pierced her. The front door creaked open, then came the gentle clink of spurs. Clint's familiar figure appeared in the doorway and his gaze darted to Mattie. Relief showed in his eyes and he sent her a barely discernible nod. Though she knew they were far from safe, her tension eased at the confidence Clint exuded.

Clint shifted his attention to Herman and his jaw muscle knotted. "You bastard," he growled at Layton.

"I didn't do anything. He did that all on his own," Layton said lightly.

Clint balled his hands into fists and took a step toward Layton. Rage rolled off him like thunderclouds coming over the mountains.

Layton raised his gun, pressing the barrel against Mattie's temple. "No you don't, Beaudry. You come any closer and I'll blow her brains out."

Clint stopped abruptly and his gaze flickered to Mattie. She could see the desperation in his eyes, the helpless fear that he was living a nightmare.

Mattie wanted to reassure him, but her mouth was so dry she couldn't speak. She lifted a trembling hand as if to reach out to him, but Layton knocked her arm down.

"Be a good girl, Mattie," he said in a steely voice.

Clint's white lips thinned. "It's me you want. Let her go and I'll do anything you say."

Layton shook his head. "She's my bargaining

chip, Beaudry. I know you got more people coming and I'm going to need her to get away. When I've gone far enough, I'll let her go." He smiled coldly and caressed Mattie's cheek with the back of his fingers. "After we get to know each other better."

Mattie flinched from his touch, her skin crawling. She knew exactly what he had in mind—the same thing he'd done to Clint's wife. She'd kill herself first or force Layton to kill her.

"Come on, Layton, she'll just slow you down," Clint said, sliding a step closer. "Besides, the folks in this town won't let you get away with it. Mattie is one of their own and they won't rest until you're hanging high."

"You've been trying to catch me for over a year, Beaudry. What makes you think a bunch of yokels can hunt me down?" Layton demanded.

"Because I'm going to come back from the grave and make sure they do," Clint said in a low, feral voice. He moved another foot closer.

Mattie shivered at his savage tone.

"*I* don't believe in ghosts, Beaudry," Layton said. He shifted the gun's aim, centering it on Clint's chest. With a distance of less than four feet, he couldn't miss. "Why don't we see who's right about ghosts?"

Layton's finger curled around the trigger.

A loud thump from upstairs startled him for a split second. Mattie shot to her feet, ramming her body against Layton's. The gun discharged, nearly deafening her. The murderer shoved her aside and she tumbled onto the couch.

Clint charged into Layton and the two men fell to the rug in a tangle of arms and legs. The revolver dropped out of Layton's hand, skittering across the floor. The sound of flesh against flesh and a few grunts punctuated the fight. Mattie pressed her hand to her mouth, frightened for Clint as she watched him absorb Layton's blows. Blood flowed from a cut on Clint's cheek.

She quickly retrieved the gun. Its cold weight felt awkward and unfamiliar in her hands. She wouldn't let Layton kill Clint. She raised the gun between her shaking hands and aimed it at the flailing men. Afraid she'd shoot Clint by accident, Mattie lowered the weapon, watching the fight with a growing sense of dread.

Clint and Layton thrashed around, exchanging more punches. Clint seemed to be gaining the upper hand with his larger body and lawman's experience.

Suddenly Layton kneed Clint in the groin and rolled away, grabbing the piece of firewood Mattie had dropped earlier. Layton swung it over his head, his intention clear.

Almost without thought, Mattie lifted the pistol and squeezed the trigger. The explosion set her ears ringing. Through the haze of gunsmoke, she watched Layton pitch forward. The log fell harmlessly to the floor beside his motionless body.

Clint's gaze flew to Mattie, his expression stunned. He pushed himself to his feet, wobbled, then stepped over Layton's unmoving body. Staying out of the revolver's line of fire, Clint reached over and wrapped his fingers around the gun, pushing it downward slowly.

Mattie abruptly released the weapon, and Clint closed his grip around the gun, taking it from her numb hands.

Her strength evaporated and she fell against Clint's powerful chest. She wrapped her arms around his waist, breathing deeply of his familiar, soothing scent. Clint hugged her tightly and she felt his trembling through her own shudders.

"Are you all right?" Clint asked huskily.

She nodded against him. "But Herman . . . he's dead." Her tears dampened his shirtfront. The tempest of emotions she'd experienced that day deserted her, leaving her feeling numb and empty.

"I'm sorry, Mattie," Clint said. "If I hadn't come here two months ago, none of this would've happened."

"If you hadn't been here, he still would've come. He was going to do to me what he did to your wife." Her voice broke on the last word, and she had to swallow before whispering, "You saved my life."

The tenderness and sorrow in his eyes made Mattie's breath catch in her throat. It would take her a lifetime to learn all the layers of the man beneath the cool exterior.

She wished she had that long.

The sound of footsteps on the porch startled Mattie, and she backed away from Clint. Green Valley's townsfolk—Kevin, Orville and Amelia Johnson, Norbert from the bank, Luther the liveryman, Ellen from the bakery, and many others Mattie had known for years—crowded into the house.

Andy shoved through the crowd and ran to her. She knelt down, opening her arms to him. For a moment, he was just her little boy again. She closed her eyes and rested her cheek against his dark hair.

"Herman's dead, isn't he?" Andy asked with a trembling voice.

Mattie tightened her embrace on her son. "I'm sorry, sweetheart."

The boy's tears dampened Mattie's shoulder as he cried. She glanced up at Clint and met his grieving eyes.

"Are you all right?" Kevin asked.

She looked up at him, noting how his face was pinched in concern. "I'm fine." She glanced down at Herman's body over Andy's shoulder and fresh anguish filled her. "I think Herman's heart gave out."

Kevin squatted down beside him, and after a minute he nodded wearily.

Two silent townsmen came forward to carry out his body.

"Is that the man . . . ?" Kevin began, looking at Layton.

"That's him," Clint said gruffly. "He's the one who ambushed me, left me for dead. He raped and killed my wife, too."

Kevin studied Clint, then nodded, almost in resignation. He stepped over to examine Layton. "He's got a shoulder wound, but he's still alive."

Though Mattie hated Layton for what he'd

done, relief washed across her. She didn't know if she could live with the knowledge that she'd taken a life.

"He'll live only long enough to be hanged," Clint said grimly. He glanced at the group of people. "Luther, Orville, get him over to the jail. Dr. Murphy can take care of him there."

Andy's crying had diminished to quiet hiccups. Clint helped Mattie to her feet and they moved aside while the two men carried Layton out. With the excitement over, the crowd dwindled.

Amelia stepped over to Mattie and gave her a hug. "I'm glad you're all right," she said, her eyes glistening. "I would've hated to lose a new friend."

Mattie gripped Amelia's hands, her throat thick. "Thank you."

The younger woman exited in the wake of her husband, leaving only Clint, Kevin, Andy, and Mattie in the parlor.

"I'd like to speak with you for a minute," Kevin said to Mattie. He deliberately glanced at Clint and Andy. "Alone, please."

Mattie looked at Andy, whose cheeks were tear-streaked and flushed. "Why don't you take Clint into the kitchen and help him clean up?"

Andy's gaze moved from Mattie to Kevin, then back. He nodded somberly. "All right."

Mattie was aware of Clint's intense scrutiny, but she couldn't meet his eyes. His wife's murderer had been caught—he'd fulfilled his promise to her. But what of her own promise to Kevin?

As Clint passed by her, he clasped her forearm

gently, the simple gesture speaking louder than words. Then he rested his hand on Andy's shoulder and guided him into the kitchen.

Mattie rubbed her brow. Her insides were raw, her feelings jumbled and confused.

"Sit down before you fall down, Mattie," Kevin ordered softly.

He guided her to the settee and lowered her to the cushion. She placed her tightly clasped hands in her lap, wondering what Kevin wanted to talk about. She was exhausted, both physically and mentally, and didn't have the energy to hide her emotions.

He cupped Mattie's cheek gently.

"I'm releasing you from your promise."

Startled, Mattie met his gaze. "What?"

"I'm releasing you from the promise you made to me about Clint's baby and about marrying me." He smiled sadly. "I heard you and Beaudry talking outside the dance hall. I never meant to hurt you, Mattie. I only wanted to take care of you."

Her head swam. "I—I can't."

Kevin moved to the hearth and stared into the fireplace, his glasses reflecting the glowing embers. "You love him, Mattie. You'd never be happy being married to me." He paused. "Comfortable, maybe, but not happy. You'd always wonder."

Part of Mattie wanted to accept Kevin's release without question, but another part of her hated to hurt him. She stood and walked to his side, then laid her hand on his arm. "What about you? What do *you* want?"

He turned back and took her hands in his. "I want you to be happy. Beaudry makes you happy." He smiled ruefully. "Though God knows why."

Mattie laughed, her tensions easing away. "Believe me, I wish I knew why, too." She sobered. "I'm sorry things didn't work out the way you wanted."

"I am, too." Kevin gave her hands a squeeze, then smiled. "I'll let the reverend know there'll be a different groom at the wedding next Sunday."

"*If* Clint's ready."

Kevin chuckled. "He's ready, Mattie." He leaned down and kissed her cheek. "You deserve this happiness."

"Thank you," she said hoarsely. She tugged off her engagement ring and handed it to him. "Give this to the woman who can love you as much as you deserve to be loved."

Kevin closed his fingers around the gold band and nodded, then turned and left.

Mattie rose to her feet and stood in the center of the parlor, listening to the faint voices of Clint and Andy in the kitchen. She glanced at the blood-soaked rug where Layton had fallen, and shivered. Then she looked toward the place Herman had died.

Her lower lip quivered, but she kept her sob at bay. She had to believe Herman was with Ruth now, that they were both at peace.

"Mattie?"

Clint's soft voice startled her and she turned to

find him standing in the doorway of the parlor. "Yes?"

"Is Dr. Murphy gone?"

"He just left."

Awkward silence filled the space between them. Clint held his hat in his hands, turning the brim around and around. "I'm sorry about Herman. I know how much you and Andy cared for him."

Mattie swallowed past the tightness. "I have to believe he's at peace now." She studied Clint, thinking that something looked odd about him. Her gaze settled on his hips. "Where's your gun?"

He shrugged, seemingly embarrassed. "I didn't have time to get it before coming here." He shifted his weight from one foot to the other. "My not having it almost got you killed, Mattie."

As much as she wished she could disagree with him, she couldn't. After shooting Layton, she understood too well the protection of a gun. "I know. It seems lately I've been wrong about a lot of things."

Clint took a step toward her. "Not wrong, Mattie." His eyes twinkled. "A little misguided, maybe, but not wrong."

Mattie snorted, then quickly covered her grin. She glanced past Clint. "Where's Andy?"

"I sent him upstairs to get ready for bed." He paused, melancholy filling his features. "He's pretty upset about Herman. Thinks it was his fault for leaving him to come and get me."

Mattie took a step toward the stairs. "I need to talk to him."

Clint caught her arm. "I already did. I told him that sometimes people we care for die, and there's nothing we could've done to save them."

She recognized his admission that he had finally released his own guilt over Emily's death, and her heart swelled. Wrapping her arms around his waist, she leaned against his chest as he drew her into a warm embrace.

"You should try to get some sleep, too," Clint said. "You've had a long day."

Though she'd been exhausted only minutes before, now she was overly conscious of Clint's presence in her house. Nervousness underlined her awareness—she had to tell him of the new life growing within her. What would he say? Would he be angry at her for not telling him before?

Maybe she shouldn't confess, and after they were married for a month or so, she'd spring it on him.

No, that was wrong. Without her promise hanging over her, she had to reveal her secret. The babe she carried was his, also.

"We need—" Mattie began.

"I have—" Clint said at the same time.

They broke off.

"You start—" Clint said.

"Go ahead—" Mattie spoke in unison.

They laughed.

"There's something I have to tell you," Mattie said quickly, afraid she'd be interrupted again and lose her nerve. Her heart raced in her chest and she couldn't seem to get enough air.

*Calm down.*

Clint could see Mattie's anxiety in the flutter of her hands, and something caught his eye. Or the lack of something. "Your ring's gone."

Mattie blinked and looked down at her bare hand. "I gave it back to him."

"Does that mean . . . ?"

"Yes." She took a deep breath. "He released me from my promise."

Elation filled Clint and he grinned. He wrapped his arms around Mattie and twirled her in a circle. Her breasts flattened against his chest, scorching him and reminding him it had been too long since he held her in his arms.

"Please put me down," Mattie said firmly.

Startled by her tone, he obeyed immediately. "What's wrong?"

"I don't feel well."

He studied her face closely—her cheeks were too pale. Herman's death and the shock of shooting Layton must be catching up to her. He cursed himself for being so callous. "Do you need to see Dr. Murphy?"

Mattie shook her head, her eyes sparkling. "I know what's wrong with me." She looked at him squarely. "We're going to have a baby."

It took a moment for her words to sink into him. *We're going to have a baby.*

He realized his mouth was gaping as he struggled for air like a landed fish, and abruptly closed it. A strange combination of happiness and anger roiled through him. "Why didn't you tell me?" he demanded. "You were going to marry Murphy, knowing it was my child?"

Anger quickly sparked her eyes and added color to her pale cheeks. "You'd left, Clint. I didn't think you'd ever come back, and when I learned I was in a family way, I didn't know what to do. Then Kevin asked me to marry him. I told him I couldn't because of the baby, but he said he'd still marry me and would accept the child as his own." She turned her attention back to Clint. "What was I supposed to do? I was unmarried, and I never expected you to return."

"But I did. Why didn't you tell me right away?" Clint demanded. Her violet eyes became shadowed and the truth struck Clint. Only one thing would have kept Mattie from telling him. "You made a promise, didn't you?" he asked gently.

Mattie blinked. "Yes. In exchange for his name and protection, I promised not to tell you about your child if you ever came back."

"And that's the promise he released you from."

"Yes."

How could he fault her for having honor? That was one of the qualities that had made him fall in love with her. He gathered her in his arms as if she were made of fragile china. "Sweet, proud, stubborn Mattie. What am I going to do with you?"

"Make me an honest woman," she teased.

Clint couldn't think of anything he'd rather do. "I think that can be arranged." He drew back, but kept her within the circle of his arms. Lowering his head, he slanted his lips across hers and Mattie melted against him. She threaded her fingers through his hair and her touch added to the spark being fanned to a bright ember within him.

They drew apart and Mattie said with throaty invitation, "Let's go to bed."

He squelched a smile and teased, "I *am* kind of tired."

"You should sleep quite well in your old room," Mattie retorted without missing a beat.

Clint threw back his head and laughed. "If you think you're getting away from me that easy, think again." He swept her into his arms, cradling her against his chest.

Mattie giggled as Clint carried her upstairs, then set her on her feet gently, but held tightly to her hand. They paused by Andy's open door and found him already asleep.

"With your permission, I'd like to adopt him, Mattie," Clint said.

Her eyes glistened and her lips quivered with a smile. "I'm sure Andy would be delighted." She rose on her tiptoes and kissed his cheek. "You're going to make a wonderful father."

As Clint watched the boy sleep, his heart expanded with something he'd never felt before. It wouldn't be long before he had a wonderful wife and two children—things he'd never even allowed himself to consider for the past year.

Not until he met Mattie St. Clair.

Clint gazed down into her upturned face. Her eyes glittered with love and acceptance. Tenderness surged through him for the beautiful, courageous woman who had saved his life in more ways than one.

He cupped her face in his palms, his thumbs gently brushing her cheeks. "I promise to love you every day for the rest of my life. And for eternity."

Tears filled Mattie's eyes, but her smile nearly tore his breath away. "And I promise to love you forever, Clint Beaudry." Her grin turned saucy. "Starting right now."

# Epilogue

**M**attie couldn't help but laugh at Amelia's mirrored look of discomfort as they were both assisted down from their buggies by their respective husbands. Although it was highly improper for two women in such advanced stages of pregnancy to be seen in public, Mattie and Amelia had conspired to attend the wedding. Mattie wasn't about to miss seeing Kevin marry a woman who truly loved him. He deserved to find the same happiness that Mattie had found with Clint.

Mattie glanced at her husband, then at Orville Johnson. In spite of their differences, the two men had become friends, too. Life had changed dramatically for Mattie when she'd become Sheriff Clint Beaudry's wife. And it was all for the better.

Andy climbed down from the front seat of the

buggy—he'd proudly driven his parents to the church for the wedding of Kevin Murphy and Ellen Willoughby, owner of the town bakery.

Clint leaned close to her. "How're you doing?"

"I'm fine." Mattie grinned impishly. "Besides, this is the best time the baby could come. Kevin's right here."

Clint chuckled, his warm breath caressing her cheek. "You're impossible."

She tickled his ribs playfully. "You weren't complaining earlier."

His warm laughter spilled across her and when his arm settled around her shoulders, she leaned into his solid body. He wrapped his other arm around his adopted son, who shook his head at both of them. Mattie couldn't help but smile at his amused tolerance.

Mattie's eyes filled with tears. She cried at the drop of hat nowadays—it was even worse than it had been early in her pregnancy. Clint didn't seem to mind. He'd usually gather her in his arms, saying her crying gave him an excuse to hold her.

Mattie had to admit that her tears were usually forgotten with his "holding."

"Afternoon," Walt Atwater called out.

Mattie motioned for the retired lawman to join them.

"We'll go save a pew for all of us," Amelia said.

Mattie nodded and watched her and Orville enter the church. After some gentle prodding from Mattie, Amelia had finally told her husband about her past. Orville hadn't been angry; in fact, he'd known about it all along. It had never mattered to him.

Mattie shook her head. Amelia and Orville were an odd couple, but the love between them was never in doubt.

"How's my favorite girl?" Walt asked, giving Mattie a careful hug.

"Bigger than a house and still growing," Mattie replied with a wry smile.

Clint grinned. "Don't let her fool you. She's never looked more beautiful."

"I always told my Sarah the same thing, but she didn't believe me, either." Walt took a deep breath and a shadow of sadness touched his eyes. "I hope she's still waiting for me."

Mattie clasped Walt's arm and squeezed it. "I'm sure she is."

Andy drew away from them. "Is it okay if I sit with Buck and Josh?"

"As long as you behave yourselves," Clint said.

"Geez, Clint, I'm not a kid anymore."

"That's right, you're not. It's Buck and Josh I'm worried about. You know how they can be."

"I'll make sure they don't get into any trouble."

Clint smiled and patted his shoulder. "Go on, then."

"Ain't those two older than Andy?" Walt asked after the boy ran off to join his friends.

"By less than a year." Clint grinned crookedly. "But I've already caught Buck kissing Gertie Swanson behind the general store."

"That boy's gonna be a handful." Walt winked. "With the ladies."

Mattie laughed. "The same could be said about two handsome gentlemen I happen to know." She lifted her arms, waiting for Clint and Walt to offer theirs.

Clint and Walt grinned at each other and obliged. With Mattie between the two men, they strolled to the church. Once inside, Walt slipped into the pew beside Orville Johnson.

"We could still go back home," Clint whispered in her ear.

She shook her head and gazed into his eyes, nearly losing herself in the love in their green depths.

"I promised my husband a waltz after the wedding." She smiled. "And Mattie Beaudry always keeps her promises."

From the author of
*Donovan's Bed*
Comes another
unforgettable love story
*The Lawman's Surrender*
by **Debra Mullins**
Filled with the power and passion
she's known for

From bestselling author
**Margaret Moore**
Comes a magnificent romance
between a man and a woman
destined to be together—
despite all odds
*His Forbidden Kiss*
It's a love story you'll
always remember!

ARM 0201